A GOSSIP'S STORY

A GOSSIP'S STORY,

AND

A LEGENDARY TALE

BY

JANE WEST

Edited by Devoney Looser,
Melinda O'Connell & Caitlin Kelly

VALANCOURT BOOKS

First published London: T. N. Longman, 1796
First Valancourt Books edition 2016

This edition © 2016 by Valancourt Books

Published by Valancourt Books, Richmond, Virginia
Publisher & Editor: JAMES D. JENKINS
http://www.valancourtbooks.com

All Valancourt Books publications are printed on acid free paper
that meets all ANSI standards for archival quality paper.

ISBN 978-1-943910-15-1
Also available as an electronic book.

Set in Adobe Caslon

CONTENTS

CONTENTS

INTRODUCTION[1]

Jane West's *A Gossip's Story and A Legendary Tale* (1796) is best known today as a possible source text for Jane Austen's *Sense and Sensibility* (1811). It may be West's fate to remain in the shadow of that more famous novel and novelist. In her own lifetime, however, Jane West (1758-1852) was by far the more famous of the two Janes, in no small part because Austen (1775-1817) published her work first as "By a Lady" and thereafter as the author of her previous novels, rather than under her own name. West, on the other hand, although she had first published some of her works using a pseudonym, eventually acknowledged and signed most of them. By the early 1800s, "Mrs. West" had become a household name, mentioned in the same breath as other great British women writers of the day, including Maria Edgeworth (1768-1849), Frances Burney (1752-1840), and Hannah More (1745-1833). West was celebrated as an author of poetry and drama, as well as of successful novels. By contrast, Austen's rise to posthumous fame as the author of six great works of fiction did not take hold until the mid-nineteenth century—an era that West herself lived long enough to see. As steadily as Austen's reputation grew during that period, West's just as precipitously fell. In the last years of her life, West would refer to herself in a private letter as "an old Q in a corner whom the rest of the world has forgotten."[2]

A Gossip's Story does not deserve to be forgotten, nor does West herself. The novel is an interesting and important one, by turns thoughtful, moving, and dryly witty. It is also a highly didactic novel—that is, it tries to shape the morality and behavior of its

---

1 NOTE: What follows contains plot spoilers. If you prefer to read without knowing the outcome of the story, you may wish to wait until you've finished the novel to return to this introduction.

2 Pamela Lloyd, "Jane West," in *An Encyclopedia of British Women Writers*, Revised ed., edited by Paul and June Schlueter (New Brunswick, N.J.: Rutgers University Press, 1998).

readers, particularly female ones. This approach is one that many readers of fiction today have little stomach for. (We now seem to prefer our didacticism in nonfiction self-help books, which themselves derive from the "conduct book" genre of the eighteenth century. This, too, was a type of writing that West published.) West's *A Gossip's Story*, describing two sisters' divergent upbringings and their coming of age, presents to readers one life path to be emulated and one to avoid at all costs. Such a fictional formula may seem rather ham-fisted to 21st-century readers, but in her own era, West was understood as an important contributor to the novel genre. As one reviewer wrote in 1812, "The merits of Mrs. West, as a Champion in the cause of morality, have long been known and appreciated."[1] The *Gentleman's Magazine*, in its 1852 obituary of West, called her a lady "whose literary compositions attained a very considerable share of popularity in the early part of the present century."[2] West was recognized in her heyday as one of the era's most important authors. Today, by contrast, she is rarely read.

To understand this complete overturning of her once-high reputation, it may be helpful to consider the literary and social context in which West wrote and published. In the late-eighteenth century, novels were generally imagined as feminine books, even if they were being read by—and, to a lesser extent, authored by—many men. The most skeptical readers of the time saw the genre as low, dangerous trash, containing escapist romantic fantasies that could brainwash polite women into having unrealistic expectations about what their futures might hold. Instead of becoming obedient wives, domesticated mothers, and competent household managers, young women readers of fiction might be led to anticipate lives of novelty and adventure. They might be led to believe that their purity, virtue, and beauty could inspire men to death-defying heroic actions and undying love. At worst, novels were thought to have the potential to encourage a naïve young woman into a romantic situation that could lead to sexual ruin—something that would not only make her

---

1 Rev. of *The Loyalists* by Jane West. *Gentleman's Magazine* (July 1812): p. 48.
2 "Obituary: Mrs. West," *Gentleman's Magazine* 192 (July 1852): pp. 99-101.

a pariah but that could cast doubt on the moral worth of her entire family. The sexual missteps of one daughter could make the others appear tainted, too, and therefore less marriageable. Since so much of the economic comfort of a privileged family depended on its making good marriage alliances for its females, sexual and monetary ruin might go hand in hand. In that sense, morally suspect novels were envisioned as very serious business.

West shared some of her culture's worries about the dangerous moral tendencies of fiction, but she was among those novelists who sought to recuperate the genre as a useful tool for women's education. As West has her fictional narrator, the gossipy spinster Prudentia Homespun, claim in the introduction to *A Gossip's Story*, she is "not ambitious of dazzling the imagination, and of inflaming the passions" (3). Instead, she has "uniformly pursued [...] meliorating the temper and the affections." Fiction, West believed, could educate properly and do a lot of good. Many of her earliest readers were persuaded that West's books promised both individual and social improvement by inculcating appropriate moral tendencies in the young.

The "good" that West envisioned was of a particular political thrust, usually described today as conservative. Some of West's contemporaries—most famously Mary Wollstonecraft (1759-1797)—believed that the problem with eighteenth-century women's education (or lack of it) was that it instructed women to become vain, overly driven by emotions, and silly, rather than rational and thoughtful. West may have agreed with Wollstonecraft that far, but for Wollstonecraft, the answer was to educate women out of some aspects of their previous gender roles. Wollstonecraft proposed educating girls in a new system that would be co-educational, and, in her fiction, she was highly critical of men's abuse of power over women in the institution of marriage. West, in contrast to Wollstonecraft, did not find systemic problems that needed to be changed in men's and women's social and marital roles. West thought, on the contrary, that women needed better to accommodate themselves to what she believed was the sound structure of courtship and marriage. Problems arose, for West, when women did not adhere *rigidly enough* to traditional

"maternal and conjugal duties," a phrase West uses apprecia-
tively in her dedication to *A Gossip's Story*. For Wollstonecraft,
the mention of "maternal and conjugal duties"—although she
certainly believed in them—would have been an occasion for
deep reflection and possible reform. Wollstonecraft emphasized
rights, where West emphasized duties.[1] The political distance
between Wollstonecraft (who is often called a "Jacobin" novelist,
due to her support of the French Revolution's leveling political
goals of liberty, equality, and fraternity) and West (often called
an "anti-Jacobin," by contrast) was in some senses profound.

At the same time, the two women writers might be said to
have a lot in common. Both ultimately published substantial
work under their own names, despite other female authors
(including Austen) having chosen the cloak of anonymity. Both
West and Wollstonecraft were successful "public women" at
a time when sustained female authorship took not only talent
and strength of character but ingenuity, as navigating a publishing world dominated by men could prove challenging. Both
women had self-confident, wry, and sharp voices on the page
that suggest no small amount of personal charisma. Both saw
themselves as author-educators of the young, particularly young
women, although Wollstonecraft was the only one of the two to
run a school and take employment as a governess. (West, having
chosen a more conventional marital path, inherited land from
her father in 1805; she appears to have had greater economic and
domestic security and therefore less need to attempt the kinds of
labor resorted to by impecunious, educated women.) Wollstonecraft has been the subject of many biographies and has become a
feminist icon, known best as the author of the important treatise
A Vindication of the Rights of Woman (1792). She is also known
as the mother who died giving birth to Mary Shelley, author
of *Frankenstein* (1818). For her part, West—although she has
recently been made the subject of a biographical dissertation by
Pamela Lloyd and of the first full-length published biography

---

[1] Gail Baylis, "West, Jane (1758-1852)," *Oxford Dictionary of National Biography*, Oxford University Press, 2004; online edition, Jan. 2008. [http://
www.oxforddnb.com/view/article/29086, accessed 28 Nov. 2010].

by Marilyn Wood—remains a far more obscure and less colorful figure.[1] That outcome might seem an obvious one to us today, but in the late eighteenth and early nineteenth centuries, the opposite would have seemed far more probable. West was poised as more likely to enjoy enduring acclaim.

If making a case for the literary importance of West fails to persuade today's readers, however, her connections to acknowledged literary greatness must remain compelling. Most critics agree that Jane Austen's first published novel, *Sense and Sensibility,* was inspired to some degree by West's *A Gossip's Story.* Although *Sense and Sensibility* was not published until 1811, it was probably begun under the title of *Elinor and Marianne* sometime before 1797—potentially right around the time the first edition of *A Gossip's Story* was first published. Thereafter, West's novel went through several editions, including a second (1797), third (1798), fourth (1799), and fifth (1804), with no substantial changes. Undeniably, *A Gossip's Story* and *Sense and Sensibility* share a great deal in terms of their plot, characters, and structure. As critic J. M. S. Tompkins put it, "There is evidence to suggest that in *A Gossip's Story* we have not exactly the source but the starting-point of *Sense and Sensibility*" (33).

Both novels are centered on two sisters, one who embodies what was known in the late eighteenth century as "sense" (solid rationality and emotional control) and the other of whom represents what was becoming the more suspect quality of "sensibility" (a kind of overtly emotional, romantic sensitivity). Both Austen and West named their heroines of sensibility "Marianne." Early on in both novels, each Marianne is dramatically rescued from physical harm by an attractive man who literally and figuratively sweeps her off of her feet. Both would-be heroes turn out to be great disappointments, as a suitor (in Austen's treatment) or as a husband (in West's). Both sister-heroines of sense, by contrast—West's Louisa and Austen's Elinor—are ultimately rewarded for their consistent, rational choices, whether romantic

---

1 See Pamela Lloyd, *Jane West: A Critical Biography.* Diss. Brandeis University, 1997; and Marilyn Wood, *'Studious to Please': A Profile of Jane West, Eighteenth-Century Author.* Donington: Shaun Tyas, 2003.

or familial. Both women of sense marry suitors who were previously and mistakenly in love with—or perhaps just infatuated with—flawed females.

If these are the similarities in the two novels, differences abound as well. As Angela Rehbein has argued, West's novel, though set in England, contains significant colonial subtexts that have ramifications for its romance plot.[1] Austen's first novel included little material with such direct global reach; her fiction would not grapple directly with colonial matters until *Mansfield Park* (1814). There are other differences, too. West's novel employs an unusual spinster-narrator, the aforementioned Prudentia Homespun, whose comic asides are nowhere replicated in Austen's omniscient narration and free indirect discourse. But even in narrative voice, some echoes of West might be found in Austen, such as in the comic treatment of the "old maid" Ann (or Nancy) Steele, Lucy Steele's older sister, or in the widowed and comical, although ultimately amiable and admirable, Mrs. Jennings.

The two novels also differ in their registers of comic expression. Austen's contains her signature irony and humor, but her comical minor characters—such as the jovial Mrs. Jennings, the dour Mr. Palmer, and his flibbertigibbet wife, Charlotte—are quite mixed, displaying both good and bad qualities. Because West is labeled as a didactic novelist, some assume that her writings will therefore be devoid of humor, but this is simply not the case. We might conclude, though, that West's forms of humor haven't traveled nearly as well over the centuries as Austen's. West's caricatured bachelors—Captain Target, Mr. Alsop, and Mr. Inkle, all of whom Miss Cardamum has her eye on—may fail to amuse many readers today. They are rather one-dimensional and flat, in comparison to Austen's deadpan Mr. Palmer or dandy Robert Ferrars. West's comic characters are clearly designed to provoke laughter through their respective and exaggerated weaknesses, foibles, and gaffes. These male characters' shortcomings are repeatedly exposed through the narrator's raillery, as well as

---

1 See Angela Rehbein, "Dutiful Daughters and Colonial Discourse in Jane West's *A Gossip's Story*," *Eighteenth-Century Fiction*, 23.3 (2011): pp. 519-540.

through the bachelors' own foolish actions; readers at the time seem to have been amused by such broad comic brushstrokes in popular fiction.

Another difference between the two novels is that West uses her fiction to focus on the well-meaning widower-father of two very different daughters; he dies at the end of *A Gossip's Story*. By contrast, Austen's *Sense and Sensibility* begins with a dying father and follows the travails of his widow and her three very different daughters. Financial problems plague both novels' survivors, but in West's case, the failed businessman-father Mr. Dudley must bear some responsibility for his fiscal problems. Austen's widowed Mrs. Dashwood, who is financially abandoned by her stepson, deserves less (or perhaps even no) blame for her challenging economic circumstances. In that sense, it may be harder to sympathize with Mr. Dudley's demise or with his earlier having given over his daughter Marianne to be raised by her wealthy, flawed grandmother. It does, however, make him a more complex character than most of West's other men. He is shown—despite his foolishly having led himself and daughter Louisa into economic disaster, and despite having put his daughter Marianne at risk by allowing her to be raised by an indulgent grandmother, to be an upright, well-meaning patriarch. Austen's Mrs. Dashwood's faults as a mother involve not asking her daughter Marianne enough questions about her supposed engagement to the false hero, Willoughby. This may seem an almost trivial parental fault by comparison to Mr. Dudley's economic ruin, but, of course, mis-educating a daughter, too, could have had dire financial consequences. This would have been particularly true if Marianne had followed in the footsteps of her fictional double and Willoughby's former lover, the second Eliza Williams, whom he impregnates and apparently abandons.

Further differences between Austen and West are also readily apparent. Austen did not interrupt any of her novels to insert long poems, as West does. For many readers, *A Legendary Tale* seems out of place in West's book, and the narrator's own defensive comments about the inclusion of a long section of verse (calling it "slightly connected with the principal story") suggests that she anticipated such complaints. The use of verse in the novel in the late eighteenth and early nineteenth centuries was perfectly customary. West herself makes reference to Oliver Goldsmith as one inspiration for her having included verse in her prose fiction, but there were many other examples she might have named. One text, Anna Seward's *Louisa* (1784), even called itself in its subtitle "a poetical novel in four epistles."[1] Seward's *Louisa* was, in effect, a "verse-novel," a progenitor of Elizabeth Barrett Browning's *Aurora Leigh* (1856). West's choice to include a substantial section of narrative poetry between the prose fiction of *A Gossip's Story* was not a technique that Austen emulated in *Sense and Sensibility*, although she did make Marianne Dashwood an appreciator of her era's poets.

Why is *A Legendary Tale* placed in the middle of *A Gossip's Story*? We might try to answer that question by looking for thematic links between the two parts of the novel. Those links certainly exist. Critics have looked to the ways in which the characters of *A Gossip's Story* responded to the reading aloud of *A Legendary Tale* as offering us further insight into the novel's principal characters. Each character finds in the long poem precisely what we might expect him or her to see. West may have included the verse section in the novel in order to try to raise the status of her "low" fiction with the then more highly regarded genre of poetry. Yet another possibility is that West was concerned that she did not have enough material in *A Gossip's Story* to make up her requisite minimum of two volumes. A novel was customarily three volumes long during this period (a so-called "triple decker"), so perhaps West sought to pad her contents with a stand-alone poem. It is difficult to know which of these explanations ought to be most persuasive to us. Perhaps all of them played some part in her choice.

West also included a verse epigraph to her novel, seen on the title page facsimile facing p. xxiv of this edition. Those lines are

---

1 It seems unlikely that West took the name of her heroine from Seward, as Louisa was a common name for a novel's heroine. Indeed, it was so common that Jane Austen, in her novel *Northanger Abbey*, has a character make a joke about the Julias and Louisas of the era's fiction.

from *Ode to Indifference* by Frances Greville (1727?-1789). Greville was a celebrated wit and a fashionable beauty, and her poem (written circa 1756-57) was widely anthologized, said to have become in the mid-eighteenth century as famous as Thomas Gray's "Elegy Written in a Country Church-Yard" (1751). Some saw the poem as an outpouring of its author's marital disappointments, its message interpreted as either telling readers not to feel too deeply for others or as suggesting not to bother trying to make others happy, lest you be disappointed by your own failure. Greville's poem prepares readers for West's treatment of sensibility. The *Ode*, too, set out to expose the dangers of romantic, overly emotional sensitivity.

A different epigraph begins West's second volume—four lines from a poem by the famed Bluestocking Elizabeth Carter (1717-1806), first published three decades earlier in her *Poems on Several Occasions* (1762). West surely admired Carter, who had made a name for herself as a poet, translator, and learned woman, having attracted the friendship of the so-called "Queen of the Blues" Elizabeth Montagu, writer Samuel Johnson, and politician William Pulteney, the Earl of Bath (1684-1764). It was the latter, the Earl of Bath, then in his late 70s, to whom Carter dedicated her volume of poems. The poem from which West's epigraph's lines come is Carter's "To the Earl of Bath." Carter's poem reflects on the benefits of age looking back on youth, in wisdom and judgment, focusing on the value of a long life's providing time for reflection, so that one could redouble one's efforts to be virtuous, godly, and Heaven-ready. The lines from Carter that West chooses for her novel's epigraph are in keeping with the perspective of *A Gossip's Story*'s spinster narrator, Prudentia Homespun. Those lines, "With calm severity unpassion'd age / Detects the specious fallacies of youth," echo West's narrator's ability to detect not her own youthful fallacies, perhaps, but also those in her own community, such as Marianne's. The next lines West quotes from Carter—"Reviews the motives which no more engage, / And weighs each action in the scale of truth"—give us a hint of what is to come by novel's end—a definitive moral. West's employing verse epigraphs to set the stage for her novel is itself a very common authorial technique in the period, but it was another convention that Austen usually eschewed. She did not use verse epigraphs. Many other differences between West's and Austen's novels could, of course, be described. Still, their connections to each other are undeniable. Reading them side-by-side offers us much that is instructive.

It is unfortunate that we do not seem to have any surviving evidence about what Jane West thought of Jane Austen. When West died, her papers went to her grandson, but he and the other executors apparently decided not to seek their publication. Although it is not out of the question that these papers may yet surface, perhaps having long been hidden in some trunk or attic, it is presumed that the bulk of West's letters and manuscripts were lost. This was an all too common fate for the papers of female authors from this period, especially those who had the misfortune to outlive their own celebrity.

There is a little more to go on in trying to determine what Austen though of West. Two references to West appear in the scant surviving letters of Austen. In one, Austen marvels at West's productivity, in light of her supposed domestic responsibilities as the wife of a farmer. As Austen wrote to her sister Cassandra in 1816:

> I often wonder how *you* can find time for what you do, in addition to the care of the House;—And how good Mrs. West cd have written such Books & collected so many hard words, with all her family cares, is still more a matter of astonishment! Composition seems to me Impossible, with a head full of Joints of Mutton & doses of rhubarb.[1]

A biographer of West refers to Austen as her "admiring reader," but this seems an overstatement (Wood viii). Austen, in an earlier letter to her niece Anna from 1814, declares that she is "quite determined" "not to be pleased with Mrs. West's Alicia De Lacy, should I ever meet with it, which I hope I may not.—I

---

1 Letter from Jane Austen to Cassandra Austen. 8-9 September 1816. *Jane Austen's Letters*. Edited by Deirdre Le Faye. New Edition. (Oxford: Oxford University Press, 1995), p. 321.

think I *can* be stout against any thing written by Mrs. West."[1] Austen's letter is a chatty and lighthearted one, but even if this statement is an exaggeration made for humorous effect, she was clearly anything but an unqualified fan of West's.

West lived a life that both she and her contemporaries took great pains to describe as uneventful and domestic. There may be a kernel of truth to this version of events, but we also ought to recognize that such details were a part of what we might now call a public relations campaign. Such PR worked very hard to paint West as a woman who was more committed to her needle (needlework) than to her pen (authorship)—a longstanding comparison and contrast used to talk about women's writing. West must have desired that her public see her as a wife and mother first and an author second, given the ideas she puts forward in her fiction. Authorship was hardly proof of a woman's doing her duty as a daughter, wife, and mother—quite the opposite. It could serve as proof of her shirking those duties.

It is impossible to know the extent to which authorship was an integral part of West's daily life. Evidence has emerged suggesting that the act of writing and of being an author was central to her identity long before she married or had children.[2] We also know that to write as consistently and as much as she did must have been a labor-intensive path and must, therefore, have been to some degree a chosen one. Still, although reassessments of West's life (and some new facts) continue to emerge, a relatively small amount of information has survived about her. Much of what we think we know is from sources that sought to paint West's life in the safest, most conventional domestic light.

Jane Iliffe West was the daughter of a tradesman—an upholsterer—a profession that carried a wider meaning than it does today. It indicates that he was a shopkeeper who sold furniture and household goods. Although she would later describe herself as a simple country girl, West's first eleven years were spent

1 Letter from Jane Austen to Anna Austen, 28 September 1814, in *Jane Austen's Letters*.), pp. 277-278.
2 Wood, *Studious to Please*, pp. 10-12. Subsequent references cited parenthetically in the text.

with her family in London (Wood 1). She moved from there to Northamptonshire and began writing poetry by age 13. Her affluent neighbors, the Hills of Rothwell Manor, became friends. The two Hill daughters, Anne (later Maunsell) and Barbara (later the Honorable Mrs. Cockayne, to whom *A Gossip's Story* is dedicated), encouraged West's writing, also providing her access to books through their father's library. By 1783, the self-taught Jane Iliffe had married Thomas West (d. 1823), a yeoman farmer who lived in the nearby town of Little Bowden. Together they had three sons, Thomas (1783-1843), John (1787-1841), and Edward (1794-1821). A quick glance at this list of dates shows that Jane West outlived her husband and all of her offspring. These deaths prompted grief-filled writing from her, including an obituary for her husband for the *Gentleman's Magazine* (Wood 106). Although she continued to write, West stopped publishing with her novel *Ringrove* (1827), which appeared when she was nearly 70 years old (Wood 112). When she died in 1852, at the age of 94, her estate was divided among six grandchildren. Her manuscripts and letters were left to her grandson, the Reverend Edward West, although to date untraced.[1] As a result, much of what we know about her consists of the literary persona she and others worked to perpetuate: that of proper wife and mother whose authorship was never as important to her as her domestic duties. She described her own verse as inelegant and crude; as she put it in a poem, she "wrote all kinds of verse with ease / Made pies and puddings frocks and cheese."[2] She called herself "Studious to please, but unrefin'd" (116). The extent to which this persona of the domestic goddess who did not take herself seriously as an author was itself a fiction we may never know.

It is with these questions, themes, and contemporary debates in mind that we as readers turn to West's second novel, *A Gossip's Story*. During her lifetime it was one of her most popular works; today it is her best-known novel. Whether anchored to Austen's *Sense and Sensibility*, read on its own, or read as part of West's

---

1 Baylis, "West, Jane," *DNB*.
2 Jane West, "To the Hon. Mrs. C-E," *Miscellaneous Poems, and A Tragedy* (York: W. Blanchard, 1791), p. 116.

vast and largely unstudied oeuvre, *A Gossip's Story* deserves re-assessment. As William Stafford puts it, "The most interesting conservative narratives of female difficulties [in the 1790s] come from the pen of Jane West."[1] Recent critical studies of West by David Thame, Eleanor Ty, Lisa Wood, Angela Rehbein, and others demonstrate a rising interest in her and her work.[2] With the publication of this edition of the novel by Valancourt Books—the first fully edited and annotated text of the novel, and the only modern reissue of *A Gossip's Story* other than Gina Luria's facsimile edition of 1974—new readers may now reach their own conclusions about West's fiction and its merits.[3] If continued critical reassessments are undertaken by the next generations of students, teachers, and scholars, then West's fiction may well regain—deservedly—some of its former prominence.[4]

1 William Stafford, *English Feminists and Their Opponents in the 1790s: Unsex'd and Proper Females*. (Manchester: Manchester University Press, 2002), p. 88.
2 See David Thame, "Cooking up a Story: Jane West, Prudentia Home-spun, and the Consumption of Fiction." *Eighteenth-Century Fiction*. 16.2 (January 2004): pp. 217-242; Rehbein, "Dutiful Daughters"; Eleanor Ty, *Empowering the Feminine: The Narratives of Mary Robinson, Jane West, and Amelia Opie, 1796-1812* (Toronto: University of Toronto Press, 1998); and Lisa Wood, *Modes of Discipline: Women, Conservatism, and the Novel after the French Revolution*. (Lewisburg, Pa.: Bucknell University Press, 2003).
3 Jane West, *A Gossip's Story and A Legendary Tale*. Introduction by Gina Luria. (New York: Garland, 1974).
4 Melinda O'Connell, who provided much of the research that went into early drafts of this introduction, is one such scholar. She began to co-edit this novel with me as an undergraduate at the University of Missouri. Both of us thank MU Ph.D. candidate Ruth Knezevich, who served as a research assistant in the summer of 2011, for her dedicated labor. Caitlin Kelly stepped in as a co-editor in 2012, helping to see the work through to fruition.

JANE WEST: CHRONOLOGY

1758 Jane Iliffe born April 30th, in a building that would later become St. Paul's Coffee House, London, the only child of her parents, Jane and John Iliffe.

c. 1780 Jane Iliffe marries Thomas West (d. 1823), a yeoman farmer from Little Bowden, Leicestershire, whose ancestors had been rectors of the parish for the previous 150 years.

1783 Jane West's first son, Thomas, born. (Two other sons were born in 1787 and 1794.)

1786 Publishes her first book, *Miscellaneous Poetry, Written at an Early Period of Life*, as "Mrs. West."

1788 Publishes *The Humours of Brighthelmstone: A Poem*, as "J. West."

1791 Publishes *Miscellaneous Poems and a Tragedy*, as "Mrs. West."

1793 Publishes her first novel, *The Advantages of Education*, under the pseudonym "Prudentia Homespun."

1796 Publishes *A Gossip's Story and A Legendary Tale*, her most successful novel, as "The Author of *Advantages of Education*."

1797 Publishes *An Elegy on the Death of the Right Honourable Edmund Burke*, identifying herself as "Mrs. West, author of *The Gossip's Story*, *Miscellaneous Poems, a Tragedy*, &c."

1799 Publishes her third novel, *A Tale of the Times* (as "The Author of *A Gossip's Story*") as well as *Poems and Plays*, volumes one and two and *The Mother: A Poem in Five Books* (as "Mrs. West," which becomes her general custom thereafter).

1801 Publishes her highly successful conduct book, *Letters Addressed to a Young Man on his first Entrance into Life*, based on letters she wrote to her eldest son, Thomas.

1802   Publishes another novel, *The Infidel Father*, as well as a short children's book *The Sorrows of Selfishness; or, The History of Miss Richmore* by "Prudentia Homespun."

1805   Publishes *Poems and Plays*, volumes three and four.

1806   Publishes *Letters to a Young Lady, in which the Duties and Character of Women are Considered, Chiefly with a Reference to Prevailing Opinions*, another conduct book, dedicated to Queen Charlotte.

1810   Publishes another novel, *The Refusal*, which claims to be the posthumously published work of Prudentia Homespun.

1812   Publishes *The Loyalists: An Historical Novel* (1812), set just before the English Civil War and featuring a character named Waverly, sometimes credited as a possible influence on Walter Scott's *Waverley* (1814).

1814   Publishes *Alicia de Lacy: An Historical Romance*.

1815   Publishes anonymously, *Vicissitudes of Life; Exemplified in the Interesting Memoirs of a Young Lady, in a Series of Letters*.

1817   Publishes *Scriptural Essays Adapted to the Holy Days of the Church of England*, a religious work.

1823   Husband Thomas West dies.

1827   Publishes her last novel, *Ringrove, or, Old Fashioned Notions*.

1843   Eldest son Thomas West dies.

1852   Jane West dies in her home in Little Bowden, having outlived all three of her sons but leaving six grandchildren. She left her papers to executors and to her grandson, the Rev. Edward West, to do with them as they wished. No one seems to have sought to publish them, and these papers appear not to have survived.

NOTE ON THE TEXT

Jane West's *A Gossip's Story, and A Legendary Tale* (1796) was a popular and successful novel, republished in multiple editions in the late eighteenth and early nineteenth centuries. A second edition appeared in 1797, a third in 1798, a fourth in 1799, and a fifth in 1804, not to mention the many copies of the novel that were republished (without any gain to the author or to West's initial publisher, Longman, in so-called "pirated" editions) in Dublin and Cork, among other places. West did not make significant additions or deletions to *A Gossip's Story* after the first edition, although she did make some changes and corrections. The source for the present text is a combination of the first and second editions of the novel, based on the two earliest versions its earliest readers would have seen. Not incidentally, these are the versions that Jane Austen may have read while drafting her novel, said to have at first been called *Elinor and Marianne*, that would later become *Sense and Sensibility* (1811).

The changes made in *A Gossip's Story* from the first edition to the second were principally in spelling, capitalization, and punctuation. It is likely that West was involved in correcting and "modernizing" the text from the first edition to the second, although we have no proof of her participation in these changes. It seems probable that West chose to update (or that her publisher recommended that she change) the spelling of many words; these cannot be called corrections *per se*. The first edition's spelling patterns were perfectly acceptable alternatives at the time, although they were then becoming seen as old fashioned. West's initial use of these more archaic spellings tells us something about her early writing style, which used variants such as "compleat" and "chearful." The editors have indicated in footnotes which of West's words were "modernized" from the first to the second edition.

With *A Gossip's Story*'s punctuation and capitalization,

however, we have chosen in general to follow the second edition. The first edition includes many irregularities in its punctuation, especially in its generous use of commas. Arguably, some of the first edition's punctuation patterns were not incorrect but were also simply practices then going out of fashion. The use of commas and semi-colons was modernized (and they were used more sparingly) in the second edition. Particularly in *A Legendary Tale*, but throughout the novel, hundreds of commas were removed in the second edition. Because the second edition more closely resembles patterns of punctuation that remain in use today, and therefore is more readable, we have elected to make the second edition's punctuation our default in this version of the text. The same is true with capitalization, in which words such as maker (referring to God) or heaven in the first edition were changed to Maker and Heaven in the second. As a result of our editorial choices, those few readers who are interested in studying West's changing use of punctuation and capitalization will need to compare for themselves the first and second editions to see examine the nature and extent of the changes. We have corrected them silently.

In addition, we have silently changed obvious errors in spelling and punctuation. For ease of reading, we have omitted the extraneous quotation marks which in the late eighteenth century were regularly used at the beginning of *every* line of quoted text. Instead, we have followed present typographical patterns, using quotation marks only at the beginning and end of quoted speeches. We have removed printer's catch-words from the bottoms of pages, as well as, of course, the long "s" of the day. We have not kept in place the practice of keeping first words of a chapter in all capital letters. Other changes from the first edition to the second have been catalogued in the footnotes, all of which have been written by the editors, as West did not include footnotes in her novel.

ACKNOWLEDGEMENTS

The editors are grateful to the University of Missouri's College of Arts and Science and its Undergraduate Research Mentorship Program. The URM Program offered Looser and McConnell the academic structure and the funding that was the impetus for beginning this project. In particular, we are grateful to Dean Michael O'Brien and to the late Professor John Miles Foley for their support.

A

GOSSIP'S STORY,

AND

A LEGENDARY TALE.

IN TWO VOLUMES.

BY THE AUTHOR OF

ADVANTAGES OF EDUCATION.

" Nor Peace nor Eafe the Heart can know,
    " Which, like the Needle true,
" Turns at the touch of Joy and Woe,
    " Yet, turning, trembles too."

GREVILLE'S ODE TO INDIFFERENCE.

VOL. I.

LONDON:
PRINTED FOR T. N. LONGMAN, PATER-NOSTER-ROW.
1796.

The following pages intended, under the disguise of an artless History, to illustrate the Advantages of CONSISTENCY, FORTITUDE, and the DOMESTICK VIRTUES; and to expose to ridicule, CAPRICE, AFFECTED SENSIBILITY, and an IDLE CENSORIOUS HUMOUR; are most respectfully inscribed to

THE HON. MRS. COCKAYNE;[1]

by one who has been long honoured by her friendship, who sincerely admires the maternal and conjugal duties exemplified in her conduct; and who wishes, by her example, to recommend them to others.

---

[1] Mrs. Cockayne was the former Barbara Hill, a close friend of Jane West's, who had married the Hon. William Cockayne, the youngest son of the 5th Viscount Cullen. The Cockaynes lived in Rushton Hall in Northamptonshire, a grand estate that Jane West must have visited often and about which she wrote poems. Barbara Cockayne died in 1838.

INTRODUCTION.

Mrs. Prudentia Homespun is infinitely obliged to the World, for the favourable reception it gave to her tale of Maria Williams, or the Advantages of Education; which more than answered her highest expectations.[1]

The World in reply thanks Mrs. Prudentia for her politeness; but assures her, it never heard either of her or her Maria.

Mrs. Prudentia in her rejoinder observes, that she must define what those expectations were. She was not romantick[2] enough to imagine, that a little novel issuing from a general repository, unsupported by puff,[3] unpatronised by friends, and even unacknowledged by its author, could rise into celebrity. There were besides some intrinsick reasons why it should not succeed, according to the common acceptation of that word. It had no splendour of language, no local description, nothing of the marvellous, or the enigmatical, no sudden elevation, and no astonishing depression. It merely spoke of human life as it is, and so simple was the story, that at the outset an attentive reader must have foreboded the catastrophe.[4] Indeed it required some attention from the reader, which in works of this kind is also a fault: for not ambitious of dazzling the imagination, and of inflaming the passions, it uniformly pursued its aims of meliorating the temper and the affections.

No pecuniary advantages, nor the applause of the million could be expected from a work like this. As to the former, Mrs. Prudentia is happily too *rich* to wish for any. Lest the word rich

---

1 *The Advantages of Education* (1793), West's first novel, also featured the conceit of a spinster-narrator named Prudentia Homespun. "Mrs." was used to refer to both married and older unmarried women in this period.

2 In the second edition, "romantic."

3 A puff was an extravagantly laudatory advertisement or review, often written by a friend of the author.

4 "Catastrophe" here means not disaster but, as in its eighteenth-century usage, the end of a dramatic piece or the dénouement, often unhappy.

should create the idea of a Nabob's[1] fortune, she explains by saying, that she possesses a clear annuity of one hundred pounds per annum, and that she calls herself very wealthy, because it is adequate to all her wishes.

The *general* approbation would not have been sufficient; for the generality of readers do not judge by the rules by which she wishes to be tried. The limited circulation of Maria Williams has afforded her the gratification she desired. She has heard, without fearing any implied flattery, the merit of the work asserted by those, who wondered who could be the author. Many ladies who, by conscientiously discharging the duties of the maternal character, may be presumed to be judges of what is best adapted for the perusal of youth, have commended it, as a work from which much real instruction may be derived. The authour's[2] highest expectations presumed upon no further applause.

She has resumed the pen with a similar intention. Happy, if while she is instructing her sex how to avoid yielding to imaginary sorrows, she can, for a moment, banish from her dejected heart, the pressure of *real* calamity, to which it is her duty to submit; or forget the friend whose approbation was the incentive and reward of her *former* labours.[3]

Some further apology may be judged necessary for introducing a Legendary Tale but slightly connected with the principal story. Were this work to be tried by the rules of an epick, the author is sensible that the episode is considerably too long: but she hopes a trifle will not be measured upon the bed of Procrustes.[4] The example of the inimitable Goldsmith,[5] and many

---

1 Nabob: a wealthy or powerful landowner; more specifically, a British man who had acquired a large fortune in India or the "East Indies."

2 In the second edition, "author's."

3 Critics have understood this as an actual reference to Jane West's life, that is, her grief over the death of her close friend Anne (or Anna) Hill Maunsell, sister of the Mrs. Cockayne to whom *A Gossip's Story* is dedicated. Anne Maunsell long encouraged West's writing and read her works.

4 Procrustes is a figure from Greek mythology, the son of Poseidon, who invited passers-by to spend the night and then stretched them out to fit the size of an iron bed.

5 Oliver Goldsmith (1728?-1774) wrote in many genres, and his novel, *The Vicar of Wakefield* (1766), included several other kinds of writing among its pages, including poetry.

later writers, who have successfully interspersed poetry with prose in works of this nature, excited a wish to gratify the publick taste by similar variety. And as moral improvement is the avowed end, descriptive poetry was not thought so *impressive* as a connected tale, which insensibly ran on to a greater length than was at first designed.

CONTENTS

OF THE

FIRST VOLUME.

CHAPTER I.

The comforts of Retirement—Rural Elegance defined by example.

As I profess myself an egotist, it will not be uncharacteristick to begin with stating the qualifications I possess, to execute with propriety the task I have undertaken.

I have been for several years the inhabitant of a small market-town called Danbury, in the north of England. As my annuity is regularly paid, and my family consists of only myself, a female servant, and an old tabby-cat, I have but little domestick care to engage my attention and anxiety. Now, as I am of a very active temper, my mind naturally steps abroad, and occupies itself in the concerns of my neighbours. Besides the peculiar advantages of my situation, I enjoy some inherent qualities, which I flatter myself render me a very excellent gossip. I have a retentive memory, a quick imagination, strong curiosity, and keen perception. These faculties enable me not only to retain what I hear, but to connect the day-dreams of my own mind; to draw conclusions from small premises; in short, to tell what other people think, as well as what they do. Other circumstances also conspire to render my pretensions to the above character indisputable.

As Danbury possesses the advantages of an healthy situation, dry soil, and pleasant environs, it has long been distinguished for the genteel connections which it affords. Many single ladies, like myself, have chosen it for their residence, and we have established a very agreeable society, which meets three times a week, to communicate the observations which the levity of youth, the vanity of ostentation, or the meanness of avarice have suggested. Our remarks have all the acumen which experience and penetration can supply, and as we exhibit models of prudence in our own conduct, it is a rule with us to shew no mercy to others.

I will not attempt to conceal the censures which the objects of our animadversion, in return, affect to throw upon us. I am not ignorant that we are termed the *scandalous* club, and that spleen, malevolence, and disappointment are said to be the idols, on whose altars we sacrifice every reputation which comes within our reach. Perfection belongs to no human institution, and I will own that sometimes we *may* be wrong. The reader must know that I am uncommonly good humoured and tender hearted; whether therefore my dissent from my lady associates proceeds altogether from a redundance of "the milk of human kindness" in my disposition, or from too great severity in theirs, time must determine.

Amongst the agreeable appendages to Danbury, its vicinity to Stannadine must be enumerated. This elegant mansion was built by a respectable gentleman, whose family falling into decay, it has since become the casual residence of several genteel people; and has thus been instrumental in promoting our amusements, not only by its pleasing embellishments and delightful walks, but by the quick succession of its inhabitants, who supply a never-failing source of observation and anecdote. I am not going to detail the commodious apartments in the house, or to describe the grounds, beautiful as they are by nature, and highly cultivated by art. A mere novice in landscape designation, I confine myself to the delineation of the lights and shades of human character; and as I conceive the history of the Dudley family may afford instruction, as well as amusement to the younger part of the female world, I shall dedicate my present history to their concerns, hinting at the same time, that it is not absolutely impossible, but that I may at some future period again treat the publick with some other delicacy, drawn from the ample stores I possess.

No sooner was the arrival of Mr. Dudley and his daughter at Stannadine announced, than our society immediately met, to determine on the propriety of visiting the strangers. This is a preliminary etiquette we have resolved never to omit in future, since by a neglect of circumspection, we had been betrayed into an intimacy with the last inhabitants of the mansion, whom we unfortunately discovered had amassed a fortune by keeping a slop-shop in Wapping.[1] The universal contempt with which we

---

1 A slop-shop was a store that sold "slop-clothing" or used clothing. Since clothing was tailored (made to order), used clothes were valuable but needed

treated them when we knew their mean origin, had indeed been the cause of driving them from the neighbourhood; but as we were all gentlewomen born, we could not easily overcome the secret mortification we had experienced.

We resolved therefore upon the present occasion to be very circumspect, and examined in full council all the intelligence which our respective Mollies and Betties[1] had been able to procure from Mr. Dudley's servants, who had arrived about a fortnight before to prepare for his reception. Little, I am sorry to say, could be discovered. He was just come from the West-Indies, and had hired most of his household in London, it was however guessed that he was rich, and his establishment was upon an expensive plan.

It was at length determined that we should depute two ladies of our body, in the character of inspectors, to inform us whether the Dudleys were *visitable* beings or not. Mrs. Medium the Vicar's lady, and Miss Cardamum the daughter of an eminent medical gentleman, were selected for the important trust. Their abilities were indisputable; as Mrs. Medium had been for many years an humble friend to a lady of quality, and Miss Cardamum constantly accompanied her papa every summer to Scarborough, it was impossible they could be imposed upon in the grand articles of fashionable appearance and intrinsick gentility.

It being necessary, not only to form a right notion of the Dudleys, but also to impress them with an high idea of *us*, we determined, though the walk was but half a mile, and the morning inviting, that Mr. Cardamum's carriage should be got ready for the occasion, and the foot-boy had orders to tye[2] on his visiting queue, brush his livery, and trim up old Bolus the favourite chair-horse. The reins also were blacked for the occasion, and all the ornaments of the buggy (I mean the capriole)[3] furbished to

---

to be refitted for subsequent owners. Wapping is a city on the north bank of the Thames in the borough of London. In the eighteenth century, it was an impoverished, filthy area, filled with maritime business, sailors, and many taverns.

1 Molly and Betty were common names or nicknames for domestic servants.
2 In the second edition, "tie."
3 Capriole or cabriolet. According to the *Oxford English Dictionary*, a "light

the brightness of silver. Miss Cardamum, dressed in an elegant new riding habit, was driver; and Mrs. Medium, in honour of the embassy, was attired in the rich brocade Lady Seraphina gave her on her nuptials, and to take off from the antiquity of its appearance, she put on a modern hat with three upright feathers. They stopped at my door, and kindly promised to give me the first intelligence of their return. The fair Belle gave the lash a smart twirl, and Bolus set off on a good round trot. Little Joe on Mr. Cardamum's poney, with his stick held perpendicular, (as was the fashion amongst the lacquies at Scarborough last season,) followed the carriage as fast as possible.

The result of the visit was communicated in the afternoon, but unhappily the ladies did not agree in their verdict. Miss Cardamum would not assent to Mrs. Medium's determination, that Miss Dudley was handsome and well dressed; and the fair spinster's opinion concerning the elegance of the furniture, and the excellence of the cakes and chocolate, was as warmly disputed by the experienced matron. The points in which they agreed did not tend to inspire us with any very high idea of the strangers. They determined Miss Dudley to be a *shy fearful thing*; Mr. Dudley, on the contrary, had a most intimidating look, which seemed to criticise every word, and to remark every action. A little incident was cited to confirm this observation. Over the chimney was the portrait of a lady, which, when Mrs. Medium admired, and observed how much it put her in mind of one in Lady Seraphina's saloon, Miss Dudley said with a sigh in a low voice, as if to prevent further enquiry,[1] that it was intended for her mother. She then stole a timid confused glance at her father, who withdrew to the window evidently discomposed. The conclusion which my friends drew from this was, that he had been a severe husband, and that his daughter would, if she durst, have reproached him for his unkindness. I ventured to hint that the fact admitted a contrary inference, but I was pressed so strongly with arguments

---

two-wheeled chaise drawn by one horse, having a large hood of wood or leather, and an ample apron to cover the lap and legs of the occupant." It was also used to mean the top or open section of a carriage.

1 In the second edition, "inquiry."

drawn from Mr. Dudley's stern manner, and from the restraint which the poor girl visibly suffered, that I was forced to give up my opinion.

After much discussion it was at last agreed, that though they promised to add but little to the pleasures of Danbury; yet as they certainly were gentlefolks, lived in style, and intended coming to our assembly, we might as well visit them. And we visited them accordingly.

CHAP. II.

The Author shews that she studies climax, or gradation of character.

As it is the duty of all authors to relieve their reader's curiosity as soon as is consistent with their plans, I shall dedicate this chapter to introductory anecdotes of the Dudley family, after having made a few preliminary observations.

The spirit of penetration or the ability to discover people's characters by a cursory glance, though arrogated by almost every body, is in reality possessed by very few. Nothing can be more intricate than the human heart, and the discriminating shades which serve to mark variation of character, are generally too minute and confused to write distinct traits upon the countenance. Even words and actions are often deceitful guides. People frequently step out of themselves. The man of sense has his weak moments, the woman of reflection on some occasions acts inconsiderately. Now though such deviations furnish very agreeable amusement to the censorious, the idle, and the malevolent; none but the thoughtless part of mankind will see these incidental defects in any other light than as a casual departure from the real character.

I confess it is my wish to hunt this said spirit of penetration out of the world, as I am convinced it is productive of many serious evils. It often teaches us to think highly of the unworthy, and meanly of the meritorious. It makes us arrogant and self-opinionated, or else exposes us to many difficulties in endeavouring to rectify the erroneous notions we have adopted. It assists the artifices of falsehood, increases the allurements of seduction, feathers the shafts of flattery, and casts an additional veil over the disguises of hypocrisy. It is one of the errors into which inexperience is most apt to fall, springing from the ingenuous confidence, sanguine passions, and prompt decision incident to young minds. Happy are they if they become less precipitate in their judgements, before[1] the consequences of their errors are fatal to their peace!

Neither Mrs. Medium nor Miss Cardamum had the apology of youth or inexperience to plead in excuse for the erroneous conclusions they had drawn. The ladies were arrived at years of maturity, and had been in the course of their lives at least one thousand times mistaken. But there are people who never will derive advantages from the past, who are happy in the art of self-excuse, and determined to think themselves always right, who place their own portion of human infirmity to their neighbour's account; and certainly, as they have so little to do in reforming errors at home, may be allowed to look abroad for employment.

To those who prefer skimming over the superficies to diving into the substance, strong features marked with masculine sense may wear the aspect of ill-humour, and severity; diffidence will appear like folly; and the reserve of polite prudence may be denominated pride. All common observers, though they love the utmost minuteness in a story, are fond of discussing abstract qualities in a compendious manner; and I have known an "Oh, Madam, it was so foolish," or "She is so ill-natured," or "Was not that extravagant," or "He is so proud," decidedly sink a character into supreme contempt, even in the short period while the speaker was dealing a hand at quadrille.[2] Indeed, exclusive of errors in point of dress or omissions of ceremonious forms, pride, ill-humour, folly, and extravagance seem to include all human vices; at least in the vocabulary of Danbury. One reason for this may be that pride and ill-humour wound our feelings, while the

---

1 In the first edition, "because".
2 Quadrille was a trick-taking card game for four players, popular in the eighteenth century.

folly and extravagance of our neighbours are implied compliments to our own good sense and discretion.

To return to the Dudleys—

Mr. Dudley possessed in an eminent degree the virtues of the head and the heart. Blessed with the early advantage of a liberal education, he united the character of the true Gentleman to the no less respectable name of the generous conscientious merchant. Having passed through many vicissitudes of life, he had learned how to form a temperate judgement, and by truly appreciating its pleasures and its pains, he knew how to reduce his desires to that moderate standard, which is most likely to produce content.

In the death of an amiable wife he had experienced a severer blow than all the former shocks of fortune could inflict. Two daughters were the offspring of an union, which, while it lasted, produced as much happiness as any sublunary connection could afford. Mrs. Alderson, the mother of Mrs. Dudley, took the youngest child immediately upon her daughter's death, with a declared intention of adopting her for her own, and making her heiress to all her fortune. Louisa, the elder, accompanied her father to Barbadoes, where he had a considerable estate, for the improvement of which he judged his presence absolutely necessary.

A mind like Mr. Dudley's, awakened to all the impressions of duty both to his Maker and his fellow-creatures, must be supposed to have possessed sufficient strength to overcome the extreme indulgence of hopeless grief. Though he found it impossible to forget that he once was most happy, he acquiesced with patient resignation in the limited enjoyments which his situation allowed, and stifling in his breast the feelings of widowed love, endeavoured to supply its place with the anxious tenderness of the paternal character. Louisa, who from her earliest years discovered a disposition to improve both in moral and mental excellence, listened with attention to her father's precepts, illustrated at times by the painful yet pleasing description of what her mother was. Instructions thus enforced by example, sunk with double weight into her retentive mind; and she early nursed the

laudable ambition of copying those amiable virtues, of which her
departed mother and living father exhibited such fine models.

As she was at the age of sixteen when she lost her mother, Mr.
Dudley's narratives were strengthened by her own recollection.
She had besides the advantage of having commenced her education under a female eye, and consequently of acquiring those soft
touches of refined elegance, which the most experienced male
instructor cannot communicate.

While Louisa thus rose into woman under her father's care,
in a climate in which the luxuriant bounty of Nature, and the
fierce contention of the elements, by producing frequent reverses
of fortune, alternately excite dissipation and demand fortitude;
Marianne experienced under her Grandmother, all the fond
indulgence of doating love. If ever the excesses of tenderness
are pardonable, they might be in Mrs. Alderson's circumstances.
She had lost an amiable and only daughter, enchanting as a
companion, and estimable as a friend; whose society afforded
her the greatest delight, whose conduct and character reflected
honour upon herself. It was natural to view the child which her
daughter had bequeathed her, with an affection rising to agonizing sensibility; to consider it as a pledge from an inhabitant
of another world, a relique snatched from the grave, a bond of
union between herself and the glorified spirit of its immortal
mother. Less firm than Mr. Dudley,[1] though not less attached
both to the living and the dead, she regarded her Marianne as
possessing a kind of hereditary claim to perfection, and almost
supposed that the necessity of culture was superseded by the
superior excellence of the parent plant.

The characters of the young ladies will be fully developed in
the ensuing pages, but unwilling to omit any thing which custom
has rendered necessary to writers of my class, I will say something of their personal attractions.

Louisa's figure was tall and elegant, her eyes expressed intelligence and ingenuous modesty. Her features were more agreeable
than beautiful, and her manner, though in general rather placidly
reserved than obtrusive or sparkling, was frequently animated by

---

1 In the first edition, "Mrs. Dudley"—likely an error.

the lively graces of youth. Yet even in those gayer moments her mirth indicated an informed, well-regulated mind. Though her education had extended to particulars not usually attended to by females, there was nothing in her conversation to excite the apprehensions which gentlemen are apt to entertain of learned ladies. Science in her might be compared to a light placed behind a veil of gauze, which, without being itself apparent, sheds a softened radiance over each surrounding object.

To all who admire beauty in its softest and most feminine dress, Marianne Dudley must have appeared uncommonly attractive. Her features were formed with delicate symmetry, her blue eyes swam in sensibility, and the beautiful transparency of her complexion seemed designed to convey to the admiring beholder every varying sentiment of her mind. Her looks expressed what indeed she was, tremblingly alive to all the softer passions. Though the gentle timidity of her temper had preserved her from the usual effects of early indulgence, it rendered her peculiarly unfit to encounter even those common calamities humanity must endure. Her natural good health had hitherto preserved her from bodily sufferings; and Mrs. Alderson had never permitted her to know a sorrow which could either be alleviated or removed.

A little time previous to the return of her father and sister from the West-Indies, her Grandmother's death rendered her possessed of a fortune of fifty thousand pounds, of which, though only nineteen, it was that Lady's dying request she should be the uncontrolled mistress. Thus blessed with youth, health, beauty, and affluence, what was wanting to render her felicity compleat?[1] I doubt not but the younger part of my readers are inclined to think that I shall describe her as *too* happy.

Mr. Dudley, though he had consented from unexceptionable motives to the separation of his children, ever lamented the circumstance as likely to check the expansion of the filial and sisterly affections. About the time of Mrs. Alderson's last illness, discouraged by the terrible devastations of a hurricane, he abandoned the schemes of improvement he had projected upon his

---

1 In the second edition, "complete."

estates, and returning with Louisa into England, offered himself to Marianne as her natural guardian and protector. That young lady's heart was too full of sensibility not to be affected by the manly tenderness of a father, and the affectionate endearments of a sister, from whom she had been so long separated. She readily accepted their invitation to reside with them, and it was with a view to her proper accommodation that Mr. Dudley engaged the spacious mansion at which in my preceding chapter I announced his arrival. Miss Marianne was not present when my sagacious neighbours decided upon the characters of the Dudleys, having determined to spend a few weeks with an intimate friend, previous to her design of fixing her abode under the paternal roof.

CHAP. III.

A fine instance of modern susceptibility introduces a delicate discussion, which is left to some brighter genius to determine.

From this excursive view of characters above the general level, I return with the delight of a bird flying to her nest, to common life, and the dear society in which I spend my hours.

I suppose it was from perceiving even the *voluble spirit* of female conversation droop when unsupported by the presence of gentlemen, that the ancient mythologists constantly grouped Cupid with the Graces, and introduced Apollo into the circle of the Muses. Though the comparison will not perhaps apply in all parts, we ladies of Danbury had our conversations enlivened by the presence of a Cupid and an Apollo too, in the persons of Captain Target, a militia officer, first cousin to a Baronet,[1] a gentleman of unquestionable honour; and of Mr. Alsop, the heir

---

1 A baronet holds a hereditary title and is called "Sir So-and-So," as is the lower-status knight. A knight's title, however, is not inherited but given as an accolade. Baronets, despite their hereditary titles, did not sit in the House of Lords. The higher-ranked peerage consisted (in rising order of importance) of barons, viscounts, earls, marquises, and dukes. West's description is certainly meant to define Captain Target negatively—as a man publicly claiming a distant heritage to someone on the lowest rung of the nobility.

of an eminent Attorney, who having amassed a considerable fortune by business, educated his son in what he esteemed the distinguishing mark of a gentleman, *Idleness*.

Against these Beaux the fair Cardamum planted all the artillery of love. She long ago, on examining her own heart upon the grand question, had determined marriage to be essential to her happiness; but on advancing to the next point in debate, who should be the man, she found herself totally unable to decide, and her heart wandered from one to the other as local circumstances directed. Every one knows that the parish church in the country answers the end of places of publick resort in London, by giving fashionable people opportunities of sporting a whim, making critical observations, or attracting the attention of the other sex. I have often seen my fair friend's eyes, even in the most pathetick parts of Mr. Medium's discourse, wander from the Captain's hat, when decorated with the military plume, to Mr. Alsop's servants in their new liveries, and pitied the perplexities which agitated her gentle bosom. If family, martial address, knowledge of the world, and an infinitude of small talk, recommended the accomplished Target; no less did the charms of youth, wealth, and great docility of temper plead in favour of the rich Alsop. Without pretending to that penetration I decried in a former chapter, it was easy to discover the present state of her heart; as it was an invariable rule to speak of the favourite of the week in terms of studied contempt or marked censure. While her affections rebounded from one gentleman to the other, I was easy; but when for several days together she talked of the conceited foppish airs Target gave himself, or of the poorest of all poor creatures, Alsop, I trembled for her peace of mind.

The rivals continued to live together in terms of perfect intimacy. I must suppose they were ignorant of the storms they excited in the breast of beauty; for had they known the state of the lady's heart, could modern friendship have been proof to the temptation of securing so invaluable a prize? I am confirmed in my opinion by reflecting, that extreme humility and superabundant diffidence are the unhappy failings of the present race of young men. They think too meanly of themselves and too exaltedly of us, to dare to aspire to the possession of the excellence they at distance adore; and though condescending sweetness and easy access are no less the characteristick of the present race of beauties, their worshippers are so apt to consider them as inexorable divinities rather than as placable mortals, that hopeless of success they retire from their altars in the dumb silence of despair.

But I will consider the case in another point of view, and propose a question which I hope some sister novelist will discuss, as it is an extremely delicate point of honour, and will bear amplifying through at least fifty pages. Supposing the gentlemen actually perceived the state of the lady's heart, could they consistently with friendship and generosity make any efforts to secure it entirely to themselves? Was it not infinitely more congenial to those refined principles and delicate distinctions, invented by several French writers, and adopted by our own, to leave her entirely to herself, and neither to do any thing transcendently praise-worthy, or to say any thing eminently clever, to influence her decision? I cannot determine this point, but will proceed in the narrative way to state, that certainly neither of them was guilty of the crime of endeavouring to detain the angel which thus hovered between them.

It would have been a solecism in good breeding, if Captain Target and Mr. Alsop had omitted to pay their devoirs to the Dudley family. The Captain only waited to know whether the cellars were well stocked, and the table hospitably supplied, to propose to his friend a morning walk to Stannadine. Mr. Alsop readily acquiesced in the proposal, though from different motives. Happy as he was in many respects, he was tormented by the attacks of a cruel invincible enemy, who, in spite of all his efforts, haunted all his waking hours. This enemy was Time. Such is the strange intricacy of human affairs. It was originally bestowed by Providence as an estimable blessing, an improveable talent, the source of present enjoyment and future felicity.

Full of the heroick design of killing this monster, my heroes sallied forth, and were received by Mr. Dudley with politeness and attention. Captain Target readily fell into conversation; they talked of the West-Indies, its important commercial advantages, and natural beauties; the military gentleman enlivening the discourse with anecdotes of several gallant officers, with whom he became acquainted during the summer encampments. Mr. Alsop was silent, contemplating the form of Mr. Dudley's buckles, and wondering if they were more fashionable than his own.

As it was the merchant's custom to banish as much as possible the little rules which etiquette unnecessarily prescribes, the strangers, though it was a first visit, consented to stay dinner, and Mr. Dudley, to employ part of the morning, led them the tour of his pleasure grounds, pointing out some little improvements he proposed to make. To these Captain Target assented with warm approbation, while the modest Alsop, though he equally understood and admired Mr. Dudley's taste, contented himself with the harmless epithets of "vastly pretty, vastly clever indeed."

From the shrubbery they returned to the drawing-room, where Miss Dudley received them with the smile of welcome and the blush of delicacy. Captain Target poured forth a volley of compliments, but could he have attended to any thing but the sound of his own voice, he might have perceived that the lady to whom they were addressed, knew how to estimate her own worth too well, to be elevated by casual attentions or superficial praise. Mr. Alsop not being so fluent in his expressions, contented himself with silent admiration, never once withdrawing his eyes from Miss Dudley, till the servant summoned them to the dining-room.

If Captain Target had been moderate in his approbation before, the present scene would have thrown him into ecstasies. Every thing was excellent; he eat voraciously, met with all his favourite dishes, with wine peculiarly adapted to his taste, and at the conclusion of his visit he entreated Mr. Dudley to allow him the honour of considering him in the light of an intimate. Mr. Alsop's bow urged the same request, to which Mr. Dudley politely assented.

On their return home, Mr. Alsop, who had pondered upon the events of the day, without being able to shape the chaos of his own mind into any determined form, resolved to sound his friend's *real* opinion, that they might at least have the happiness of agreeing in the same story. A prudent scheme, and the more necessary, as the absence or presence of the applauded persons frequently produced a wide difference in the Captain's sentiments. Finding him however sincere upon the present occasion, he commenced a warm admirer of the family at Stannadine, and heroically resolving to defend the cause of injured merit, called upon Miss Cardamum the next morning with the express design of telling her that he really thought Mr. Dudley a very good sort of man, and his daughter a pretty agreeable young lady; adding as a clencher, that Captain Target said so too.

Whoever considers how rude it is to dispute any opinion which a lady has advanced, or how highly affronting it is to commend the features of another in the presence of a sister belle, may form a faint idea of Miss Cardamum's resentment, heightened by the painful sentiments which love and jealousy excited. She darted on Mr. Alsop a look of fiery indignation, which on recollection she turned into the smile of sarcastical contempt, complimenting him upon his *superior* share of discernment. Then turning to some ladies who were present, she expatiated upon the merits of young Mr. Inkle the new draper,[1] declared he was not only well bred, but handsome, and so respectfully civil in his deportment, that she should not at all wonder at his marrying a woman of superior education and large fortune. Amongst Mr. Inkle's merits, his never contradicting any body was pointed out with such marked encomiums, that poor Mr. Alsop, though not very acute in his feelings, could not but observe how highly he had offended; and feeling his courage unequal to the task of endeavouring to mitigate her resentment, confusedly withdrew. As he was not at the card assembly that evening, I presume he spent it alone in all the agonies of distress.

Happily our sex is of too gentle a nature to suffer our resentments to be as lasting as they are violent. Miss Cardamum met both gentlemen in her walk next morning, and curtsied[2] with her usual affability: nay, her kind consideration led her still further,

---

1 A draper is a manufacturer of woolen cloth.

2 In the second edition, "courtesied."

for anxious to prevent any ill consequences arising from her late encomium on Mr. Inkle, she took care to tell her companion Miss Dorothea Medium, loud enough for the gentlemen to hear, that though the man was very well in his shop, and behaved civil to his customers, it would be very wrong to treat him in the same manner as one would genteel people; for tradesfolks were very apt to give themselves airs, if genteel people took notice of them.

CHAP. IV.

Containing what may be termed a literary curiosity, being an extract from the journal of an old maid.

Before the character of the elder part of the Dudley family could be decided upon in a satisfactory manner, a new star arose in the horizon. I almost doubt whether the first appearance of Helen at the Court of Priam excited more wonder and surprise amongst the Trojan ladies,[1] than did the lovely Marianne Dudley, when in the full blaze of natural charms, aided by all the graceful appendages which tasteful art could bestow,—she burst upon us at our monthly assembly in full splendor. So incontestable was *her* claim to the praise of beauty, that even the invidious were hurried into applause. Miss Cardamum was the first who recovered from the general consternation. She ventured to observe that though her features were very regular, she thought they were rather deficient in expression. Mrs. Medium pursued the hint, and lamented the want of a certain dignity of manner and look, of which Lady Seraphina was immensely fond, adding, "Now there's my Dorothea, though a plain girl, (hold up your head my dear,) she has more of that turn of countenance which her poor dear Ladyship so much admired."

The incertitude of publick opinion has been exemplified by histories of degraded heroes and persecuted patriots. I choose

---

1 Helen, a figure from Greek mythology, was a beautiful woman whose abduction by Paris (son of Priam, the King of Troy) was said to have prompted the Trojan War.

to illustrate it by an instance from common life. As it was very natural for enquiry to be busy about an object that so strongly arrested attention, we soon discovered Marianne's independent fortune. Rumour on this occasion acted in her usual way, increasing it to at least one hundred thousand pounds; for the many-tongued goddess always enlarges the possessions of the wealthy, in the same proportion as she diminishes the resources of the unfortunate.

We were likewise told that Mr. Dudley and Louisa were almost dependent upon Marianne, who, like most favourites of fortune, was capricious, vain, and haughty; and returned their kind solicitude to please with whimsical indifference. No sooner did we know that the former objects of our dislike were less happy than we supposed, than all their good qualities burst in a flood upon us, and we alternately pitied and admired the modest, the sensible, and affable Louisa.

These tender sentiments were confirmed by fresh news from Stannadine. John the errand-man, had told Betty at the Post Office, that a fine gentleman was expected as a suitor to the younger Miss. Every lady in Danbury was now out of patience that such a little chitty face should be preferred to her elder sister: it furnished several pathetic dissertations on the bad taste and mercenary temper of men, and brought back to the remembrance of our society the golden days of youth, when female merit, unless obstinately bent on a single state, was sure of procuring the regard of the other sex. Mrs. Eleanor Singleton and myself enlarged upon the difficulty we had to avoid being actually worried into matrimony, in spite of our avowed declarations to the contrary.

I have often lamented the situation of many good ladies, who like myself may be said almost to subsist upon news, and are often forced to devour very unwholesome aliment. The events which *really* happen in a small neighbourhood, are not sufficient to furnish the supplies conversation eternally requires, without the aid of fiction. I have often, though encumbered with my umbrella and pattens,[1] carried a piece of intelligence round the town

---

1 Pattens are overshoes that are used to raise the foot above muddy ground.

in the morning, which in the evening I was again forced to step out and contradict. An extract from my weekly journal will prove this observation.

MONDAY.

Mr. Pelham is come to Stannadine—They will soon be married, for the mantua-maker[1] went over this morning, doubtless to receive orders about wedding-clothes. Memorandum. Miss Cardamum says they will have the clothes from a London warehouse, and that the groom went to town yesterday about them.

TUESDAY.

Not quite certain which of the ladies Mr. Pelham addresses. He was seen walking this morning with Miss Dudley.

WEDNESDAY.

Miss Marianne has positively refused him—She may be a long time before she has another offer.

THURSDAY.

It is very odd, if he is refused, that he still stays at Stannadine. Perhaps he intends to offer himself to Louisa.

FRIDAY.

We have all been mistaken. The Housekeeper told my butcher when he went there for orders, that Mr. Pelham is not come as a lover, but only as an old friend of the family.

Finally, after Mr. Pelham's person and character had run through all the changes of handsome and ugly, young and old, rich and poor, amiable and disagreeable, we sent him back to his own habitation on Saturday. Now though we could not discover the mystery, there really was something in Mr. Pelham's visit.

Ever since Marianne's arrival at her father's, Miss Dudley perceived an unusual gravity in her air and manner; and with true sisterly affection as well as delicacy, endeavoured to encourage her to reveal the cause by a soothing tenderness of behaviour, rather than by a prying curiosity, which indeed never deserves, and seldom possesses confidence. The timid Marianne at length

---

1 A mantua-maker is a dressmaker.

ventured to unbosom herself to her sister, by owning that during her visit at Lady Milton's, she had received declarations of love from Mr. Pelham, her Ladyship's nephew, a gentleman of handsome fortune and unblemished character.

Louisa congratulated her upon so respectable a conquest, and expressed the transport she would feel at seeing her placed under the protection of a worthy husband; but added, that probably she was not yet able to judge, whether Mr. Pelham really possessed the requisites that were essential to her ideas of happiness.

Marianne's uncertainty upon this subject did not arise from any doubt she entertained respecting the gentleman's merits, or the possibility of her approving him. She was fearful lest Miss Milton's affections should have been engaged by her cousin, in which case she would die a thousand deaths before she would be the cause of blasting the tender blossom of her Eliza's latent love. She had not indeed any grounds for this suspicion, but the friendship which subsisted between the ladies was of a romantick kind, and consequently was too refined in its hopes and fears to be adapted to ordinary capacities.[1]

Louisa was not casuist enough to determine the intricate question, whether Marianne ought to reject Mr. Pelham, on the possibility that Miss Milton might be in love with him. Knowing no other rules of action than the plain laws of equity and honour, how could she decide on a point, which I may say was finely obscured by surrounding difficulties? Had she pleaded for Mr. Pelham, Marianne had a variety of instances of high heroick virtue to produce, not drawn indeed from actual observation of life, but from her favourite studies. She had long been an attentive reader of memoirs and adventures, and had transplanted into her gentle bosom all the soft feelings and highly refined

---

1 Romantic friendship is said to have been commonplace among women in the eighteenth century and may have involved declarations of love and passion and deep emotional and perhaps even physical intimacy. It was not, however, understood by the culture as sexual, transgressive, or threatening. In fact, there is evidence that it was understood as a culturally acceptable precursor to heterosexual marriage. See Lillian Faderman's *Surpassing the Love of Men: Romantic Friendship and Love Between Women from the Renaissance to the Present* (1981).

sensibilities of the respective heroines.[1]

After several days of cruel perplexity, in which she at length resolved to sacrifice love (for she doubted not her own regard for Mr. Pelham) upon the altar of friendship; a servant arrived with a packet from Lady Milton. The first letter addressed to Mr. Dudley I shall transcribe.

'SIR,

'Though many years have intervened, since your departure from England terminated an acquaintance from which I received the sincerest pleasure, I do not doubt your recognising the writing of an old friend with joy. The warm esteem which your excellent wife ever expressed for me and my late sister Pelham, and the happy hours we passed together in early life, induces me to urge my present request with an air of confidence. The many excellencies of your younger daughter have made a deep impression upon my nephew's heart; I flatter myself, Sir, that upon enquiry you will find both his morals and fortune unexceptionable. Should he be so fortunate as to obtain the approbation of the young lady and yourself, I cannot express the transport I shall feel at receiving the child of my most valued friend into my family. My daughter, who loves her Marianne with more than a sister's fondness, is in raptures at discovering her cousin's attachment, and laments bitterly that a disorder in her eyes prevents her from addressing her dear correspondent upon the subject. Mr. Pelham writes by the same conveyance. Allow me, Sir, to hope that his proposals will be as agreeable to you, as the sweet object of his affections is to us, and that you will fix an early day for the visit he requests permission to make. With respectful compliments to yourself and Miss Dudley, with whom I hope soon to renew a personal acquaintance, and kindest love to my dear niece elect, (pardon the freedom of that expression,) I remain,

'Dear Sir,

'Yours affectionately,
'E. MILTON.'

---

1 The "female Quixote" (that is, the woman who mistakenly believed things she read in works of fiction provided sound ways to interpret reality) was a popular character in the 18th century. See, for instance, Charlotte Lennox's *The Female Quixote* (1752). Marianne is here revealed to be quixotic.

CHAP. V.

Female irresolution may proceed from too much as well as from too little refinement.

A mind disposed to enjoy all the agreeable circumstances this world affords, would have considered the letter with which I concluded my last chapter as a pleasant event, at least as an indisputable proof that the Miltons actually desired the proposed alliance. But Marianne Dudley was too refined to be thus easily satisfied. She doubted not that her Ladyship stated, as far as she knew, the real cause of Eliza's distressing silence, but could delicacy, while labouring under the pangs of hopeless love, do otherwise than endeavour to conceal its tortures, under the assumed air of indisposition? No, it was too evident; Eliza was certainly in love.

Such were the reflexions which agitated her bosom, when her father with a smiling air delivered the letter for her perusal. Louisa had informed him on his consulting her about their contents, that she believed her sister was not indifferent to Mr. Pelham's merits; how then could he account for the strong distress visible in Marianne's countenance: she however, recollecting that her sorrows were of too delicate a nature for her father to understand, thought it right, if possible, to keep them from his observation, and hurried out of the room just in time to conceal a flood of tears.

Mr. Dudley turned to Louisa to explain this extraordinary circumstance, who perhaps thinking her sister a little whimsical, disguised her knowledge of the real cause, and pleaded the perplexing terrors an ingenuous and reflecting mind must feel at the idea of intrusting its happiness to a stranger's care. She took an opportunity of following Marianne to her dressing-room as soon as she could, and found her just recovered from a profound reverie. A happy and heroical thought had occurred. By receiving Mr. Pelham's addresses she would be enabled to judge of the state of Miss Milton's heart; and if by her pining despair her latent love was confirmed, generous friendship might at any time renounce its own happiness, and even at the altar resign the expectant bridegroom, who, if unwilling to accept the substituted charmer, would be *no* hero.

She communicated this plan to Louisa, who, happy that a treaty so agreeable to her father might at any rate commence, informed him immediately of her sister's acquiescence. A letter of invitation was in consequence dispatched, and the happy lover soon appeared at Stannadine.

If an open, ingenuous countenance, manly sense, and easy accommodating manners may allowably inspire the beholders with a sort of intuitive esteem; Mr. Pelham, who possessed all these advantages, had a claim to the warm affection with which Mr. and Miss Dudley received him. They felicitated each other on the agreeable prospect which the proposed acquaintance offered; and forgetting that the tie of relationship was not yet confirmed, received him with all the kindness of a brother and son. He brought Marianne a letter from Miss Milton, dictated with such apparent ease and heartfelt satisfaction, that even her fertile imagination could scarcely start any fresh doubts on that head.

Yet she was not happy. She now began to be apprehensive that Mr. Pelham was not the kind of character with whom she could enjoy that perfect and uninterrupted felicity which she was certain the union of two kindred minds afforded. In the first place, he seemed much more gay and lively than was consistent with the painful suspence in which courtship ought to keep the lover's heart. His manner was unembarrassed, which was wrong; he was comfortable in her absence; her presence indeed seemed to give him satisfaction, but not of the transporting kind she expected. He maintained his own opinions in conversation, and though he treated her with respect, yet not with deference. In his addresses as a lover, he fell far short of that kneeling ecstatick[1] tenderness, that restless solicitude, that profound veneration, in

---

[1] In the second edition, "ecstatic."

short, those thousand nameless refinements, which some call absurdities and some delicacies, but by which men, who really love, aspire to gain the woman of their heart. Consequently might she not fear that his attachment was not of a kind to render their future lives a state of paradisiacal bliss?

If my readers suppose that the lady's fastidiousness arose from vanity, arrogance, or spleen, they mistake the character I mean to delineate. It was long ago observed that the virtues lie between two opposite vices; thus is all our attention awakened to keep the strait path of rectitude, as the least deviation leads us into one of the extremes. From over-strained humility, from gentleness which had encreased to timidity, and from sensibility indulged till it became a weakness, from these causes I say, and from a wrong estimate of life, the errors and sorrows of Marianne Dudley are to be derived.

In her character I wish to exhibit the portrait of an amiable and ingenuous mind, solicitous to excel, and desirous to be happy, but destitute of natural vigour or acquired stability; forming to itself a romantick standard, to which nothing human ever attained; perplexed by imaginary difficulties; sinking under fancied evils; destroying its own peace by the very means which it takes to secure it; and acting with a degree of folly beneath the common level, through its desire of aspiring above the usual limits of female excellence.

Lest an objection should be started, that the exhibition of such a character may be of disservice to the general cause of morality, I shall urge my reasons for maintaining a contrary opinion. I have looked on life with deep attention, and foresee no evils likely to ensue from impressing upon the minds of youth, as soon and as deeply as possible, just notions of the journey they are about to take, and just opinions of their fellow-travellers. I am persuaded that the imaginary duties which the extreme of modern refinement prescribes, are never practised but at the expence of those solid virtues, whose superior excellence has stood the test of ages. I conceive that the rules prescribed to us as social and accountable beings, are fully sufficient to exercise all our industry while in this transitory state. I wish to ask the fair enthusiasts who indulge in all the extravagance of heroick generosity, romantick love, and exuberant friendship, whether they really suppose it possible to improve upon the model which Christianity (our best comfort in this world and sure guide to the next) presents for our imitation. If not, I would tell them, that simple but inestimable code presents no puzzling question to tear the divided heart by contrary duties. It speaks of life as a mutable scene, and it admonishes us to enjoy its blessings with moderation, and to endure its evils with patience. It tells us that man is as variable as the world he inhabits, that imperfections mingle with the virtues of the best; and by the fine idea of a state of warfare, urges us to constant circumspection and unwearied attention. From this mixture of good and evil it directs our pursuit after the former, by teaching us to *curb* our passions, and to *moderate* our desires; to expect with diffidence, enjoy with gratitude, and resign with submission. It commands us, conscious of our own failings, to be indulgent to the errors of others. Upon the basis of mutual wants, general imperfection, and universal kindred, it builds the fair structure of candour and benevolence.

And do these writers, whose works generally fall into the hands of the younger part of the softer sex, *indeed* suppose that they serve the interests of this divine institution, when they excite the dangerous excess of the passions, by representing the violence of love, grief, despair, and jealousy, not only as amiable frailties, but as commendable qualities? Ought suicide ever to be introduced by a Christian author, but as a brand of infamy to mark characters peculiarly detestable? Should the love of a man to a married woman ever be softened into an innocent attachment, or described as a tender weakness which he *cannot* conquer, consequently rather as the error of nature and necessity, than of choice? Why is the young mind led to form hopes which cannot be realized, and thus, by barbing the shafts of disappointment, to add to the already ample stock of human calamities? In youth we start upon a race, in which the difficulties of the way generally increase as we draw nearer to the goal; and instead of strengthening the resolution, and bracing up the soul for the contest, modern writers generally teach us to shrink at the first shock of evil; to melt in tender softness at woes of our own creating, and thus to turn with disgust from life before the sun of our existence has advanced to its meridian.

These romantick notions indeed generally leave us on our journey; but what is the consequence? Repeated disappointments sour the temper, we grow querulous complainers, disagreeable to others and burthensome to ourselves; and at last, not unfrequently do we arraign the wisdom of Providence for not having rendered this world a perfect, instead of a probationary state; for not having given us the felicity it never promised, or for having implanted in us desires which we ought to subdue, since our Creator meant them rather as trials of fortitude than as sources of gratification.

CHAP. VI.

The Author endeavours to get rid of the serious humour which contaminated the last chapter.

To those who have had the courage to follow me through the serious conclusion of the last chapter, no apologies for its contents will I hope be necessary; and I am certain all my well-bred readers will exercise their usual privilege of skipping over the uninteresting page. For their sakes, therefore, I shall immediately resume the narrative, premising, to conciliate their regard, that though I live in retirement, I know too much of the manners of the world, ever to expect even momentary attention to a moral reproof, when it attacks a reigning foible. And indeed, since youth and affluence generally protect their possessors from many real calamities, and as a certain portion of sorrow seems necessary in the composition of human affairs; it would perhaps be cruel to persuade the gay world to forget the many *pretty little* subjects of complaint, and all the agreeable vicissitudes which the fairy regions of *imaginary* distress amply supply.

In returning to my history I shall illustrate this position. Can the calm satisfaction a young woman, who thinks and acts in a common way, would receive from the addresses of such a lover as Mr. Pelham, be half so enchanting as the sweet perturbations, the delightful emotions, which a superior turn of sentiment excited in Marianne's breast? Now elevated by the hope that he would refine into an Orondates,[1] now agonized by the idea that he had nothing of true sensibility in his composition. From her early childhood she had maintained a voluminous correspondence with Miss Milton; but on the present occasion she was deprived of all the consolation which pouring out her soul to her Eliza would have afforded, by that young lady's warm esteem for her cousin. Miss Dudley's sincere affection and acknowledged prudence pointed her out as a proper confidante, but unfortunately she wanted the grand requisite, for Louisa had so little sentiment, that she was more inclined to laugh at her sister's apprehensions, *than to pour balm into the wound*. Marianne was therefore compelled to confine her sorrows almost wholly to her own bosom.

On the contrary, Mr. Pelham was so thoroughly satisfied with his reception that he impatiently wished for an alliance with a family truly estimable in all its branches. The romantick turn of his fair mistress did not indeed escape his penetration, and he once dared to rally her upon the subject; but perceiving it only encreased the seriousness of her features, he carefully avoided again introducing it. He had delicacy enough to be tender of the failings of the woman whom he loved, and enough of love to be convinced, that the sweetness of her temper and the goodness of her heart would conquer the little errors which a romantick propensity had engrafted upon her inexperienced mind; at least would prevent them from ever giving pain to an affectionate husband. He hoped a little commerce with the world, to which

---

1 Oroondates was the romantic hero of Madeleine de Scudéry's *Artamene, ou Le Grand Cyrus* (1649-53). At two million words, it is one of the longest novels ever written. Popular in the seventeenth and early eighteenth centuries, by the late eighteenth century the novel was seen as something akin to today's soap operas, and its emotionally sensitive, overwrought, and lovelorn warrior-adventurers had become, for most, a source of ridicule. Marianne here demonstrates her foolishness by believing that perhaps Mr. Pelham may grow into that kind of a lover.

she was almost a stranger, would divert her thoughts from their present train, and he anticipated the agreeable prospect of her laughing in a few years at her former enthusiasm.

Soon after he left Stannadine he was invited to Milton-Hall,[1] to join in the festivities which were intended to welcome the return of her Ladyship's only son from the Indies; where he had resided several years in a military station, and amassed a fortune sufficient to restore that ancient family to the respectability it formerly possessed. At this happy meeting, Mr. Pelham's agreeable prospects were discussed amongst other family topicks. He spoke of the merits of Mr. and Miss Dudley in such warm terms of recommendation, that Sir William Milton's impatience to be introduced to these estimable characters, could not confine its desire of gratification till after his cousin's nuptials. The privileges allowed to an accepted lover, seemed to justify a request to accompany him on his next visit to the Dudleys, and Mr. Pelham, not a little proud of his Marianne's attractions, had no objection to introduce her to his friend.

Nature indeed had been far less liberal to Sir William than to the other gentleman. To judge by his countenance, a gloomy suspicious soul seemed to lour[2] from under his dark bent eye-brows, and the air of conscious hauteur, which accompanied all his actions, rendered even his condescensions painful and mortifying. He had been too long accustomed to the servile adulation of the east, to recollect that freeborn Britons are seldom inclined to admit the claims of wealth and arrogance, if men possess no superior title to respect and esteem. So striking was his appearance, that even the candid Louisa told her sister, that, if Mr. Pelham's countenance had been as unpleasing, she would have considered her apprehensions of future unhappiness to have been rational.[3]

But though Miss Dudley drew these unfavourable conclusions from Sir William's manner, he saw in her's an enchanting grace which enforced his approbation. Never did easy sweetness

---

1 In the second edition, "Milton Hall".

2 Lour meant a gloomy look, such as a frown or a scowl.

3 Many in the eighteenth century believed that personality could be read by observing countenance or demeanor.

of temper, modest sense, polished affability, and strict propriety of expression and behaviour, appear more amiable than in the worthy Louisa. These were the qualities which he most desired in a companion for life, and conceiving the proposals he had it in his power to make too ample to admit of hesitation, he soon requested a private conference with Mr. Dudley, and asked his permission to address his elder daughter.

The fond father would have rejoiced, if the man who aspired to the justly esteemed darling of his heart had been more apparently amiable. He answered with hesitation. His daughter's choice was free, and he should limit his interference to the character of an adviser; but he added, the liberality of Sir William's proposals required at least frankness on his part. It might be expected from his style of living, that Louisa's fortune would prove adequate to the expectations Sir William Milton might justly pretend to. It was unhappily the reverse. Indeed on declining the mercantile business, he imagined he had secured an handsome income, but the destruction of that part of Barbadoes in which his estate lay, together with the doubtful credit of a great mercantile house, in whose concerns he had from motives of private friendship rashly embarked all his personal property, rendered his daughter's fortune at best but problematical; and he feared he could rate her value at little more than a mind, which would not be destitute of comforts, even in depressed circumstances.

Sir William was more gratified than disappointed at this discovery. The idea of laying a wife under an obligation was rather flattering to his pride; and since his own fortune was too large to confine his views in plans of expenditure, he was desirous of marrying a woman who having no claim of her own to affluence, might enjoy the wealth to which he gave her a title, with exultation and gratitude. He told Mr. Dudley, that thanks to fortune and his own exertions, he had no reason to consider pecuniary conveniences. Miss Dudley was the woman he should prefer to all others, and he even wished her to bring him nothing more than her merit and her affections.

There was such an air of generosity in the above declaration, that Mr. Dudley condemned himself for having yielded to erroneous and uncharitable prepossessions. He promised to introduce him to his daughter, as an admirer whose pretensions met his approbation; and then retired to consider of the most likely means to render his mediation successful. He recollected that when they discussed the characters of their visitants the preceding evening, Louisa had spoken of Sir William in terms of such strong disapprobation, and drawn a parallel between him and Mr. Pelham so manifestly to Sir William's disadvantage, that Mr. Dudley thought proper gently to check her warmth, as rather indicative of the rashness of a precipitate conclusion, than of the dispassionate, candid judgment he wished her to form. She yielded with placid submission to his reproofs, and allowed the force of the extenuating circumstances he urged in Sir William's behalf; but, reflecting upon the circumstance, Mr. Dudley thought he perceived her acquiescence had rather proceeded from deference than from conviction.

CHAP. VII.

Extremely dull.

Mr. Dudley hastened to Louisa's apartment, impatient to discuss the important subject which occupied his attention. He intended to state with emphasis and precision the reasons which induced him to accede to Sir William's offers, and to exert his own influence over Louisa's mind to ensure their success; but ere he had proceeded far, the young lady's apprehensions took the alarm. She sunk upon her knees, and clasping her father's hands, with eyes swimming in tears, and looks full of anxiety and consternation, exclaimed, "My dearest Sir, do not marry me to Sir William Milton."

To give pain to that bosom which had been the faithful repository of his secrets and sorrows; to afflict the dutiful and amiable child, to whose love and sympathy he had ever fled as a refuge from injury, and a cure for disappointment; was more than Mr. Dudley's resolution could support. He tenderly raised her, assured her of his unremitting tenderness; and hurried out of the room to give vent to the expression of that concern his swelling heart could scarcely retain.

When alone, and removed from the influence of her powerful tears, he recollected that till she was in possession of the whole argument, her decision could not be just. The sentiments respecting filial confidence which she had always entertained, the known propriety of her conduct, and the calm command she had ever possessed over her affections, left him no room to suppose that her dislike to Sir William proceeded from the addresses of a preferred, though unacknowledged lover. He at least determined to make another attempt, and fearing again to expose his resolution to the influence of her soft distress, had recourse to his pen, and wrote the following letter:

'TO MISS DUDLEY.

'However lively my dear child's reluctance to read this address may be, it cannot exceed what I feel, while by writing it I discharge a certain, though painful duty. Let a similar inducement urge you, my Louisa, to weigh my arguments with attention. When you have done this, with all the temper and consideration of which you are mistress, I give you my word that your answer shall be decisive. The subject in discussion shall never more be revived, if you persist in your refusal.

'Have I too highly rated your confidence in me, by supposing that you are actually free from the impulse of a prior attachment, and consequently at liberty to govern your heart by the dictates of your judgment? If, my love, from exuberant delicacy or extreme timidity, you have concealed from me a secret of such importance, this is the moment of discovery. To urge you in favour of Sir William, while you feel a preference for another, would at once be cruel and unjust. Fear no upbraidings from a father: my arms are open to embrace you, my heart confirms your pardon, and my best advice and assistance are ready any way in which you shall require their exertion; but till you assure me to the contrary, I will suppose you absolutely disengaged.[1]

---

1 By "absolutely disengaged" Mr. Dudley means that he believes Louisa's heart is not predisposed ("engaged," meaning attached) to another suitor.

'Did all men see you with my partial eyes, I should have a proposal to announce, at least as unexceptionable as that which awaits the acceptance of your happy sister. I do not scruple to own that neither the person or manners of Sir William Milton are conciliating. His virtues appear to be of the stern rather than of the amiable cast, and I should conceive, that like our first King Charles, he would soil the gloss of generosity by an ungracious method of bestowing favours.[1] But when the heart is right, candour will excuse the rest. Were you less happy in the prudent gentleness of your own temper, I would not recommend an union with one who will probably claim indulgence. I depend upon the influence of your sweetness, to soften his asperity, or at least to enable you to support its effects with patience and chearfulness. You have too much good sense to expect perfection either in character or situation, and though an accommodating temper is essential to happiness in most marriages, I think my Louisa might be happy if her husband possessed it but in an inferior degree.

'I build my hopes on the just sense he has of your merits. He generously supposes them an ample equivalent for all the advantages wealth can bestow. How flattering is this opinion to a doating father! How satisfactory when he reflects that his darling child's virtues are of a cast that will bear the scrutinizing eye of inquiry! That they will realize the expectations of love, and elevate it into esteem! Am I too sanguine in supposing that a man, who can make the liberal offers he has done, will be influenced by the sweet and candid partner he has purchased with his liberty and his fortune?

'You are, I know, above pecuniary motives; on this head, however, I shall introduce myself. Unwilling to disturb your peace, I have as much as possible diminished my fears for the security of the fleet, in which the little property I could preserve from the wreck of my fortunes in the West-Indies, is embarked.[2]

---

1 A reference to King Charles I (1600-1649), who was king from 1625 until his execution in 1649. Many believed his failures and missteps brought about the English Civil War.

2 Mr. Dudley is afraid that the ships carrying over to England the remainder of his wealth from the British colony of Barbados will be lost or pirated.

I have also wholly concealed my doubts, which are now almost certainties, respecting the responsibility of the Messieurs Tonnereaus. Sir William knows on what a doubtful contingence your fortune depends, and I never shall forget the air of pleasure his countenance assumed at the discovery; as if he till then doubted the validity of his pretensions to you. Consider, my child, if my apprehensions are just (and I assure you I did not lightly entertain them) how I am to support the thought that my rash and fatal confidence has reduced you to penury. You will, I know, endure adversity with dignity and patience, but every smile in which you meekly dress your countenance to receive me, will be a dagger in my conscious heart.

'To you, who have been bred in affluence, the perplexities of a limited fortune are inconceivable while at a distance; but when experienced they will be most poignantly felt. I knew them, my child, in my early years. My excellent father possessed every desirable blessing except a competence. He was, you know, a Clergyman, living upon small preferment.[1] His numerous family was at once his delight and his perplexity, the source of all his pleasures, and the object of all his fears. Even his firm philosophick mind and steady confidence in Heaven, sometimes yielded to the distresses which the numerous wants of his children occasioned; and the fear of leaving his almost adored wife, and his orphans destitute, to the mercy of the world, grew as his health declined almost insupportable.

'From such pangs, my Louisa, I would secure you, by an union with a worthy, though perhaps not an highly amiable man. Personal considerations are beneath your attention. Defect in character is the unavoidable lot of humanity. If you have discovered no reasons for disapprobation, stronger than those you stated last night, and your heart is *totally* disengaged, I trust your affections may be taught by gratitude to flow in the channel which judg-

---

1 Members of clergy in the Church of England during this era subsisted on "livings"—yearly sums that were awarded to a parish's clergyman, who was chosen for his post (often for life) by the principal landowner of the parish. Mr. Dudley's statement implies that his father was never able to secure a generous living. Instead, he had a "small preferment," a modest amount he secured for an appointment to a minor position in the Church.

ment prescribes. If your repugnance is still insurmountable, do not add to your perplexity by the apprehension of my displeasure. The reasons which influenced my child are at least entitled to my respect. Whether I possess a cottage or a palace, my Louisa is most welcome to the comforts it affords. The companion of my prosperity shall teach me to support adversity: her happiness not her aggrandisement is the wish of her

'Most affectionate father,

'RICHARD DUDLEY.'

CHAP. VIII.

An attempt at novelty. Louisa reluctantly consents to admit the addresses of a rich young baronet.

Miss Dudley had scarcely recovered from the involuntary shock, which the first intimation of Sir William Milton's attachment had occasioned, when her father's letter arrived. She had persuaded herself that either entreaty or fortitude might prevent the dreaded tie. The contents of the letter would at least have convinced her, that something could be urged in justification of Mr. Dudley's wishes; but the sentiments of love and confidence with which it was replete, forcibly appealing to her heart, and calling forth the mingled sentiments of filial piety and strong reluctance, too much agitated her mind to allow her to reason. She sat a few moments trembling and silent, and then burst into tears.

Marianne, who at that moment entered the dressing-room, was shocked at her sister's pale and agitated countenance. She flew towards her: "You are ill, my dear Louisa, for Heaven's sake, speak." Miss Dudley faintly attempted to smile. "My disorder," said she, "is nothing but an apprehensive mind; you have a claim to my confidence. Sir William Milton has made proposals respecting me to my father, which I am grieved to say he approves."

"Ah, my love," exclaimed Marianne, "how similar is our fate!

I have endured too much not to pity you; but what are your resolves?" "If possible, to comply with my father's wishes," returned Louisa. "Heroick girl! The resolution is worthy of yourself. I have at last brought my mind to the same determination. Hearts like ours, my Louisa, can never know felicity but in the converse of a kindred soul; yet though our future lives must pass in one sad joyless tenour, it will be a support in our sufferings, to reflect that we have complied with the paternal injunction. This thought will be a balm to all our woes, and will at last render the bed of death easy. I have long ago given up every hope, except what I derive from your affection. My sister in blood and now also in affliction."

Louisa was too seriously discomposed to answer this address in any other way than by a tender pressure of her hand. She begged to be alone. "I must," said she, "be prompt in my reply; as it will be decisive, I ought to deliberate." Marianne expressed how deeply she felt for her, and withdrew.

Louisa now exerting all her natural fortitude, again perused her father's letter. "Shall I," said she, "shrink from a duty, when encouraged by example as well as precept?"

To her father's enquiry[1] respecting a pre-engagement, she fancied she could give a clear and satisfactory negative. She had not entirely escaped the addresses of lovers, but neither their assiduities nor their offers ever excited more than a momentary attention. How then could she explain the violence of her aversion to Sir William? And yet the more she probed her heart, the more sensible she was of her reluctance.

Her father's observation in the succeeding paragraph, respecting the superior merit of her happier sister's lover, brought Mr. Pelham before her eyes, in all that strong light of contrast in which her fancy had often exhibited him. Her imagination winged by the wish, that he, instead of Sir William, had been the lover Mr. Dudley proposed, did not easily return from its excursive flight, to recollect that wishes are the weak resort of a querulous, impassioned mind. Her soul was above envy, and though the brightness of Marianne's prospects seemed to

---

1 In the second edition, "inquiry."

deepen the gloom of her own, she perceived her sister was not in reality happier. By her, the real excellencies of Mr. Pelham's conduct were overlooked, while she continued in fanciful pursuit after an imaginary undefined good. Louisa again endeavoured to avoid the fault she saw in her sister, and to make the best of her own lot; but in endeavouring to think of Sir William, the idea of Mr. Pelham again returned. Her cheek glowed, and perhaps for the first time she had cause to arraign the rectitude of her heart. Deceived by the native openness of her temper, she supposed she was only cultivating the friendship a sister ought to feel for a sister's lover, when her attention was rivetted to all Mr. Pelham's words and actions. Without her own concurrence, or indeed knowledge, her thoughts during her hours of retirement had been chiefly appropriated to him. Conviction flashed upon her soul, and she felt a momentary humiliation. I say momentary, for no sooner did she discover the state of her heart, than she determined that Sir William Milton should not owe his rejection to the preference she secretly entertained for a gentleman, who would soon probably be her sister's husband. Marianne's whimsical irresolution[1] afforded her neither hope nor justification; Mr. Pelham's attachment was avowed, and his mistress must, if true to her own happiness, reward it. At least honour, delicacy, sisterly love, all forbade her to indulge a passion, which could only end in guilt or disappointment.

On returning to the letter, her father's sentiments confirmed her noble resolution. He praised her prudence; ought she to disgrace his judgment? He spoke of her as his dearest consolation; and should she add to his griefs or his embarrassments? What a transport to be able to support an unfortunate but almost adored father! Could love, even innocent happy love, supply a more exalted bliss? Determined, with all the laudable diffidence of an ingenuous mind, not to trust her resolution to the chance of an hour, she resolved to write to her father, and to inform him of her acquiescence with his wishes. There are some secrets which scarcely admit of being disclosed even to ourselves. Louisa's was of this nature. Resolved to eradicate an attachment it would have

---

1 In the first edition, "resolution."

been criminal to avow, she judged it unnecessary to mention to her father the reason which most forcibly determined her; since virtue, discretion, and self-command told her it would not long exist.

'TO MR. DUDLEY.

'Dear and Honoured Father,

'Have you from my earliest infancy to this moment ever given a stronger proof of your affection for me, than the letter I now hold to my throbbing heart? You bid me, Sir, be sincere; I have bathed it with tears of veneration, gratitude, and reluctance. The last was the least painful emotion.

'I acknowledge no prior attachment, and I trust I shall be able to bestow my heart where your wishes point. At least, the gentleman whom your superior penetration is disposed to favour, may be sure of acquiring my esteem. Be pleased to inform Sir William Milton that I will endeavour to deserve his generous preference: our acquaintance has been so recent that he will not expect me to say more. To you, my father, I will own that the unbounded affluence he possesses has to me no other charm, than that it will enable me to relieve every anxious care which oppresses your heart. You invite me to partake of your cottage. Oh, for a sanctuary safe from every misfortune in which I might inshrine you!

'LOUISA DUDLEY.'

The agitation of Miss Dudley's mind was too great to permit her to write with a steady hand. Mr. Dudley, upon receiving it, hastened to her apartment. "I have," said he, tenderly embracing her, "received a letter which does honour to your filial piety and virtue. The pleasure I received from it would have been unmixed, could I have forgotten that what gave transport to my heart, was perhaps the source of bitter pangs to yours."

"You have convinced my reason, Sir," replied Louisa; "and if I did not attempt to act according to its rules, I should deserve contempt rather than pity. But does Sir William know my answer? I trust he does not press an immediate interview."

"I have avoided Sir William," said Mr. Dudley, "and for the present shall. You have rather told me what you wish to do, than what you are able to perform. It is not necessary that he should be immediately accepted, but after he is, it is highly important that he should not be able to tax your conduct with levity or caprice. Recollect yourself, my child: the subject in debate respects your future happiness, yet it is not more important to yourself than to me. If the pleas I have urged give you pain, forget them."

"Your tenderness," said Louisa, melting into tears, "is less pleasing, as it implies a want of that confidence in my strength of mind, which I wish to inspire. Have I, Sir, forfeited your esteem? I mean to be ingenuous; Sir William shall know my errors and defects. I will tell him at our first interview, that, perhaps I can never return his disinterested regard with warm attachment; but that he shall possess my duty, esteem, and gratitude. If this declaration satisfies him, I will be his."

"And shall I prepare him, my love," said Mr. Dudley, "by telling him that at the apprehension of that interview you trembled, turned pale, and eagerly caught hold of my hand? My dear child, you never appeared more deserving of my esteem than at this moment. But be not precipitate; if your resolution is well founded, it will be the same to-morrow morning. We shall, you know, have company to dinner; resume your composure, and judge of your lover's behaviour. Trivial circumstances sometimes prove a true index to the heart, and may his be worthy of yours!"

Mr. Dudley pressed his daughter's hand between his, and withdrew, rightly judging that she would be better enabled to tranquillize her mind by reflection, than by a further discussion of the painful subject.

CHAP. IX.

A conversation piece, concluded by a song.

The benignant smile with which Miss Dudley performed the honours of her father's table this day, was not the satisfactory glow of a delighted heart, but the placid sweetness of a dignified and benevolent mind. Politeness and attention were so habitual to her, that it was impossible for any of the guests to complain of neglect, though her bosom was throbbing with sensations of the most painful nature. Determined to give the pleasure she could not feel, she smothered her sighs with such care, that even Mr. Dudley's watchful eye could not discover her serenity to be only assumed; and he congratulated himself that the alliance which promised to support his tottering fortunes, would also confirm his Louisa's happiness.

The next interesting figure in the groupe was Mr. Pelham, but as he really was as much at ease as he appeared, his merit must rank below the mild chearfulness[1] of Miss Dudley. His lively sense and attentive good-humour, while it seemed only solicitous to call forth the various talents of the company, enjoyed the reverberation of the pleasure which he excited. Every body went away satisfied, and persuaded that, next themselves, Mr. Pelham was the most amiable and best-informed person of the party. Swift observes, "that the person whom all agree to pronounce deserving of the second place, deserves in reality the first:"[2] I shall not controvert this opinion.

The fair Marianne was not so universally admired. After she had left her sister's dressing-room, to divert the sympathizing pain she really felt, she had recourse to her studies. The novel selected for the morning was of the mournful cast, and after attending the heroine through four long volumes of sentimental misery, the ideas of soft distress were so familiarized to her mind, and so heightened by Louisa's sufferings and her own perplexities, that during the whole evening she appeared more like the weeping April than the smiling May.

Sir William Milton exhibited a different cast of character. On his entrance into the room, he cast an observing glance from under his bent brows, on the company, which, though it consisted of all the *genteel* people of Danbury, he considered to be utterly beneath his notice. Wrapping himself, therefore, in his own conscious importance, he sat silently enjoying the superior-

---

1 In the second edition, "cheerfulness."

2 This is not a precise quotation. In the dedication to his *A Tale of a Tub* (1704), Jonathan Swift (1667-1745) wrote, "it is a maxim, that those, to whom every body allows the second place, have an undoubted title to the first."

ity he felt. At intervals he threw his eyes upon Louisa, not to see how much she surpassed the objects around her, but to wonder why she would take pains to render herself agreeable to *such* people.

I do not hold forth this conduct as prudent. Few people are so stupid as not to perceive when they are despised, and fewer yet have sufficient servility to submit to contempt. Those who appear to do so are guided by interested motives, and it would lower the hauteur of arrogance to reflect, that the inferiors on whom they exercise their ill-humour, expect to be repaid for their forbearance. Wealth and rank have many natural advantages; mankind only asks permission to applaud and to admire them. A nod from his Grace, a bow from my Lord, or smile from the Squire, are a sort of checque drawn upon our own vanity, which we punctually discharge with a large quantity of commendation. All my neighbours went determined to like the Nabob; yet even Captain Target, though he had resolved to visit him at Milton-Hall,[1] returned without being in raptures. To own the truth, every body was too much piqued, to confess their own peculiar disappointment, but very kindly pitied other people's; and the unamiable description of Sir William's haughty reserve concluded with, "To be sure *I* should not say so, for he was very civil to me, but quite rude to Mr. and Mrs. such-a-one."

No sooner had the party broken up, than Marianne began to pity Louisa; "I trembled for you, my love, the whole day," said she. "How embarrassing! to be forced to entertain strangers, while your heart was torn with such cruel apprehensions."

"I could have wished," replied Louisa, smiling, "that you had been a little better able to assist me. I was concerned to see you so out of spirits."

"And did you observe it? O you are just such a kind attentive friend as my dear Grandmamma was! But sympathy, the boast of women, has no place in the bosom of men. You must now acknowledge that I am right. If Mr. Pelham loved me, he never could have been so chearful[2] and volatile while I was so

---

1 In the second edition, "Milton-hall."
2 In the second edition, "cheerful."

depressed. Sir William's behaviour was strikingly different; he hung upon your looks with the air of a man, who only lived in your presence. His silence too and dejected air were highly expressive of the anxious unaccepted lover. Indeed, Louisa, you will rule every movement of his soul."

"I had rather be less important to him, or else discover something more amiable in his manners," returned Louisa. "His fixed attention disconcerted me, but perhaps time may render him less alarming. However, as you are become the panegyrist of my admirer, let me speak in favour of yours."

"Giddy insensible creature," replied Marianne.

"How," cried Louisa, "can you call him insensible, who took this morning, unknown to any one, a walk of five miles to relieve a worthy family in distress? He is chearful[1] and agreeably animated indeed, but did you ever see his mirth offend the laws of decorum, politeness, or humanity? With what respect does he speak of serious and sacred subjects? His behaviour to Mr. Medium to-day is in point. How generously did he rescue that diffident man from the frothy jests of Captain Target? What consequence did he give him in the eye of every one present, by the attentions he himself paid? I trust I should not have been negligent, but it would have been impossible for me to overlook the dignity of the clerical character, while such a Mentor was present. How delicately did he divert from Miss Cardamum the commonplace raillery upon old maids, at the instant too that Mr. Alsop was preparing a laugh at the Captain's jokes? Every one was delighted to see the man of wit look infinitely more ridiculous, than the poor persecuted spinster."

"My heart was not sufficiently at ease to observe them," answered Marianne, half smiling. "But I am rejoiced to see you could. It certainly is a good omen for Sir William."

"I do not doubt," returned Louisa, recollecting herself, "but that I shall soon be able to discover many latent good qualities in *him*; and then my present reluctance to his addresses will disappear."

---

1 In the second edition, "cheerful."

"Not if you are like me," sighed Marianne. "Mine encrease[1] every hour."

"Then, for Heaven's sake, why not immediately refuse Mr. Pelham?"

"Can you, who set me such a pattern of heroism, ask, or need I answer? Filial piety forbids."

"You certainly mistake my father," returned Louisa, "he leaves you absolutely free: he does not even influence you by giving his opinion."

"And can you imagine me ignorant what that opinion is?" said Marianne. "His eyes have told it me, every commendation he utters convinces me of his wishes, and to those wishes I devote myself a sacrifice. I might even ask you, why he should be so solicitous to see you married, and yet indifferent how I am disposed of?"

Louisa, who recollected that her father did not wish to depress her sister's mind, by discovering the misfortunes which threatened him, knew not how to reply. Marianne, who misconstrued her embarrassment, passionately exclaimed, "Speak, your silence is more distracting than certainty. If there be any reason, it must be that I have less of his affections, and if so, lost, undone Marianne!" "You yield to a causeless alarm," returned Louisa. "Do, my dear girl, endeavour to conquer these keen sensibilities. Be assured you have a full share of my father's heart. Let me persuade you to entrust to him all your troubles. His tenderness will relieve, and his discretion will direct you. He has all the delicacy you can wish for in a confident;[2] he will encourage you by his condescension; and support you by his firmness. When you have opened your heart to him, you will no longer doubt his lively affection. Tell me, Marianne, will you take courage? Shall I prepare him for the interview?"

After a little hesitation Marianne consented, and retired to consider what her troubles and sorrows really were.

In the morning Miss Dudley met her father in the library. Her smiling aspect induced him to tell her, that, encouraged by the

---

1 In the second edition, "increase."
2 That is, confidant.

unconstrained ease of her behaviour yesterday, he had acquainted Sir William Milton with her determination; which he was the more solicitous to do, as he perceived the young Baronet hurt at being kept in suspence. He concluded with saying, that the favour of an immediate introduction had been requested. Louisa had sufficient presence of mind to avoid trembling, and again catching hold of her father's arm, she walked to the window, and in a few moments said she would retire to her dressing-room after breakfast, and would then see Sir William.

She now recollected her sister's request, and stated, as well as she was able, the irresolution and terror under which Marianne laboured. Mr. Dudley, who had long thought his younger daughter one of the peculiar favourites of fortune, was astonished to find that she also was suffering under "the penalty of Adam."[3] He readily promised his assistance, but had Louisa been in a livelier humour, 'tis[4] possible they might have mutually laughed at the peculiar nature of the fair mourner's embarrassment.

I formerly gave a reason why I avoided dwelling upon love scenes; and indeed that which passed between Miss Dudley and Sir William was not very well calculated to do credit to the describer. The gentleman was consequential, the lady was confused. The swain, at the moment he declared his high sense of his mistress's excellencies, took care to place his own advantages in a striking point of view; and the nymph, when he took leave, could not help wishing that he might appear to greater advantage at his next interview.

Considering it wrong in her present situation to indulge reflections to his disadvantage, Miss Dudley strove to banish them, by adapting the following stanzas to her harpsichord:

---

3 The phrase "penalty of Adam" appears in Shakespeare's *As You Like It*. West, in using the phrase, is both referencing a familiar Shakespearean quote and referring to Adam's situation after being expelled from the Garden of Eden and cast into the flawed world beyond it. West seems to suggest that the "penalty of Adam" is the moment at which one finds that life is no longer easy, when human sorrows begin, or in which life's harsh realities are made clear. It is a phrase West uses several times in her published fiction and conduct books.

4 The second edition changed "'tis" to "it is."

SONG.

I.

Th' Idalian[1] boy with frolick mien,
And Cytherea,[2] changeful Queen,
　　To Hymen's[3] shrine advance;
Hope beckons to her fairy band,
With these the Graces, hand in hand,
　　Unite in festal dance.

II.

Pleasure attunes her silver shell,
Of ever-during joys to tell,
　　Which mutual love supplies;
And sanguine youth, enwreath'd with flowers,
Transported views the white-rob'd hours,
　　That bright in vision rise.

III.

But not for me the joyful train
Bids Pleasure sound that raptur'd strain,
　　For me no Graces play;
Th' Idalian boy bends not his bow,
Nor does the torch of Hymen glow
　　On me with gladsome ray.

IV.

Be firm, my heart, the conflict dare,
A father's grief, a father's care,
　　Thy wish'd assent beguiles;
And powerful Virtue! be thou nigh,
Chase the fond dew-drop from my eye,
　　And dress my face in smiles.

---

1 Idalium was a mountain city in Cyprus, where Aphrodite, Greek goddess
of love and beauty (called Venus in Roman mythology), was worshipped.
2 Aphrodite is also known as Cytherea (Lady of Cythera).
3 In Greek and Roman mythology, Hymen was the god of marriage, rep-
resented as a young man carrying a torch and veil. Hymen's band indicates
marriage or wedlock.

V.

Nor let me with desponding gloom
Confine my prospects to the tomb,
　　Or pine with mortal care;
When conscience whispers mental peace,
Shall not the war of passion cease?
　　To guilt belongs despair.

CHAP. X.

*Humbly dedicated to the improvement of all fair
Quixotes in heroism.*

Lest the affection of my readers should be wholly engrossed
by the calm dignity with which Louisa reconciled her mind to
whatever was unpleasant in her situation, I shall dedicate this
chapter to Marianne, who was now immersed in a sea of troubles.

She so deeply pondered on the probable consequences of the
interview with her father, that her mind was rendered too weak
to derive any benefit from it. She alternately threw herself upon
the sopha, and reclined upon the bosom of her confidential maid
Patty.[1] She now feared she should never support herself in the
expected conversation, and then again fortified her resolution
with hartshorn.[2]

Mr. Dudley, at his first entrance into her dressing-room, perceived his daughter's terrors, and endeavoured to divert them.
He praised the docility of a bull-finch, which, at her bidding,
chanted the tune of "Ma chere amie." He next commended the
elegant fancy, with which she had decorated Miss Milton's portrait, by connecting it to her own by a broad blue ribband, on
which the words, "The bond of friendship," were embroidered

[1] It was a stereotype in romantic novels that a heroine would confide her
troubles in a trusted female servant. Patty is also a common nickname for a
"maid" or servant.

[2] Hartshorn is a kind of smelling salt. Marianne is concerned that the conversation will make her faint.

in silver foil. By thus leading her attention from the subject, he enabled her to recover herself; and in a little time she found courage to tell him, that she wished to have his opinion whether it would be improper for her to dismiss Mr. Pelham.

Of that, Mr. Dudley answered, she must be the best judge, as she knew what kind of encouragement she had given him.

"None, upon her word," she replied, "except permitting his visits."

"The dismission of a lover who has received only that mark of attention," resumed Mr. Dudley, "is rather an embarrassing affair; since it proves that the person you thought worthy, when at a distance, is not so eligible upon a nearer view. Will you, my dear, state your objections to Mr. Pelham?"

Marianne began her customary complaints. "Their sentiments did not coincide, their tastes were materially different, there was no similitude of soul, nothing to form that strong tie of sympathy which you know," said she, "must exist, or else there can be no certain expectation of felicity."

"Perhaps, my love," replied Mr. Dudley, "you will alter your opinion when you have heard what I am going to tell you. I have not entirely depended upon Mr. Pelham's very prepossessing countenance, nor the amiable urbanity of his manners, in forming a favourable opinion of his intrinsick worth. I have taken the liberty Lady Milton proposed, and have made repeated enquiries respecting his character. The result is highly satisfactory. I am told that his morals are unexceptionable, and that his reputation for probity and goodness stands very high. He is respectfully treated by his superiors; a proof that he is free from the contemptible meanness of fawning servility. His equals esteem him, and he is idolized by his dependents; I should therefore think his benevolence and agreeable temper unquestionable. In fine, I am told that he is a kind master, an indulgent landlord, an obliging neighbour, and a steady active friend."

"Yet, Sir," said Marianne, "you are only describing what I should call a good sort of person. These are merely *common* virtues. How detestable would he be if destitute of them."

"Take care, Marianne, how you treat a good sort of man, as

you term him, with contempt, or despise the person who conscientiously performs the ordinary duties of life. Providence has ascertained their value by their hourly recurrence. A man's family is the theatre wherein he can exercise every laudable quality. If he fail to practise them daily at home, he will never perform them gracefully before the eye of the world. Believe me, my child, the *common* virtues, as you stile them, are most essential parts of the human character. They do not indeed dazzle our senses; but they gladden our hearts by a mild uniform lustre. To your question, what Mr. Pelham would be, if destitute of them, I will answer, that many men are, who impose upon the world as the possessors of superior merit; and who peculiarly attract the attention of the superficial part of your sex."

"Do not speak with severity, my dear Sir," said Marianne, her eyes swimming with tears. "Your voice and look intimidate me."

"My voice and look then belye[1] my heart," rejoined her father, "which at this moment overflows in tenderness for you. Proceed, my love; have you any thing else to state?"

"Many things, my dearest father. Yet turn aside your face. Spare my blushes. He is not, indeed he is not, the tender, respectful, sympathizing lover, which my heart tells me is necessary for my future repose. He does not love me, at least not with that ardent affection, that deference, that assiduous timidity—But you smile, Sir."

"I did, my dear, to see by what a false romantick standard you estimate your lover's worth. Have you observed so little of real life as not to perceive, that the kind of address you talk of, is chiefly practised by the designing part of mankind, upon the woman whose person or fortune is the object of their desire? You must know that marriage divests you of all this assumed consequence.[2] Law and custom leave the husband master of his own actions, and in a certain degree arbiter of his wife's. Whether your lover was a sentimental sniveller, or an artful designer, the

---

1 In the second edition, "belie."
2 When Marianne (or any heiress) marries, her property becomes her husband's, by law, unless there is a separate prenuptial arrangement for her keeping a portion of it at her own disposal.

mock majesty with which you were invested could not continue in the married state. The romantick part of love quickly evaporates, and the soonest with him who has been the most visionary in his expectations. Think yourself happy if the kneeling slave does not change into the Tyrant, and compel you, in your turn, to endure without complaint, the whimsical indifference of caprice, or the sudden burst of petulance. Do not let my long lecture tire you; but I must observe that Mr. Pelham's character as a man, is of much greater consequence to your future peace, than his behaviour as a lover. The latter distinction will soon be laid aside, on the former you must depend through life; and he who practises the other relative duties, will seldom act wrong in this more intimate and interesting connexion."

"But, Sir," said Marianne, "even in your circumscribed and limited idea of love, some portion of it is necessary. Three years ago I passed the summer with Mr. Pelham at Lady Milton's; if I *really* made an impression upon his heart, would he have concealed his passion till my Grandmamma's death had ascertained my fortune? I then thought he appeared most attentive to Miss Milton."

"If you, Marianne, are serious in this objection, your age affords the best answer. The character of a girl at sixteen is not sufficiently determined, to allow a prudent man to look forward to a permanent connexion. Nature has been liberal to your person, and I perceive you are fond of making impressions at first sight; yet would you not wish your lover to say with Juba,

"'Tis not a set of features, or complexion,
The tincture of the skin, that I admire;
The virtuous Marcia towers above her sex?[1]

Till you are certain that the discovery of similar perfection in your character, has not secured to you Mr. Pelham's affection, I should advise you not to think him mercenary. Besides, recollect he was then a minor, consequently he could not with propriety think of marriage; and an attempt to engage you in the many in-

---

1 The character of Juba (Prince of Numidia) appears in Joseph Addison's play *Cato* (1713). West leaves out several lines in her partial quotation.

conveniencies of a long entanglement,[1] however consistent with the narrow views of self-indulgence, has little of the generosity inseparable from my idea of true love."

Marianne asked, with some degree of eagerness, whether true love could discover any faults in the object of its affections?

Mr. Dudley was of opinion that it could, as well as true friendship, for as the object of either of those passions was a fallible being, it was a proof that we indulged them to a blameable excess, when they precluded us from the exercise of reason. "I recollect," continued he, "the circumstance to which I dare say you allude, and will only tell you, that if you do not renounce your romantick notions before you have been a wife a twelve-month, I shall think very *highly* indeed of your husband's politeness, or very *meanly* of the sincerity of his attachment to you."

"I shall never be converted, Sir," replied Marianne with a faint smile. "The picture you have drawn of a married life, has determined me never to enter into it. My heart tells me that if my husband were to omit any of those thousand delicate attentions, those pleasing assiduities that won me to be his, despair and death must be the consequence."

"If you speak seriously, my dear child, I shall advise you by all means to adhere to your resolution. Your motives for rejecting what I think a most eligible offer, prove that you have cherished instead of suppressed those painful sensibilities, to which your sex owes its severest miseries; are you, my love, who tremble at a breeze, fit to encounter the storms of life? If you feel yourself unable to support a casual unkindness, in which perhaps the heart has no share, or a casual error from which the mind, on recollection, revolted, endeavour to contract your sphere of action, and to make yourself happy with fewer blessings, as you cannot encounter their attendant sorrows. Marriage, like all other sublunary connexions, mixes the bitter with the sweet. Mutual confidence and esteem compose the latter, and mutual forbearance must be exerted to palliate the former. The similitude of soul,

---

1 By "long entanglement," Mr. Dudley means a long engagement. Once Pelham reached age 21, he would no longer have needed parental consent to marry.

of taste, and of sentiment, which you talk of, is not necessary. The strong tie of sympathy often cannot exist; and the delicate attentions and pleasing assiduities of the lover so rarely appear in the husband, that if these circumstances *still* seem essential to your peace, do not commit your happiness to the slender chance of finding a human phœnix, but confine your sensibility to the calmer enjoyments of friendship. A mistake *there* will neither be so irretrievable, nor so excruciating."

Marianne only answered with a deep sigh, and Mr. Dudley, after conjuring her to give the whole argument a fair discussion, withdrew.

CHAP. XI.

A specimen of an Abigail's eloquence. Marianne appears in various points of view.

Immediately after Mr. Dudley was gone, Mrs. Patty entered the dressing-room. From the circumstance of having attended her young lady from her infancy, she imagined herself intitled to give her opinion upon every occurrence, and by virtue of listening had made herself mistress of some part of the foregoing conversation. She was particularly shocked at the cruel advice given against matrimony; nor could she have endured greater consternation, had her lady's last present been spoiled at the dyer's, or had any one assured her that the butler had sent a billet-doux to the housekeeper. Those, who consider how advantageous a young lady's love affairs are to an Abigail, the certainty of possessing all the old wardrobe, when the fair bride puts on her nuptial paraphernalia, and the possibility of further presents; must have hearts of adamant, if they do not excuse Mrs. Patty's passion, and forgive her, though she should be a little illiberal to Mr. Dudley.[1]

---

1 An "Abigail" is a female servant. Patty is concerned that Marianne's unwillingness to marry will mean that her mistress won't buy new wedding clothes. This would mean that Patty would not get any hand-me-down clothing from Marianne. It was customary for women of means to give their servants old clothing for refitting.

"Oh, Patty," exclaimed Marianne, "I am not equal to the troubles I must undergo. I am weary of life."

"A great deal too good for the people you are *consarned* with, Madam," replied Patty.

"Oh no, I am a poor helpless, weak, inconsistent, creature."[1]

"But if I were you, Madam, I would not be *so* long. Mr. Frank tells me as how his master is quite resolved about it, and means to put the question this very time; and I know *I* should not *argufy* long. I never knew no good come of *shilly-shally* doings, I'd have him at once."

"I never will," said Marianne, "nor any one else. I detest the sex. My father has inspired me with an abhorrence of all men."

"Never did I hear of any thing so barbarous," cried the indignant Patty. "I am sure you never should have seen him this morning, if I had thought what he was going to say. Just as if it was not natural to be married, and as if people then could not be happy if they like. I am sure it is their own faults if they *arn't*. Hate all men, indeed! why the poor young gentleman will go mad. Pray, Ma'am, don't use such sad words any more, for you frighten me to death. But I know what our old gentleman would be at, I can see as well as another."

Marianne, who sat deeply musing upon what her father had urged, did not hear one word of Patty's eloquence; but passionately exclaimed, "O my Grandmamma, if your fatal partiality had never distinguished your unhappy child, I should have had no cause to doubt the sincerity of my lover's attachment. Fortune, thou idol of mercenary souls, I detest thy pageant incumbrance!"

Mrs. Patty, who thought money a very good thing, and was seldom withheld from answering by not clearly comprehending her lady's meaning, readily replied, "Why, certainly Ma'am, when people love one another, there is no need for money to make them happy, and to be sure, young Mr. Pelham is very rich, and you may not like to keep much company. But then cannot you live quite retired, and do a great deal of good, and be *vastly* generous to every body about you."

---

1 In the first two editions, the two preceding paragraphs were printed as one but have been broken up here for clarity.

"I repeat that I hate him, that I am determined against him," exclaimed Marianne.

Patty, who thought it impossible her mistress should, of her own accord, hate such a good-humoured looking gentleman, was out of all patience with Mr. Dudley; to whom she supposed this determination was owing, and resolved to relieve herself from the burden of the secret, which she had faithfully concealed *three* hours. "Shame upon them," said she, "for a parcel of crafty folks, and Heaven forgive me for speaking rash, but I can tell why he does this. Why, Ma'am, I did not mean you should know any thing about it, and to be sure I promised Thomas not to say a word, but it is very true for all that. Your Papa has outrun the constable I find, and as sure as you are alive wants you never to marry, that you may take care of him, and *the* Miss Louisa he is so fond of. Thomas told me this very morning that things were in a sad poor way. His master gets no sleep, but is walking about his room, or else writing, and looking over accounts. And he found a bit of an old letter, so he is sure there will be a crash soon. But I know if I were you, I never would be made a tool of, and all to please a favourite sister."

As wise people often defeat their aims by too great caution, cunning also frequently overshoots the mark by too much craft. Patty's speech, instead of awakening the angry malevolent passions in the bosom of her gentle mistress, as she designed it should, inspired the kindest sorrow for her unfortunate father; mingled with a regret too tender to be called envy, that his preference for Louisa was so visible. Her heart was really excellent, and she resolved not meanly to supplant, but heroically to emulate her sister. Miss Dudley's motive for encouraging Sir William was now apparent, and stimulated by her example, Marianne formed the resolution of never marrying, while her father's circumstances continued perplexed, but to dedicate the fortune she had just quarrelled with to his support.

The heart is never so easy as when sustained by conscious rectitude, and though the romantick turn of this young lady's mind, taught her to overlook little duties, it impetuously urged her to perform high acts of virtue. To increase the merit of the sacrifice, she resolved to conceal the motive, and after severely chiding Patty for her impertinent invectives, (which she, with the true adroitness of her profession, excused by exuberant declarations of regard for her dearest lady,) dispatched her to beg a second interview with Mr. Dudley.

She met him with a smile, which beaming through her tears, bespoke the triumph of fortitude in a feeling heart, and told him, she had weighed his arguments, and felt determined against marriage.

Mr. Dudley begged her to form no resolutions which might restrain her judgment respecting a future connection. A lover might appear better adapted to her taste; but as Mr. Pelham had not sufficient influence to induce her to change the single state, his dismission became unavoidable.

Marianne told her father her motives would ever hold in force: "You will," said she, "be left without a companion when Louisa marries Sir William. Allow me to fill *her* place in your affections, and to dedicate my life to you."

"You will ever preserve your *own* place," said Mr. Dudley, clasping her to his bosom, "and I trust my beloved girls will only leave me to secure to themselves more tender and affectionate friends, whose protection will continue when mine is terminated by the law of nature. Time, my Marianne, will, I hope, diminish that dangerous susceptibility which wars against your peace, and then, like your sister, you will increase my happiness, by giving me a son[1] worthy of my tenderest affection, if deserving of you."

Marianne's transport was unbounded. Filial piety taught her to glory in the praise of such a father, while conscience increased her joy, by suggesting the honest pride of having deserved it. The only task remaining, was to dismiss Mr. Pelham politely, and Mr. Dudley reluctantly undertook the painful office.

That gentleman's mind was indeed prepared in some degree for this mortification. He perceived the little progress he had made in his charmer's heart; and as his attachment rather increased than declined, he felt the severest concern. Desirous

---

1 Mr. Dudley means he would be given a son-in-law, should his daughters marry.

of securing a woman, interesting even in her eccentricities, he would willingly have framed his addresses to her taste; but as it is very difficult for a man of honour to adopt the character which he despises, or to speak a language foreign to his heart, his unfortunate attempts at sighing Strephon[1] were so remarkably unsuccessful, that they only gave the idea of an ironical caricature; and convinced Marianne that he rather designed to ridicule than to flatter her opinion. But, though equally unhappy in his natural and assumed character, he still kept lingering near her, fascinated by the hope which love supplied, that time might work some change in his fortune. A hope which the favourable regard of Mr. and Miss Dudley certainly strengthened.

The regret he felt at being deserted by this poor support, was too severe to be softened by the warm expressions of esteem with which Mr. Dudley qualified his daughter's refusal. He repeatedly enquired if her determinations were positively fixed; if entreaties might not prevail upon her at least to postpone his rejection; at length recollecting himself, and fortifying his mind by the proud (or shall I say by the prudent) consideration that marriage could promise little happiness, unless founded on the basis of *mutual* regard, he determined to submit to his fate. At taking leave of Stannadine he impressed every one with grief for his departure, except the person whose approbation he had been most solicitous to obtain.

---

1 Strephon was a traditional name for a lovesick youth in the pastoral and romance traditions. Repeated sighing was considered a physical sign of being lovesick.

CHAP. XII.

Extremely useful to the author, giving her an opportunity of filling her book, contrasting her characters, and displaying great critical acumen.

The mythological fable of the combat between Hercules and Antœus,[1] may allude to the pertinacity with which the human mind reverts to its first designs. When our plans are thwarted and disconcerted, the moment of apparent defeat is that in which we most zealously form the project of a fresh attack. My classical readers will thank me for this allusion, if it be only applied to a waiting-maid.

In short, the redoubtable Patty, though one offer of marriage was absolutely negatived, was still resolved to defeat her master's supposed design, of fortuning Miss Dudley with her lady's property; and thinking numerous lovers must at least unsettle her intention of living in "blessed singleness," she began to debate upon the ways and means of raising her an army of admirers.

The world is ever so generously inclined to rescue a rich beauty from the vile durance in which she is kept by an avaricious, tyrannical, or capricious father, that Patty had only to tell her poor mistress's hard fate, in order to succeed. Even Danbury was not without somewhat of the chivalrous spirit, and two Knights-errant issued forth to rescue the captive Damsel. I chuse[2] to speak according to the *real* intentions of the parties, for ostensibly it was only one Knight, and an attendant Esquire.

Captain Target encouraged Mr. Alsop to make proposals, promising to second him with all the powers of his address and

---

1 Antaeus was a Greek mythological giant who made everyone he came into contact with wrestle with him. He killed all opponents until he was defeated by Hercules, who figured out the secret of Antaeus's power. Hercules held Antaeus off of the ground, which made him weak, and crushed him in a bear hug.

2 In the second edition, "choose."

eloquence; which, to say truth, he meant to employ to his own advantage, if occasion offered. Let those who censure this as a breach of friendship, consider the fascination of youth, wealth, and beauty, and they will, at least, allow that the Captain did not act an *uncommon* part.

As it was very material to the success of their projects, that Mr. Dudley should not be apprized of them, reserve in his presence became indispensably necessary; and Mr. Alsop depending upon his friend for explanation, was not sufficiently pointed in his devoirs to Marianne, to enable her to discover, whether the frequency of these gentlemen's visits was owing to the attraction of her own charms, or the good arrangement of her father's table. There was something so unique in them both, that without any share of coquetry it was allowable to indulge a laugh at their expence; and *Louisa* often diverted her mind from the gloom of her own prospects, by rallying her sister upon her conquest, not only of young meum and tuum, but also of the veteran son of Mars.[1] Except the amusement which they afforded the ladies, their presence added little to the pleasures of Stannadine. To a man like Mr. Dudley, possessed of resources in his own mind, what is commonly called a good neighbour is rather a formidable character; and Sir William Milton, now almost an inmate in the family, never spent an hour with our Danbury beaux, without discovering some new quality to excite contempt. Neither of *my* friends were skilful in making discoveries of the mortifying kind; Mr. Alsop knew no other criterion by which to discover dislike, than the blunt expression of "Sir, I do not want your company," and the Captain was persuaded that Mr. Dudley enjoyed his long military details, and that his happy, easy, unencumbered, attentive manner had quite conquered the Baronet's reserve; because he often condescended to laugh at his jests; but Captain Target was not blessed with the clearest penetration.

Conversation is a delicacy of that peculiar nature, that to pre-

---

1 Meum and tuum is Latin for "mine and thine." This is a cutting reference to Mr. Alsop's materialistic tendencies. Mars was the Roman god of war, so the veteran son of Mars is a humorous label for Captain Target, who puffed up his military exploits and knowledge to impress others.

serve all its agreeable pungency, many uncommon ingredients are necessary. Mr. Dudley often felt distressed how to amuse his guests, and one evening, to prevent the rising yawn, without having recourse to the sameness of cards, he proposed the perusal of a Legendary Tale, which had afforded him entertainment a few days before. Marianne seconded the motion, declaring herself an enthusiastick admirer of poetry. Her echo Alsop repeated her words, with the addition that he loved it so much, that he always used to read the pretty things in the papers to his papa, and his aunt Peggy; and the Captain enjoyed tales and stories to his heart. It was at first proposed that Louisa should be orator, but she, with graceful diffidence, desired leave to propose an abler substitute, and delivered the manuscript to Sir William, with a smile which almost divested[1] his countenance of its usual austerity.

As my narrative is not now at a very interesting period, I am inclined to hope my critical readers will allow me the Gossip's privilege of digression. I will promise them, that my poetical episode shall be as conducive to *forward* my main plot, as secondary characters and flowery illustrations are, in the most approved productions of my contemporaries. Besides the usual advantage of filling my volumes, those, who choose to skip over adventitious matter, will at one glance know where to begin again. The moral may recommend it to the few, who still love to see nobility clad in the respectable robe of virtue; and eminent rank described in unison with dignified sentiments and generous actions.

RODOLPHO, EARL OF NORFOLK;

A

LEGENDARY TALE.

Wisdom and Fortune combating together,
If that the former do but what it can,
No chance can shake it.   SHAKSPEARE.[2]

---

1 In the first edition, "devested"—likely an error.
2 These lines are from William Shakespeare's tragedy *Antony and Cleopatra* (1623).

PART I.

'Twas at the hour when evening's pall
    Hangs lightly on the vale,
The songsters of the grove were mute,
    Hush'd was each ruder gale:

The weary swain had sought the path
    Which toward the hamlet goes,
To take his hard-earn'd frugal meal,
    And snatch his short repose:

When by the tufted oaks that throw
    Long shadows o'er the mead,
The brave ill-fated Edgar led
    His much o'er-wearied steed.

Bruis'd was his buckler, deeply bruis'd
    The cuirass[1] on his breast;
And many a hostile blow had fall'n
    Upon his batter'd crest.

Affliction o'er his graceful form
    A soft attraction threw,
As damask roses seem more sweet
    When wash'd by morning dew.

As sad he mus'd on pleasures past,
    On crosses that annoy,
And every bitter ill that taints
    The cup of human joy;

Sudden a tumult in the wood
    His startled ear alarms,
The shriek of terror and surprize,
    The clang of hostile arms.

Nor did the generous Edgar doubt
    His succour to bestow,
His heart, tho' full of sharp distress,
    Still felt another's woe.

---

1 A cuirass is a piece of armor that covers the torso.

Now, near the spot, he view'd a scene
    Which might the brave affright,
Six ruffians join'd in murderous league
    Against one gallant Knight:

That Knight with inbred courage warm'd
    Full on th' assailants bore;
A faithful servant at his feet
    Lay bath'd in mortal gore.

Resistless as the lightning's flash,
    His faulchion[1] Edgar drew;
Nor does the dreaded bolt of Heaven
    Descend with aim more true.

Two quickly fell; the stranger Knight
    Th' unhop'd-for succour blest;
New vigour nerv'd his sinewy arm,
    And fortified his breast.

Sharp was the conflict! dire the scene!
    But Heaven is virtue's guard;
By arduous conflict proves its worth
    To justify reward.

All lifeless fell; the rescu'd Knight
    Survey'd them on the ground;
And knew them well, an outlaw'd band
    For desp'rate deeds renown'd.

And now he snatch'd brave Edgar's hand
    With frank and courteous mien;
"How dear," he cried, "I prize my life,
    Hereafter shall be seen.

No low-born peasant hast thou sav'd,
    No base unthankful churl;
Rodolpho is my name, a Knight,
    And now of Norfolk, Earl.

---

1 A falchion is a single-edged sword.

But let us to my castle haste,
 In yonder vale it lies;
And lo, to speed our tardy steps,
 Night's deeper shades arise."

They left the wood-crown'd hills, and swift
 The winding vale explor'd;
And here a train with lighted brands
 Came forth to meet their lord.

Their vestures of rich cloth of gold,
 Shone glittering in the light,
And soon the castle's spacious walls
 Burst full on Edgar's sight.

The ample moat, the lofty spires,
 Each work of Gothick art,
Proclaim'd at once the master's wealth,
 And spoke his liberal heart.

Observant of his honour'd will,
 The servants crowded round,
And Edgar saw the stately board
 With tasteful viands crown'd.

Rodolpho took a golden bowl,
 Mantling with cordial wine,
And graceful to his gallant guest
 Consign'd the draught divine.

Then to his train, "Whilst we with food
 Our wasted strength restore,
Go, bid the minstrel's sweet-ton'd harp
 Some soothing ditty pour."

The bard obey'd; love's woes he sang,
 And then that descant clear,
Whose theme, the wars of ancient days,
 Enchants the chieftain's ear.

But as the wat'ry halo veils
 The splendor of the moon,

So look'd Sir Edgar's tearful eyes,
    Pain'd at the martial tune.

Rodolpho stopp'd the thrilling song,
    Then thus his train addrest,
"That yet I live to thank your care,
    Be this brave hero blest.

Had not his arm from robbers fell
    A sure defence supply'd,
I now had lain a lifeless corse,[1]
    By faithful Osbert's side."

He ceas'd; and through the spacious hall
    The burst of transport reign'd,
Which, plainer far than study'd speech,
    Great Norfolk's worth explain'd.

On Edgar each the ardent eye
    Of grateful blessing threw;
It spoke the feelings of their hearts,
    It spoke their virtues too.

The tumult ceas'd: now all retir'd,
    Save Norfolk and his guest;
Again the Earl grasp'd Edgar's hand,
    And tremulous address'd:

"Fortune around my favour'd head
    Has all her gifts diffus'd,
Nor yet has Love, to bless my life,
    Her sweeter hopes refus'd.

My father from the Norman shore
    With Royal William came;
He shar'd the dangers of his lord,
    He shar'd alike his fame.

Proportion'd to his soldier's worth,
    The King rewards bestow'd;
And, since my father's death, to me
    Hath Royal bounty flow'd.

---

1 An archaic spelling of corpse.

His honour'd patronage I boast,
   His confidence possess;
I use my pow'r to punish wrong,
   To mitigate distress.

Thou brave preserver of my life,
   Or let me call thee friend,
My tongue would speak my heart's warm wish,
   But fears it may offend.

In ev'ry gesture, ev'ry look,
   Thy lofty soul I trace;
The dignity of conscious worth
   Informs thy meaning face.

Yet have I mark'd thy frequent sighs
   Which tho' in part suppress'd,
Awake a fear that fortune's wrongs
   Have oft thy soul distress'd.

Say then, in all the ample store,
   The power, the wealth I bear,
Is there a blessing thou wouldst deign,
   At my request, to share?

Nor fear to ask: Rodolpho's life
   Is not of value base;
Some ample boon, some princely gift,
   Should its preserver grace."

He paus'd; o'er Edgar's glowing face
   A deep suffusion pass'd;
And now his eye was rais'd to Heaven,
   And now on Norfolk cast.

"Oh soul of honour!" he exclaim'd,
   "Too high the chance you rate;
Which haply led me to behold
   Thy late disastrous state.

For he who had a moment paus'd,
   Yet seen th' unequal strife;

Must have a heart as base as those
    Who sought thy sacred life.

Great Earl! as at thy festal board
    Observant I have sate,[1]
And seen thy menials with delight
    Thy honour'd mandate wait:

My soul hath mus'd on all the wrongs
    I unregarded met,
From those who, tho' they share thy rank,
    Its duties still forget.

If to a poor man's simple tale
    Thou canst indeed attend,
And to a lost and friendless wretch
    Thy favouring arm extend;

Know then, that Edgar is my name,
    And tho' of humble birth,
I boast a parentage renown'd
    For uncorrupted worth.

My father, whose ingenuous mind
    Confess'd fair glory's charms,
Inspir'd his dear and only son
    With love of arts and arms.

Fair was the promise of my youth,
    Beyond my rank or years;
In studious lore, in manly sports,
    I rose above my peers.

Impassion'd memory with delight
    Yet recollects the days,
When all was pleasure, all was hope,
    Encouragement, and praise.

Destructive to this scene of joy,
    Love wak'd its fatal flame;
Rob'd in an angel's smiling form
    The dear delusion came.

---

1 Archaic spelling of sat.

Thou say'st, Rodolpho, thou hast lov'd,
    Thou wilt not then disdain
To hear me, tho' from grief diffuse,
    My tale of woe explain:

A Saxon lord, whose lofty tow'rs
    O'erlook'd the vale he[1] plough'd[2],
To grace his daughter's natal day,
    Conven'd a festal crowd.

The martial sports, the conqueror's prize,
    My swelling heart inflam'd;
I went, and victor in the joust,
    The promis'd honour claim'd.

I follow'd with exulting step
    The vassals of the lord,
To where the mistress of the feast
    Bestow'd the wish'd reward.

High on a rustick throne she sate,
    With woodland lilies crown'd,
Her simple vest of virgin white
    A cord of silver bound.

O'er her fair neck, whose snowy hue
    Her garland did upbraid,
Half falling from a silken net
    Her nut-brown tresses stray'd.

She turn'd on me her radiant eyes,
    Bright as the star of love;
She smil'd; so sweetly breaks the morn,
    In yon blue vault above.

But each fine feature to describe,
    Demands superiour art;
Suffice it, their remembrance lives,
    Deep graven in my heart.

---

1 The first edition uses "we." The second edition changes to "he."
2 In the second edition, "plow'd."

In tones, harmonious as the spheres,
    My wish'd success she hail'd:
I should have answered, but at once
    The pow'r of language fail'd.

Kneeling I took the proffer'd prize,
    In humble awe I gaz'd;
A courtly victor would have spoke,
    A colder lover prais'd.

Blushing she sought the festal hall;
    There 'mid the virgin choir,
Obedient to her father's will,
    She chaunted to her lyre.

The hopes of virtue were her theme,
    Its perils, and its praise;
Her heav'nly looks might speak herself,
    The subject of her lays.

O blest transcendently! she cry'd,
    And worthy to be blest,
Are all who through the maze of life,
    Keep virtue's pure behest.

Hard is the task, but toil and pain
    Invigorates the mind,
Which, sinking on the couch of sloth,
    Feels all its pow'rs confin'd.

Heaven ne'er meant that man with ease
    His wishes should obtain,
He must from labour's strenuous grasp
    The palm of triumph gain.

Oh gen'rous youth! if e'er thy heart
    To glory dares aspire,
Let active merit's guiding ray
    Direct the great desire.

By virtue, to the happy few
    Who love her laws, is giv'n

Heartfelt tranquillity on earth,
    And happiness in heav'n.

She ceas'd; the numbers on my soul
    New energy bestow'd;
At once love wak'd its thrilling flame,
    And emulation glow'd.

I felt the buoyant gale of hope
    A rising fervour breathe;
Vast was her worth, but sanguine love
    Can miracles atchieve.

Arms seem'd the nearest path to fame;
    I rous'd my rustick bands,
And rescu'd from an outlaw'd chief
    Her father's richest lands.

I conquer'd, but with generous pride
    All retribution wav'd;
I only sought my charmer's smile,
    And scorn'd the lands I sav'd.

But soon her father's piercing ken
    My latent love descry'd;
Still will the conscious eye disclose
    Those truths the heart would hide.

Musing on every favouring hope
    Her gentle smiles convey'd,
As pensively one day I sate
    Beneath a poplar's shade,

Her father came; Dar'st thou, he cry'd,
    Of rustick birth, aspire
To gain a beauteous lady's love,
    Who calls a Baron sire?

Presume not on the little fame
    Thy sword by chance hath won,
Far nobler deeds, far ampler praise,
    Must grace my future son.

But to disguise thy daring love,
    No mean denials seek;
E'en now it flashes in thy eyes,
    And blushes on thy cheek.

My vengeance, yes, my veng'ance, boy,
    Can arrogance restrain;
Dare not beyond to-morrow's sun
    Abide in my domain.

He ceas'd—I trembled; 'twas not fear,
    A glow of honest shame;
A painful consciousness of worth,
    Which yet I scorn'd to name.

My ready hand had grasp'd my sword,
    But love the purpose stay'd;
It was the father of my fair,
    I sheath'd the half-drawn blade.

Yes, at thy bidding I will go,
    From England I will fly;
Thou hast insulted me; 'tis well
    I frame no fierce reply.

Hereafter thou perchance may'st hear
    Of my success in arms;
My country's foes shall know how well
    I prize thy daughter's charms.

I turn'd—the glow of injur'd pride
    Suppress'd each mournful thought;
I flew not to my father's arms,
    But Robert's banners sought.[1]

Exulting, on my arm the cross
    Of Palestine I bound;
Nor doubted quickly to return,
    With martial honours crown'd.

---

1 "Robert's banners" refers to Robert the Bruce, King Robert I, a warrior who successfully fought the English for Scottish independence in the 14th century.

How well I fought, let envious spleen,
    Let calumny proclaim;
My native courage caught from love
    Enthusiastick flame.

By those I rescu'd, hated, scorn'd,—
    Ah! spare the painful tale—
I saw the hopes of youth and love,
    Of truth and candour, fail.

Tir'd of a scene where low-born art
    Could merit's dues command,
Harass'd with toil, with sorrow worn,
    I sought my native land.

These bruised arms and Knighthood's rank,
    In six long summers won,
I bear; to soothe[1] a father's grief
    For his unhappy son.

Yet still I feel the fear of love,
    But why that fear deplore?
It is the inmate of a heart
    Where hope exists no more."

END OF PART I.

PART II.

    "Blest are those
Whose blood and judgment are so well commingled
That they are not a pipe for Fortune's fingers
To sound what stop she pleases. Give me a man
That is not passion's slave, and I will wear him
In my heart's core, aye, in my heart of heart."

SHAKSPEARE.[2]

---

1 In the second edition, "sooth."
2 From William Shakespeare's tragic play *Hamlet*, a speech by Hamlet himself, spoken to his friend Horatio in preparation for testing his uncle's guilt in the death of his father.

To Edgar then Rodolpho spoke;
   "What insolence deny'd,
By gen'rous friendship's grateful hand
   Shall amply be supply'd.

And if the charmer of thy soul
   Thy high desert can move,
Her haughty father shall be forc'd
   To court thy slighted love.

Oh! Edgar, I have heard thee tell
   The story of thy woes,
And felt that int'rest in thy fate
   Which sympathy bestows.

Scorning the snares which for my rank
   Ambitious beauty threw;
No artful smile, no studied glance,
   My cold attention drew.

Anxious from every base reproach
   My tow'ring fame to shield,
In science I amusement sought,
   And honour in the field.

As foremost in the royal chase
   I urg'd my rapid steed,
One day I met a lovely maid,
   Attir'd in sorrow's weed.

Slow she approach'd; when near, she rais'd
   Her long, disorder'd veil,
And show'd a face divinely fair,
   But through dejection pale.

Wilt thou, she cried, Oh gallant Knight!
   A Damsel's fears allay,
And swiftly to my lord the King
   My anxious steps convey?

I have a tale of woe to tell,
   Would I could access find!

All righteous Heav'n, who knows my grief,
    Will move the royal mind.

I would have sooth'd the fair distress'd,
    But converse she delay'd:
I led her to the green wood tent,
    Where still the monarch staid.

There in that eloquence of phrase
    Which sorrow can bestow,
Prostrate at royal Willliam's feet,
    She told her tale of woe.

Her father, injur'd by a lord,
    Rank'd in the royal train,
Had dar'd to utter his complaints
    In treason's guilty strain.

With purpos'd insurrection charg'd,
    Imprison'd and arraign'd;
He saw his ancient honours seiz'd,
    His fair demesnes[1] distrain'd.

And still th' inexorable law,
    By mercy unconfin'd,
Had to attainder of estate,
    Life's deadly forfeit join'd.

The weeping beauty did not fear,
    Tho' want prepar'd to seize
Her, whom luxurious grandeur rear'd
    On the soft lap of ease.

She fear'd not scorn, tho' scorn with joy
    The bow of satire strung,
To spoil the shrine where flattery late
    Its gilded off'rings hung.

Her gentle frame contain'd a soul
    In filial duty brave;
A father's life was what she sought
    From fortune's wreck to save.

---

1 Demesnes means his domain or real estate in his possession.

Stern is our royal master's soul,
    The guardian of the law;
Decided by the harsh decree,
    No lenient grace he saw.

Thy sorrow for thy father's crimes,
    He cry'd, shall ne'er atone;
Unpunish'd, shall rebellion's voice
    Insult the sacred throne?

Oh! Edgar, never can my eyes
    Forget the awful scene;
The horror of the lady's look,
    Her wild disorder'd mien.

Then must he die? she beat her breast,
    She groan'd in deep despair:
Then must my father die? she shriek'd,
    And rent her flowing hair.

Oh! save *him*, William! take *my* life,
    Let justice have its due!
You had a father, but, alas!
    Your sire you never knew.

Whilst thus through all the echoing tent
    The stream of horror rung;
At once compassion, wonder, love,
    Within my bosom sprung.

If e'en the monarch's eye austere
    With pity seem'd to melt,
Oh think how deep my softer soul
    Its thrilling impulse felt.

I risq'd[1] my hopes; but let me spare
    To tell each various art,
By which, to mercy by degrees
    I mov'd great William's heart.

---

1 In the second edition, "risk'd."

The pardon gain'd, I flew with joy
    The mourner to console,
And in her father's prison met
    The mistress of my soul.

By time subdu'd, her pious grief
    Seem'd fix'd, but yet resign'd;
And to despair's pale hollow cheek
    The calm of patience join'd.

She knelt beside her contrite sire,
    For him to Heav'n she pray'd;
Can beauty ever look more sweet
    Than thus in tears array'd?

I gave the pardon—then my heart
    A painful bliss confess'd;
When the rapt father's eager arms
    His fainting daughter press'd.

Recov'ring from her trance of joy,
    I saw her transport speak,
Irradiate her yet doubtful eye,
    And flush her changing cheek.

Assur'd, confirm'd, with winning grace
    Around my knees she clung;
She blest me, but her eyes by far
    Outspake her fault'ring tongue.

Now passion swelling in my soul,
    A sudden impulse mov'd;
I caught the charmer to my heart,
    And told her that I lov'd.

At once I claim'd her sire's assent,
    And told my rank and state;
Boasting what blessings I design'd
    Should worth like her's await.

Edgar! I know a lib'ral mind
    Will own a terror here,

Lest gratitude on gen'rous hearts
    Should lay a task severe.

I should have waited till her eyes
    A soft esteem confess'd;
Ere e'en in private to her ear
    I had my love express'd.

I err'd, my friend;—my pensive heart
    Does oft its error own
When 'stead of love's impassion'd voice
    I hear cold duty's tone.

To-morrow's sun (but can I then
    Taste fullness of content?)
She seals with me the nuptial oath,[1]
    Oh may her heart assent!

E'en when I left her yesternight,
    And fondly breath'd adieu,
And of the morrow talk'd, her cheek
    Assum'd a paler hue.

Cold she withdrew her trembling hand,
    And as she turn'd aside,
I saw a tear, the tears of love
    Would she attempt to hide?

If to her sire I breathe a doubt,
    He talks of virgin shame;
Of timid diffidence, which checks
    Chaste beauty's bashful flame.

Still as I listen to his words,
    Each sad suggestion flies,
And all my future hours of life
    In prospect sweet arise.

O gallant Edgar! think me not
    The slave of jealous fear;
The doubt that hangs upon my heart
    Is caus'd by love sincere.

---

1 Tomorrow they are to be married.

Might but to-morrow make her blest,
　　How welcome were the day!
But while in talk we waste the hour,
　　The night wears fast away.

My brave preserver; from thy breast
　　Dismiss this gloom of woe;
And with thy friend, on festal mirth,
　　One happy day bestow."

"Blest be thy morrow," Edgar cry'd,
　　"The first of happy days!
But shall my father say his son
　　At bridal feast delays?

Six annual suns have seen his cheek
　　Bedew'd with constant tears;
Nor shall those sorrows cease to flow,
　　Till Edgar's self appears."

"Go then," Rodolpho rising, cried,
　　"If such thy kind desire,
Within my castle rest to-night,
　　To-morrow seek thy sire.

Yet when his fond impassion'd arms
　　Shall suffer thee to stray,
Reflect that Norfolk owes a debt
　　He lives but to repay."

The parting warriors now again
　　The hands of friendship join'd;
And Edgar, guided by a page,
　　Sought out the room assign'd.

They pass'd through many a marble hall,
　　And many a lofty dome,
With cedar lin'd, or richly grac'd
　　By Antwerp's costly loom.[1]

---

1 Antwerp (Belgium) was known as a place where fine lace was produced
during this period.

The wish'd apartment gain'd, the Knight
    Again admiring gaz'd;
For here, the wall with portraits hung,
    The mimick pencil prais'd.

On one fine painting, full in sight,
    He cast a startled view;
A woman's form; his beating heart
    Confess'd the likeness true.

"Know'st thou that lady?" to the page
    Impetuously he cried;
"It is Albina," said the youth,
    "My master's destin'd bride."

"Thy master's bride, Albina, say—
    The Baron Siward's heir!"
"The same, but scarce the painter's art
    Could sketch the peerless fair."

The page retir'd—the Knight alone
    Stood motionless in thought:
His lov'd Albina! For whose sake,
    He Robert's banners fought.

The hope that Norfolk's friendship rais'd,
    On her alone rely'd;
Albina! soul-distracting thought!
    Is Norfolk's destin'd bride.

Beneath a canopy of state,
    Which grac'd the proud alcove,
In vain the downy couch invites
    The frantick slave of love.

Still gazing wild with folded arms,
    The portrait full in view,
He drives love's arrows in his heart,
    And barbs their shafts anew.

Yet from Rodolpho's boding fear
    A dawn of hope may break,

The tear that pain'd the gen'rous Earl
    Might flow for Edgar's sake.

"Oh blasted be that impious hope!
    Shall I the villain prove,
And steal from him I most esteem,
    The idol of his love?

No, from this moment every wish
    Despairing I forego;
'Tis better to be curs'd myself,
    Than cause Rodolpho's woe.

Albina, tho' I must till death
    Thy lovely form adore,
Thy lovely form, thy angel face,
    Shall feast these eyes no more.

The story of my hapless love
    Shall ne'er thy ear offend,
Nor fondly wake the pitying sigh
    That wrongs my gen'rous friend.

That dear remembrance once bestow'd,
    Thus from my arm I tear;
Would I could tear her from my heart,
    But she is rooted there."

Now from his arm the string of pearl
    He eagerly unties;
The string of pearl Albina gave,
    His youthful valour's prize.

"Go, bracelet, to Rodolpho's soul
    A love like mine convey;
But teach the genial flame to burn
    With more auspicious ray.

Go, when he binds thee on his arm
    An equal joy impart,
As once I felt, when first the smile
    Of beauty touch'd my heart."

So pass'd the tedious night, now faint
    Approaching morning gleams;
And e'en sad Edgar's woe-worn breast
    Receives its gladd'ning beams.

One wish remain'd, it was to sooth
    The anguish of his sire;
He hastens to the castle gate,
    There meets Rodolpho's Squire.

To him the bracelet he consigns,
    To bear it to his friend;
And with it say, that Edgar's prayers
    Will still the Earl attend.

But pensive visions of the night
    Had wak'd the ill-omen'd dread,[1]
That fresh distresses ripen'd hung
    O'er Edgar's fated head.

"Howe'er severe on me," he cries,
    "The blow of anguish falls,
May peace and happy love secure
    These hospitable walls."

Then, all his dearest hopes resign'd,
    Upon his horse he sprung;
The courser's hoofs re-echoing loud,
    Upon the champaign rung.

The Earl arose; he sought his friend,
    Then at his absence sigh'd;
And pensive, on his arm the pledge
    Of parting kindness ty'd:

And now his bridal train he call'd,
    And vaulted on his steed;
'Twas snowy white, of faultless form,
    And sprung from gen'rous breed.

---

1 In the first edition, "illumin'd," an apparent error.

Exulting on Rodolpho's cheek
　　Sate expectation warm;
And dignity and manly ease
　　Seem'd blended in his form.

Rich was his vesture; o'er his horse
　　Embroider'd trappings flow'd;
But worth disclaiming outward pomp,
　　The Earl conspicuous shew'd.

At Siward's castle now arriv'd,
　　The joyful Baron came
To meet the splendid cavalcade,
　　And bless Rodolpho's name.

"Thou gen'rous friend, to whom I owe
　　My fortune and my life,
Come, ever welcome!" he exclaim'd,
　　"Behold thy destin'd wife."

Slow was the fair Albina's step,
　　And pensive was her air;
Her face was pallid as the veil
　　Which held her beauteous hair.

Tho' deck'd in bridal robes of state,
　　Yet still her looks express'd
The victim of unhallow'd rites,
　　For mournful orgies dress'd.

"Receive, my child," her father cried,
　　"Thy virtues to reward,—
Receive from thy fond parent's hand
　　This brave and worthy lord.

No longer let thy maiden fears
　　A coy reserve impart;
Avow the love that heaven approves,
　　And give him all thy heart."

Albina now her pensive eyes
　　On brave Rodolpho threw;

And when they met his ardent gaze,
    They timidly withdrew.

He snatch'd her hand; "What! still, my fair,
    This cold and distant fear?
Does my Albina doubt my love,
    Or why distress'd appear?

"Oh! rest assur'd, thou dearest trust
    That Heaven on earth can give;
'Tis but to make my charmer blest
    That now I wish to live.

"But yesternight, when robbers fell
    My evening walk assail'd,
Lifeless on earth the servant sunk,
    Who to defend me fail'd:

"When from my tir'd o'erpower'd arm
    Its wonted vigour fled,
And death's eternal gloomy shade
    Seem'd falling on my head:

"Memory, amid the tumult wild,
    Thy lovely image drew;
And thy soft woes, in fancy seen,
    Restor'd my strength anew.

"When rescu'd by a gallant knight
    Whom heav'n to save me sent,
Life seem'd a nobler gift, since life
    Would now with thee be spent.

"But wherefore should I bless the hand
    That did the gift bestow,
If from thy fix'd, thy cold disdain,
    I only anguish know?"

"Let not my lord," Albina said,
    "Such painful doubts suggest,
Nor think his merit fails to move
    Albina's conscious breast.

"Can she forget, when scorn'd, refus'd,
    In vain she mercy crav'd,
When, at the moment of despair,
    His gen'rous pity sav'd?

"If then his kind, but partial eyes,
    Deems her a meet reward,
Duty shall prompt her grateful heart,
    To bless her honour'd Lord."

END OF PART II.

PART III.

"I am not of that feather to shake off
My friend when he most needs me. I do know him
A gentleman, that well deserves a help,
Which he shall have."

                                  SHAKSPEARE.[1]

Now, while th'attendant train carous'd,
    And drain'd the festal bowl,
While musick's various pow'rs combin'd,
    Entranc'd each joyful soul,

Rodolpho, whispering to his love,
    His Edgar's worth express'd,
And shew'd the bracelet he receiv'd
    From his departing guest.

Instant her looks, her trembling frame,
    Confess'd a wild alarm;
While her fix'd eyes, with frantick gaze,
    Dwelt on her lover's arm.

Vain was each effort to conceal
    Surprize so highly wrought;
She fainted; but Rodolpho's arms,
    The sinking beauty caught.

---

1 From William Shakespeare's *Timon of Athens*, a difficult play usually classed with his tragedies.

Their lovely mistress to support,
    Th' attendant handmaids flew;
Reluctant from her opening eyes
    The thoughtful Earl withdrew.

Cold o'er his soul each doubt confirm'd,
    Its painful influence flung,
And heavy on his bended arm
    His head recumbent hung.

When Siward, whose presaging heart
    The cause too well divin'd,
With agitated pleading look,
    Rodolpho quickly join'd.

Now all retir'd; a pause ensu'd;
    To break it Siward try'd;
Check'd by Rodolpho's look, which spoke
    Stern honour's wounded pride.

At length he said, "Let not my Lord
    Suspect a passion base:
Did e'er my daughter's guiltless heart,
    With mean desire debase?

"A rustick stripling[1] at a joust
    With victory was crown'd,
And gain'd the bracelet, which is now
    Entwin'd thy arm around.

"My daughter's hand bestow'd the prize,
    But he audacious grew,
And dar'd, with bold presumptuous love,
    Thy promis'd bride to view.

"I drove him from my wide domain,
    And many a year is pass'd,[2]
Since in the wars of Palestine
    I trust he breath'd his last.

---

1 In the second edition, "strippling," a newly introduced error. A stripling is
a young man.
2 In the second edition, "past."

"But when Albina on thy arm
    The well-known bracelet view'd,
Her shame and scorn at Edgar's love
    Were painfully renew'd."

"There need no pleas, I rest assur'd,"
    Rodolpho answer'd mild;
"But this young Edgar, only once
    Did he behold thy child?

"No plea of merit had the youth?
    Was love his only claim?"
He paus'd, and Siward's conscious cheek
    Confess'd the blush of shame.

"His courage," Siward cried, "my lands
    From lawless ruffians sav'd;
But when I offer'd him reward,
    His pride the offer wav'd.

"Yet till his manner, voice, and look,
    His latent views express'd,
Within my castle he abode,
    My brave acknowledg'd guest."

Th' indignant Earl now check'd the tear
    Which unpermitted stole,
And to the rigour of his fate
    Compos'd his manly soul.

"Go, o'er thy daughter's grief," he cried,
    "Drop pity's soothing balm,
Whilst I in yon sequester'd grove
    Regain a mental calm."

But not the still sequester'd grove
    Could calm Rodolpho's soul,
Still on his mind Albina's tears
    And Edgar's anguish stole.

Now beauty in the net of love
    His heart close captive held;

Now grateful friendship's manlier force
    The Syren's snare repell'd.

"Did less of beauty, less of worth,
    Around Albina blaze,
Less were the torture to resign,
    But less would be the praise.

"For this did Edgar from my head
    A certain death remove,
That I should sever from his breast
    The last faint hope of love?

"Did but his soul for fortune pant,
    Or sought he pow'r to gain,
How would I gratify each wish!
    Yet still the fair retain.

"Retain the fair! retain her! how?
    What now her vows demand?
Know that another has her heart,
    Yet seize her captive hand?

"Forbid it, Pity! Honour, scorn
    Indelible disgrace!
Love may with tortures tear my heart,
    But shall not make it base."

He call'd a page:—to Edgar's house
    He bade him point the road:
Not distant, in a grassy vale,
    Appear'd the plain abode.

A hawthorn hedge the garden bound,
    'Twas fill'd with many a flow'r;
A woodbine round a maple twin'd,
    Compos'd a sylvan bow'r.[1]

And there the aged Orcar oft,
    His talk of labour done,
Gaz'd on the spangled arch of heav'n,
    And mus'd upon his son.

---

1 A sylvan bower is an idealized rustic cottage.

There too, that gallant son return'd,
 He sought his griefs to calm;
And pour'd upon the wounds of love
 Consolatory balm.

"Ah! whither, dear unhappy boy,
 Does thy distraction tend?
Far swifter than yon sailing clouds,
 Life hastens to its end.

"Still as our steps, advancing, verge
 On its declining stage,
The prospects faint and distant grow
 Which did our youth engage.

"Our passions, as we bend to earth,
 Imbibe a sombre gloom;
And length'ning with our setting sun,
 The shadows reach the tomb.

"Then chief on those who patient tread
 An irksome path of woe,
Bright bursting from an happier clime,
 The streams of glory flow.

"Nor urge *my* disappointed hopes,
 I do not *now* complain:
When I beheld thee, one embrace
 Repaid each former pain.

"I ask'd not for my darling wealth,
 Virtue was all my pray'r;
And Heav'n did limit other gifts,
 To be more lavish there.

"Yet, Edgar, if thy patient soul
 The taunt of pride repell'd,
Patient endur'd the soldier's toil,
 Yet saw his rights withheld;

"Oh! bid it, in one trial more,
 Invulnerable prove,

And triumph o'er the envious shaft
    Of disappointed Love."

"Envy! Oh, father," cried the youth,
    "My heart the term disdains;
That heart, where next, bright maid, to thee,
    The brave Rodolpho reigns.

"Had any suitor cross'd my hopes,
    With merit less replete,
I would have check'd his gay career,
    Or perish'd at his feet.

"Father, thou know'st Albina's face,
    Far lovelier was her mind;
While Siward favour'd, I full oft
    With her in converse join'd.

"And still the maid would tell the joys
    On virtuous love conferr'd;
Deceiv'd by sanguine hope, I thought
    Her theme to me referr'd.

"Rodolpho now, with purest joy
    Shall listen to that theme,
Feel each licentious wish confin'd,
    Yet taste a bliss supreme.

"For him she weaves the martial scarf:
    For him the garland wreathes:
Strikes at his call the soft-ton'd harp,
    And strains soul-piercing breathes.

"Oh! let us seek some distant spot;
    My love I will suppress;
The father, whom till now I griev'd,
    Henceforward I will bless.

"For thee, and thee alone, I'll stay
    The purpose of despair;
Conscious that man is born to woe,
    Those woes I'll firmly bear."

He said, and with a sickly smile
    The drooping Orcar cheer'd,
When sudden at the wicket gate
    The gen'rous Earl appear'd.

He saw his friend, a painful thrill
    Seem'd ev'ry thought to check,
'Till brave Rodolpho's outstretch'd arms
    Were circled round his neck.

Long paus'd the Earl, then fault'ring spoke,
    " 'Twas much unkind to go,
To leave me on this awful day
    Did little friendship show.

"I come to lead thee to the hall,
    The feasts, the sports attend;
And ev'n Albina's self requests
    The presence of my friend."

"Does she request it?" Edgar cry'd,
    And fix'd his glaring eye;
"She doth request it," said the Earl,
    "Can'st thou the fair deny?"

"No, I will go!"—Forth from the bow'r
    With frantick speed he sprung;
His troubled soul to phrensy'd rage
    By fancy'd wrong was stung.

Now whilst upon his panting breast
    His mail he firmly ties,
Orcar on pensive Norfolk turn'd
    His mild persuasive eyes.

"Great Earl, shall not that youth's despair
    Thy kind concern engage?
He is my son, my only child,
    And lo! I droop with age."

"Oh venerable sire! no wrong
    Thy Edgar shall annoy;

But follow, and prepare thy soul
    To meet a scene of joy."

Silent and swift, across the vale
    The tortur'd friends return'd;
Dejection sunk Rodolpho's heart,
    With anger Edgar's burn'd.

"This low-born sneer, this mean device,"
    Thus to himself he said,
"Shall all her former virtues blast,
    And all her charms degrade.

"I thank her, for I now am free,
    My heart each fetter breaks;
From visions of ideal worth
    My wond'ring soul awakes.

"With smiles of cold contempt I'll meet,
    Her proud exulting eye;
My heart may in the conflict break,
    But it shall never sigh."

Now broke upon his loathing view
    The castle's turrets white;
Those turrets which in happier days
    Inspir'd a gay delight.

Far diff'rent now, each lofty spire,
    And gaily swelling dome,
Increas'd the horrors of despair,
    And deepen'd all its gloom.

Now joyful, at the Earl's return,
    The portals were unbarr'd;
The bridal train in order stood
    Within the castle-yard.

Rodolpho fair Albina sought
    Within the hall of state;
Affrighted, trembling, and dismay'd,
    The mournful beauty sate.

Silent her father stood, his looks
    Spake horror's pale presage;
Ambition's sullen gloom, the scowl
    Of disappointed rage.

Now Edgar on his long-lov'd maid
    Throws his disdainful eyes;
But when he sees her grief of soul,
    Far diff'rent passions rise.

"Those clasped hands, that solemn look,
    Do they insulting prove?
Thine, Norfolk, was the mean device,
    Thou tyrant in thy love!"

His trembling hand now grasps his sword,
    But honour, soon alarm'd,
Determines yet to spare a foe,
    Unguarded and unarm'd.

"Yet, haughty Earl, the hour shall come,
    Nor distant is the time,
When bursting from each vein, thy blood
    Shall expiate thy crime.

" 'Till then, with insolent delight
    My heartfelt anguish view."
So thought the youth, and o'er his face
    His beaver[1] sternly drew.

Radiant as in a night of frost
    Beams Cynthia's silver car,[2]
Albina look'd, through chilling grief
    Each charm seem'd lovelier far.

Rodolpho took one parting gaze,
    A long and deep farewell;
It seem'd at once eternal love
    And fix'd regret to tell.

---

1 The lower portion of the face-guard of his visored helmet (*OED*).

2 Another reference to classical mythology, as the goddess Artemis or Diana (the poem's Cynthia) is imagined in her role driving a silver car (here cart or carriage) across the sky.

Her father seiz'd her hand, she rose,
    To Norfolk's Earl she came;
Reluctant was her ling'ring step,
    And terror shook her frame.

"Canst thou," she cry'd, "the sudden pang,
    Which reason blam'd, forgive?
I never more shall see the youth,
    Yet suffer him to live."

The Earl receiv'd the proffer'd hand
    That Siward had resign'd;
"Thou givest her to me," he said;
    "I do," the Sire rejoin'd.

"Then thus with her I pay the debt
    Which I to valour ow'd;"
He turn'd, and on his frantick friend
    Th' angelick maid bestow'd.

Then whil'st o'er all his glowing face
    Benignant transport broke,
Thus to the agonized pair
    The gen'rous Noble spoke.

"Sweet mourner, turn, Rodolpho yields
    To Edgar's claim thy vows;
Turn, lovely maid, with tender smiles
    Now greet thy destin'd spouse.

"Fortune and merit both combin'd,
    Thy passion shall approve;
Nor thou, brave Edgar, doubt the friend
    That gives thee e'en his love.

"Siward, if still thy narrow heart
    Can humble worth disdain,
Know, Edgar from this hour is lord
    Of many a fair domain.

"Soon o'er the lands which I bestow
    His lib'ral care shall shine;

Give rapture to his father's heart,
    And self-reproach to thine.

"Nor, Edgar, let a friendly fear
    Thy present bliss decrease;
Approving virtue cheers my soul,
    And all within is peace.

"Charm'd by the joys, which heav'n around
    Benevolence hath thrown,
I share the blessings I impart,
    Nay, make them all my own.

"Hereafter in some pensive hour
    Should selfish thoughts offend,
To banish every mean regret,
    I'll seek my happy friend.

"There as he shines, in fortune, fame,
    In love, in virtue blest,
The musick of his grateful voice
    Shall harmonize my breast."

Continuation of the 12*th Chapter of*
The Gossip's Story.

When Sir William Milton had finished the long manuscript, Captain Target, who had with great difficulty refrained from paying his respects to Morpheus[1] during the recital, began to rouse his faculties by emphatical commendations, which he happily divided between the story and the reader.

Marianne, whose eyes swam with tears, rejoiced that the lovers were at last made happy together, of which she had once many doubts.

Mr. Alsop applying every word which Marianne uttered in favour of love, to his own advantage, took courage, and ventured to give his opinion; which was, that it was very cleverly brought about to make my Lord give up some demesnes to Edgar, for he

---

1 Morpheus was the Greek god of dreams.

thought the *Old Gentleman* never would have allowed his daughter to marry a man, who was not only of low birth, but who had no *fortune*.

"Mr. Alsop," said Sir William contemptuously, "overlooks the circumstance which ennobled Edgar; he bore arms in Palestine."

Captain Target could not suffer a hint in favour of the military line to pass unnoticed. He bowed profoundly to the Baronet, and declared himself happy in entertaining the same honourable sentiments of the character of a soldier; adding in a theatrical style, "None but the brave deserve the fair. Is not that your opinion, Miss Dudley?"

"I hope, Sir," said Louisa, colouring at this unexpected reference, "I shall not offend your allowable partiality for your *own* profession by observing, that I am glad Rodolpho is not left unhappy. Indeed I think he is placed in the most enviable situation, since the consciousness of having performed a highly generous action, must afford a perfect delight to an exalted mind. But Edgar labours under the weight of an obligation, which he never can repay; besides, he may fear that his transports are the cause of distressing his benefactor."

"My sentiments, Madam, respecting the sublime pleasures of generosity entirely coincide with yours," said Sir William; "but I am sorry to hear you speak of gratitude as a *painful* sensation."

"Not absolutely so," replied Louisa, distrest at an observation which was accompanied by a look of angry penetration. "I only think Rodolpho's is the most enviable lot. He is placed in such a favourable point of view that had I been Albina, I should have felt half sorry to resign such a worthy lover."

"Not if you had been previously attached to Edgar, sister, and recollected what he had suffered for your sake," said the gentle Marianne. "True, Madam," exclaimed Alsop with a deep sigh; "but every body don't know what true love is."

"Indeed, sister," returned Louisa, laughing, "Mr. Alsop is a better adept in love affairs than I am: but let us change the subject of conversation. It grows too interesting."

Mr. Dudley now observed, that if the manuscript had entertained his friends, it answered the purpose for which he had

introduced it. Its merit, he said, consisted in its simplicity, and he
was going to make some observations on the studied ornaments
with which many modern poets overload their productions, till
they obscure the sense, and disturb the harmony of the language;
when the entrance of a servant to announce supper happily
relieved the Danbury gentlemen from a literary discussion, of
which, to say the truth, they were not very fond.

On their return home, Mr. Alsop asked his friend's opinion
respecting the present state of his affairs. The Captain swore
they were in an admirable train, and mentioned Louisa's laughing at him, as a convincing proof that she was apprehensive of his
influence over her sister's mind.

In short, things were thought ripe for the grand attack, and
it was agreed that a letter should be written expressive of Mr.
Alsop's passion, which his confident promised to deliver. They
then separated for the evening; the Captain to fabricate a speech,
intimating a struggle between love and friendship; and Mr.
Alsop to read the Polite Letter-writer,[1] prior to the composition
of his intended epistle.

---

1 Mr. Alsop plans to consult a book of a type popular in the eighteenth
century—one that taught readers the etiquette of composing letters, often
by offering examples of a particular type of epistle. One such title (a very descriptive title!) was *The newest and most compleat polite familiar letter-writer.
On the most important concerns in life, both with regard to love and business; in
which is included letters giving an account of the political state of England, with
several letters of the most celebrated authors, both antient and modern, viz. Pliny,
Cicero, Voltaire, Locke, Balzac, ... King of Prussia, &c. &c. With a collection of
the newest and most polite message cards. A collection of select moral sentences,
extracted from the most eminent authors both antient and modern, directing
not only how to think, but to act justly and prudently in the common concerns of
human life. And ten precepts, which William Lord Burghley gave to his second son
Robert Earl of Salisbury. To which is prefixed, a large introduction, containing
directions and proper forms to be observed in writing familiar letters on all occasions, and addressing persons of eminent rank and station. For the use of young
gentlemen, ladies, tradesmen, &c. The second edition, with large additions and
amendments*. By John Tavernier, Esq. (1760).

CHAP. XIII.

*A letter (but not the one the reader was induced to hope for) calls
forth some very antiquated notions.*

The post arrived at Stannadine soon after the departure of the
visitors, and Mr. Dudley on receiving a packet from his London
correspondent, wished his daughters a good night, and retired to
his chamber.

The intelligence it contained was of the unpleasant kind. It
certified the report, that the French had detached a squadron to
lay wait for the West-India fleet; which was destitute of adequate
means of defence against an unexpected attack; it also added,
that the capture of a ship in which they had hoped to receive
large remittances, had precipitated the ruin of Mr. Tonnereau's
firm, which had that day stopped payment.[1]

While Mr. Dudley sat meditating on his misfortunes, with
the deep regret of a man sensible that he had been guilty of an
irretrievable error, Louisa entered the room. Mr. Dudley's agitated mind was strongly impressed on his countenance; but his
daughter was in too much disorder to regard it. Pale, trembling,
and unable to speak, she gave him a letter which *she* had just received; and while he perused it, she sunk into a chair. I shall copy
this alarming epistle:

'TO MISS DUDLEY.

'Madam,

'I make bold, though a perfect stranger, to trespass upon your
goodness. I am told that you are shortly to be married to Sir

---

1 France and Great Britain were then at war, so this was a calculated attack
on a British ship from the West Indies by the French. Mr. Dudley's property
on the ship was pirated by the French. As we were told earlier, Mr. Dudley's
remaining assets were invested in a friend's great mercantile house, here
revealed to be Tonnereau's. As a result of the ship's capture, Tonnereau's firm
had to stop paying its creditors and investors—in effect going bankrupt. Mr.
Dudley is financially ruined.

William Milton. I must say, Madam, from all I have heard of you, I wish you a better husband than such a villain. I am a poor widow woman, who keeps a coffee-house in —— street, and a few years ago my daughter (a very handsome, well-behaved young woman) went to the Indies, in hopes to make her fortune. She there met Sir William, then only Captain Milton, and he fell in love with her, and she with him. He promised to marry her, and so at last ruined her.[1] But he kept her like a Princess all the while she staid there. Poor creature, the worse for her now. For at last he quarrelled with her, and left her behind him when he came to England, and would do nothing for her, and she is come home in great distress indeed. She has two children, Madam, and I have hard work to maintain myself these bad times. So I hope you will persuade Sir William to do something handsome, and I shall be bound to pray for you; from

'Your humble servant,

'MARY MORTON.

'N.B. He ought to do something for his children, they are too young to affront him.'

Mr. Dudley, after perusing the letter, cast his eyes upon his daughter, and asked her what could be done.

"Can I, Sir," said Louisa, bursting into tears, "vow to love and to honour a man who labours under such an imputation? Cruelty is added to licentious perfidy. My dear father, forgive me! My very soul revolts against this union."

"Oh worthy of thy excellent mother," said Mr. Dudley: "No, Louisa, you cannot. I am far from thinking so lightly as some people do of the vicious irregularities in which many young men indulge: but to abandon the unhappy creature he has seduced, to the horrors and temptations of poverty; to make no provision for his innocent, helpless offspring! Rather would I see thee a beggar, than suffer thee to contaminate thyself by participating in his guilty affluence. He capable of a generous affection! Impossible!"

---

1 Here "ruin" means sexual ruin. Milton is revealed to be a libertine and a heartless one at that. Some men of means provided financially for their bastard children, but Milton did not do so for his offspring with Miss Morton.

"You have relieved my anxiety," replied Miss Dudley; "yet why should I doubt that my dear father would see the atrocity of such an action in as strong a light as myself? But, Sir, you have had letters from London. Not distressing ones I hope."

"They are not consolatory, my child," resumed Mr. Dudley; "but we must first decide upon this affair."

Louisa, who perceived her father agitated by a contrariety of passions, guessed at the intelligence he would not communicate, and regretted that she had rushed into his presence, to overwhelm him with the additional weight of her own sorrows. She strove to compose herself, and again perused the letter from Mrs. Morton. She began to think it possible she might have been betrayed by her secret prejudices, to adopt a severe opinion without sufficient proofs; and, determined not to trust to her own judgment, asked her father, if the letter did not bear evident marks of being dictated by strong resentment.

Had Mr. Dudley seen what passed in his daughter's mind at that moment, he would have contemplated the triumph of filial piety, desirous of giving up every thing but its integrity, to ward the shafts of misfortune from him. He would have admired the virtue that warred with even the innocent and allowable propensities of the heart, and still more would his daughter's character have risen in his eye, from her attempt to hide the intended sacrifice from his observation, by giving to the excuses she was forming, the air of extenuating love. He was ignorant of these circumstances, and when Louisa asked him, if it would not at least be just to allow Sir William an opportunity of justifying his conduct, he supposed it possible the dislike his daughter at first expressed against her lover, had subsided; and was succeeded by a degree of attachment.

But since love, though indulged to the degree of dotage, would not, in Mr. Dudley's opinion, obviate the many evils incident in an alliance between a virtuous woman and a profligate man; he only wished, from the supposed state of Louisa's affections, that Sir William might be able to justify himself from the severe imputations cast upon his character. On reading the letter again, he thought it probable that spleen, violence, and disappointment might aggravate the offence. "But depend upon it, my love," said he, "the charge has some foundation. It would be wrong not to hear what he can plead in his defence, and indeed you cannot now decline his addresses, without giving him a reason for your conduct. I will speak to him to-morrow morning."

Louisa now pressed her father to discover the purport of his intelligence from London, but he eluded enquiry,[1] determined that she should know nothing more of his misfortunes, till Mrs. Morton's accusation was either refuted or confirmed. He rightly thought, that though pecuniary circumstances may influence a woman's choice, when no solid objections can be made to the lover; innocence, if bribed by the wealth of the universe, should shrink from a connection with vice. He therefore pretended the ease he did not feel, and reminding her of the lateness of the hour, with a fervent caress dismissed her to repose. It was a blessing which neither of them enjoyed that night: besides the pressure of their own sorrows, each of them laboured under the apprehension of what the other endured; for the filial and paternal ties are at least as susceptible of these emotions, as either friendship or love.

CHAP. XIV.

A wealthy lover is dismissed by a family upon the eve of bankruptcy, for what the world may style spirited conduct.

Miss Dudley rising early next morning, as was her usual custom, to superintend domestick affairs, met Sir William in the passage leading to the breakfast-room. He had an unusual degree of urbanity in his aspect, and seizing her hand with an air of gallantry, begged the favour of a few minutes' conversation: Louisa reluctantly assented; and he gave her a letter he had just received from his mother, in which her Ladyship expressed her eagerness to receive a daughter of her late beloved friend, in a yet *more* endearing point of view, than that in which her nephew hoped

_____

1 In the second edition, "inquiry."

to have presented one. She concluded with begging, that his amiable mistress would sacrifice a few scruples of punctilio to her earnest entreaties. Her health, she said, was apparently declining, and she felt all a parent's anxiety to see the happiness of her son secured, and to participate in his transports, while she was yet able to enjoy them. Sir William strengthened this argument by urging his own impatience; he flattered himself he had not been wholly undeserving her favour; settlements he was ready to discuss with Mr. Dudley; but as he meant by their liberality to prove his high sense of her merits, no objections could arise on that head. He concluded with hoping, that as female coquetry had no part in her character, she would shorten the time of probation, and favour him with an early day.[1]

Louisa, with streaming eyes, perused Lady Milton's letter, and from the maternal tenderness visible in every part, was led to wish that she could gratify the kind request. She started from her reverie at Sir William's last words; the proof of his unworthiness flashed upon her mind, and while her soul overflowed with veneration for the mother, it shrunk in abhorrence from her son. She attempted to speak, but was unable. She turned aside her face glowing with confusion, and clung to the arm of her chair as if to support her trembling frame. Sir William, who construed her behaviour into maiden delicacy, was going, by declarations of everlasting love, to deliver her from her embarrassment; when Mr. Dudley entered the room. Louisa never beheld her father approach with more pleasure; she instantly rose, and referring her lover to him for an explanation, hastily withdrew.

Though the young Baronet would have preferred receiving from his mistress the desired consent, he was not thrown into despair by this reference. He gave Mr. Dudley his mother's letter, and informed him that he had been urging Miss Dudley to favour him with a speedy union. Lady Milton's consent was, he said, of no consequence in one point of view, as his fortune was perfectly independent, and in his own possession; but as it implied a just respect for the Lady he so highly esteemed, he

---

1 Milton hopes that Louisa will not play hard to get or insist on a long engagement.

could not but rejoice in every tribute that was paid to his Louisa's virtues.

Mr. Dudley, after observing that he was the last man upon earth to whom apologies for filial deference were necessary, declared his grateful sense of Lady Milton's favourable sentiments of his family. He then hinted, that before the proposed alliance could take place, a very painful subject must be discussed.

Sir William, supposing he meant settlements, replied, that in all pecuniary concerns, Miss Dudley's wishes should be the only bound to his liberality.[1]

"I do not doubt your generosity on that head, Sir William; it was to another circumstance I alluded. But let me premise, that you see before you a man of bankrupt fortunes; one who has ruined himself and his child by a fatal confidence; one who has nothing but his integrity left. Be pleased, Sir, in our future conversation to remember this circumstance."

Sir William, grasping Mr. Dudley's hand, protested the intelligence gave him no pain except upon his account. He would with pleasure afford him all the assistance which his ample fortune could bestow. He would settle upon him what income he should judge necessary for his support; and as to his Louisa, the enjoyments of wealth would be doubled to him by her consenting to share them. He thanked Heaven he had no occasion to bound his expences by parsimonious rules, and liberality was the darling passion of his soul.

Mr. Dudley bowed with the air of one who would rather avoid than court the favour of proud munificence. Anxious, however, to avoid offending the haughty youth he intended to reprove, he expressed a lively sense of his generous promises. "Indulge me, Sir," said he, "with the privilege our present situation claims, and suffer me not only to act the part of a father to my girl, but of a

---

1 Marriage settlements were agreed on by both parties (often the fathers or the husband and the wife's father) and were generally drawn up as contracts by lawyers. These contracts included matters such as how much money the wife would bring to the marriage, whether she would be allowed any "pin money" (spending money), and what part of the marital fortune would go to her, rather than to their potential offspring, if the husband were to die before his wife (her "jointure").

real friend to you. A report has reached us which has given us both pain; and a just regard for Louisa's future peace compels me to ask the nature of your connexion with Miss Morton?"

A stroke of electricity could not have more sensibly affected Sir William Milton. A deep suffusion stole over his gloomy features, which was soon succeeded by a livid paleness. There needed no skill in physiognomy to exclaim, "Guilty, upon mine honour."

Mr. Dudley, who hoped his silence was at least a proof of contrition, proceeded: "It is not my wish, Sir, further to distress you; I see and pity your confusion. Few of us can walk in the unerring path of rectitude; and perhaps a sincere endeavour to reclaim our wandering steps is all that can be expected from human infirmity. Though licentious indulgencies ever were and must be criminal, I am willing to allow something for the impetuosity of youthful passions; the influence of dissipated society; and the unrestrained freedom of manners in which Europeans indulge themselves, in the luxurious climate of the East. But there are some circumstances in the distressing account which shocks credibility, and I doubt not but that you will exculpate yourself from *them*."

"Name them," said Sir William, in an imperious accent.

"That you have abandoned the unhappy creature you seduced, to want and all its horrid temptations. Nay, that you have neglected to provide for your own helpless, unoffending offspring."

"You must give up the author of this report," resumed the Baronet, in a loud, authoritative tone.

"Not till you in a satisfactory manner refute the charge."

"I scorn to answer anonymous scandal," said Sir William. "If you esteem me a villain on slender proofs—retain your opinion."

"I should rejoice in your vindication; but this warmth is no step towards it. The consequences of my thinking you a villain, is my daughter's rejection of your address."

"You speak, Mr. Dudley, as if the obligations were on *your* side. I have a due sense of your daughter's merit; but love has not so blinded my reason as to make me undervalue my own pretensions."

"I perceive, Sir," said Mr. Dudley, "that you *remember* my poverty: but I am still rich in my child, nor dare I entrust you with my only remaining treasure, till I am assured I commit her to the protection of a man of principle and honour. You frown, Sir; I cannot be silenced by a frown. The man who can so far preserve his equanimity of mind during the ruin of his fortune, as to ask nothing of the wealthy, is too rich to fear their resentment."

"Did you, Mr. Dudley, formerly find this intellectual wealth a good marketable commodity?" interrogated Sir William. "I rather suspect you did not fully appreciate its value, till you retired from mercantile pursuits."

"If by reminding me of the profession I once followed, you mean to throw any reflection on the general character of a British merchant, you rather expose your own want of information respecting the resources and wealth of this empire, than discredit me. I glory in having stimulated the industry of thousands; increased the natural strength of my country; and enlarged her revenue and reputation, as far as a private individual could. My fall has not been accelerated by vice, extravagance, or dishonesty: but we wander from the point. Disputes of this nature are only unnecessary aggravations. If you continue to refuse the desired explanation, I can no longer consider you as Louisa's lover; and whatever my sentiments of your conduct may be, it is only in that character that I can claim any right to inquire into it."

"I question," said Sir William, "if *that character* gives you the right to which you pretend. But it is not from *you*, Sir, that I shall take my dismission. I must see Miss Dudley, I will know how far you have prejudiced her against me. She may perhaps explain *your* motives for this extraordinary interference."

"I have no improper ones," replied Mr. Dudley, rising to ring the bell. Then addressing the servant who came in, he desired that Louisa would immediately attend. The gentleman remained sullenly silent till she entered the room.

"My dear," said Mr. Dudley, "Sir William Milton wishes to speak to you, perhaps he will favour you with the explanation he has refused me." He then attempted to withdraw; Louisa fixed her pleading eyes upon him, as if intreating[1] his stay; but he determined to resist their silent language; till Sir William observed that he had nothing to urge to Miss Dudley which it was improper for her father to hear.

"I find, Madam," said the haughty lover, "that I have forfeited Mr. Dudley's esteem. I wish to know if *you* too consider me as a base seducer; the betrayer of innocence; one who meanly abandons the creature he has plunged into guilt: nay, who deserts his own helpless, unoffending offspring? Are you too, Madam, resolved to withhold from me the name of my accuser?"

"If my father," replied Louisa, "has informed you of the charge, you must know in what light I consider it. I should desert the female character if I was destitute of delicacy and compassion: and unless you wish to *disprove* these censures, of what use can it be to discover from whence they proceed?"

"I perceive," returned Sir William, "(I wish I could say with indifference,) the slender hold I have of your affections. Perhaps, Madam, it was the splendor of my offers alone that procured me *even* a momentary attention."

"Had you, Sir, appeared to me at first in the light you now do, not even your *splendid* offers would have excited a moment's hesitation. I cannot reconcile my heart to an husband deficient in moral principle."

"And may I ask," exclaimed the peremptory lover, "what that high standard of perfection is by which those who aspire to you must be measured?"

"The standard after which you enquire,[2] Sir William, does not exceed moderation: it is humble like my own deserts. But we only agitate each other; permit me to withdraw."

"No, by my soul, I cannot lose you!" cried Sir William, in violent emotion. He would have bent his knee, but recollecting that Mr. Dudley was present, refrained from the undue condescension. He gazed upon her a few moments, and then in a low tone said, "You could not treat me with this indifference if you ever loved me. But even at this moment you scornfully enjoy my agony."

---

1 In the second edition, "intreating."
2 In the second edition, "inquire."

"As these censures," resumed Miss Dudley, "are merely intended to evade a charge you do *not* deny, I need not labour to reinstate myself in *your* good opinion. Yet I could wish to preserve Lady Milton's, and will entreat as a *last* favour, that, when you inform her of what has passed, you will give as candid an account of me as can consist with your own vindication."

"Sovereign contempt, by Heaven! But, Madam, you mistake me if you think to awe me into supplicatory submission. However highly you may rate my love, I can borrow some of your philosophy to conceal its pangs. May you find a worthier lover, or at least one who is a better adept in the disguises of courtship."

Sir William then ordered his horses, and Mr. Dudley, after an invitation to stay breakfast, which was coolly declined, did not oppose his departure.

CHAP. XV.

Calamity frequently expands a generous heart.

Mr. Dudley attempted to fortify his daughter's mind with those principles, which not only blunt the keenest arrows of disappointment, but convert them into blessings. "Your dream of happiness, my love," said he, "appears to be terminated: yet from the calm consistency of your conduct, I trust that you are not destitute of those mental supports, without which all that the world calls good is but splendid misery. You feel, my Louisa, that you have acted as you ought, and that reflection will enable you to support even the painful discovery of the unworthiness of a favoured lover." "It was your recommendation, Sir," replied Louisa, "which first induced me to accept Sir William Milton's offers. I relied upon your judgment, and felt assured that the good qualities you ascribed to him would excite my esteem, my gratitude, and my love. I have every reason to rejoice that we have been convinced of the defects in his temper and conduct, before it became my painful duty to endure them. But I fear, my dear father, that the termination of this connection may be of serious consequences to you?"

"When your mother died," replied Mr. Dudley, "I lost my high relish for the comforts and pleasures affluence bestows. I trust my heart has not been tainted by misanthropy, but I have been so accustomed to seek for my pleasures and comforts out of my own mind, that to renounce society, and to seclude myself from the world, will scarcely excite a sigh upon my own account.[1] For you, my child, I deeply feel; your spirits have not been broken by repeated trials, and rising into life, you look upon it with all the sanguine preference of youth. Anxious to preserve to you the prosperity you have hitherto enjoyed, I considered Sir William's apparent generosity with too favourable an eye; but no more of him. Amidst the ruin of my fortunes, I rejoice that the little estate your grandfather left you in Lancashire for pocket-money will preserve you from indigence. You have not to thank me for this reserve, it was happily secured from my indiscretion, and consequently could not be sacrificed to an artful, ungenerous friend."[2]

"My dearest father," said Miss Dudley, "do not afflict me by these self-upbraidings. I owe you a debt I never can discharge. Not to mention the thousand kind attentions which have hitherto made my life a round of delights, it is from you I have received a superior education; you instilled into my infant soul principles which, unless my own fault, must insure my present and future happiness. Why, Sir, for I will speak proudly, should not *your* daughter be able to find pleasure and comfort in the resources of her own mind as well as yourself? We shall live very comfortably upon that dear little estate you talk of. I always had a turn for œconomy and management; am quite a cottager in my heart, I assure you. The few friends we possess will continue to

1 Mr. Dudley will no longer have the money to maintain any standing in the world or to pay the costs associated with making visits or receiving visitors. His poverty will force him to "renounce society"—that is, the gentry and pseudo-gentry routine of visits, attending entertainments, and so on.

2 "Pocket-money" is independent spending money, which could be used at her own discretion. In other words, this estate from her grandfather does not generate enough income for an upper-middle-class family to live on, afford a carriage and a household of servants, and entertain visitors, but it was given to Louisa to spend on the fashionable activities it was assumed she would be raised to enjoy. The "artful, ungenerous friend" is Tonnereau.

esteem us in any station; and as to general acquaintance, I never considered them important to my happiness."

"A cottage life, my love," resum'd[1] Mr. Dudley, "is not so pleasant in reality as in theory. Like every other state it has its vexations, even for those who were born with no higher hopes. To them who have been accustomed to the elegant enjoyments of life, it presents evils that patience and fortitude may teach us to support; but which are doubtless evils. To you they will be less painful than to a light frivolous mind, and this is all my consolation."

Mr. Dudley then asked if Marianne had been informed of his perplexities? Louisa answered in the negative; but owned that her sister had lately made some enquiries to which (from an idea that it would be most agreeable to her father) she had given evasive answers.

Mr. Dudley commended her prudence. "When your grandmother took Marianne," said he, "it was with the express condition that she should exclusively be considered as *her* child. I trust you possess her friendship, and will occasionally receive substantial proofs of it: yet to be wholly cast as a dependant upon her bounty would not, I think, contribute to the happiness of either. She is dutiful, affectionate, and generous; but her feelings are peculiarly lively; and as is the case with most people of strong sensibility, there is some degree of uncertainty in her conduct. For my own part, there is scarcely a misery I would not sooner endure, than pension myself upon my child, with an apprehension that by so doing I might prevent her from forming such connections as her fortune and merit might otherwise attract. Had Mr. Pelham been agreeable to her, I think I could have been happy in the protection of such a son. I have judged from her cast of character, that a single life would be most conducive to her happiness; but as even candour itself could hardly acquit me of interested views, were I to urge such advice in my present situation, I have only to hope that I shall be able to conceal from her the present state of my affairs, until she selects some worthy admirer for her husband. Our expences at Stannadine indeed are

---

1 In the second edition, "resumed."

considerable, yet I think continuing them a few months longer, from the hope of her forming a suitable attachment, is justifiable. I shall not scruple applying to her for a share of them; besides my love, (here Mr. Dudley faintly smiled,) perhaps a publick enemy may prove more favourable to me than an insidious friend."[1]

Miss Dudley acquiesced in these opinions, and Marianne soon joined the party, anxious to know the cause of Sir William Milton's hasty departure. Her father was happy to hear her, after the perusal of Mrs. Morton's letter, express strong detestation of libertine principles; a sentiment which, I will affirm, is natural to a delicate unvitiated female mind.

Mr. Dudley then informed his daughters, that some unexpected business would call him to London. He lamented that he should lose the society which was so delightful to him; but yet would not be so selfish as to desire them to resign the country, while glowing in the richest robe of summer, to accompany him to a dirty, deserted town.[2] Louisa guessed at her father's real motives for declining their company, acquiesced in the pretended one; and Marianne was too much enamoured with purling streams, and moss-grown dells, to endure the thought of leaving Stannadine.

CHAP. XVI.

An interesting adventure. The purblind God of Love dispatched upon two different errands, commits an irreparable mistake.

The interesting particulars I have been relating afforded the greatest treat to my neighbours that they had enjoyed for many years. Two lovers at first encouraged, then hastily dismissed, opened a fine field for conjecture. Curiosity, which had hitherto been employed in successively detecting the extravagance, parsimony, careless negligence, and suspicious watchfulness of Miss

---

1 The public enemy is Sir William Milton. The insidious friend is Tonnereau.

2 The wealthy who were able to do so left London for the summer for a country estate. That is why Mr. Dudley describes London as "deserted."

Dudley's domestic management, was entirely diverted from family arrangements, to consider what *could* be the cause of these revolutions. After many debates, we at last finally determined, that Miss Marianne refused Mr. Pelham, because her father gave him a bad character; and that Sir William Milton *flew* off, when he discovered Louisa had no fortune.

The frequent visits of Captain Target and Mr. Alsop to Stannadine were another inexhaustible topic of conversation. I observed that this summer proved the healthiest I had ever known. None of my friends answered my enquiries with complaints of *feeling* they did *not know how*: not one creature had a nervous attack or was out of spirits. Sometimes we dispatched a nobleman in a coach and four to fetch off Marianne, and then again created a group of bailiffs, armed with an execution, to drive out the whole family.[1] For my own part, I made a very prudential use of this general solicitude. Whenever I laboured under any of those little perplexities which mistresses of a family sometimes feel, I introduced the Dudleys, and can truly say, that more than once it prevented my party from discovering that my coffee was cold, and my silver waiter dreadfully tarnished.

My friendship for Miss Cardamum would have given me pain, on account of the evident dereliction of her beaux; but happily that lady had accompanied her papa to Scarborough, from whence she wrote very sprightly letters to Mrs. Medium, obliquely intimating, that she had danced with two of the first gentlemen of fashion there, who had said very *soft* things to her. She enquired with perfect *nonchalance*, whether Alsop or Target had run away with Marianne Dudley yet; declaring either of them were very likely to draw in a raw young creature, who had seen nothing of the world. I considered these observations as an unquestionable proof that they had totally forfeited her good opinion.

I am however willing to hope that the reader's regard is not so

---

1 In other words, the town gossips imagine Marianne marrying a nobleman at one moment and imagine Mr. Dudley being forced from the estate and having his property confiscated as a debtor (and perhaps taken to debtor's prison) in the next moment.

wholly withdrawn from them, but that curiosity is still anxious to know the event of the letter, which we left Mr. Alsop composing in the twelfth chapter. It was indeed a very unfortunate performance, for though written in a fair legible hand, and very correctly spelt, it was so long in finishing, that before it was ready to present, Mr. Dudley had set out for London. As it began with stating, that the reason which determined him to that mode of address was to avoid the jealous attention of her father, the very basis on which it was founded being subverted, the unhappy edifice fell to the ground; and thus the offspring of the Loves and Graces was smothered in its birth. But still the heroick Alsop was not discouraged. How persevering and indefatigable is love!

To account for the confidence which swelled his hopes, I must disclose a secret which my Betty told me: namely, that by means of Miss Lappel, the millener,[1] a secret correspondence had been entered into between the aspiring lover and Mrs. Patty.[2] Every one who has clandestinely addressed a rich heiress knows that it is of great consequence to secure the waiting-maid; and I would not be so disrespectful to Mr. Alsop's learning, as to hint that he was deficient in such necessary knowledge. Mrs. Patty's zeal to have her lady married was too warm to be very nice about the intended husband; and no sooner did Miss Lappel tell her how deeply Mr. Alsop was *smitten*, and how very rich he was, than Patty thought it might do very well. They agreed indeed that he was *no wit*, and rather slow in conversation; but then he was good-natured, and Patty observed with a wink, that the *sharpest* men did not make the best husbands. In fine; by a prudent disposal of a few yards of Valenciennes edging,[3] Mr. Alsop secured an able assistant, and Patty entertained her lady with encomiums

---

1 A variant eighteenth century spelling of "milliner," a person who makes or sells hats for women.

2 Betty is Prudentia Homespun's (the narrator's) waiting-maid. Mrs. Patty is Marianne's waiting-maid. A waiting maid was a personal attendant who assisted a woman of means in getting dressed, doing her hair, etc., hence their assumed (and indeed, often actual) intimacy.

3 Valenciennes edging was a decorative French lace. Mr. Alsop has "bought" Mrs. Patty's assistance in his courtship with Marianne with a few yards of lace.

upon that gentleman's great merit, as often as she dared to enter upon the subject. The trusty Abigail too, whenever she wanted a little article at Miss Lappel's, took care to tell the happy lover, that her lady seemed more and more pleased when she told her about him, and that she was sure it would *do* in time.

Relying upon this intelligence, and feeling a degree of suspicion whether his old friend Target would play fair, for which doubt, to say truth, he had some reason, Mr. Alsop determined to trust all to his own person and eloquence; therefore, one fine hot morning in July, he set out, like another Paris,[1] to conquer or die. Not, indeed, attired like the young Trojan, when he challenged the gruff, ill-behaved king of Sparta to the lists of war; but in clean silk stockings; and a new pink padusuay[2] waistcoat; his hair loaded with powder; and the lower part of his face so enveloped in an enormous beau dash, as to threaten suffocation.[3] He wore a large bouquet of myrtles and geraniums, whether with an emblematick design, I will not say, and tossing a light rat-tan in his right hand, tripped nimbly over the meadow. I do not compare him to any ancient god, or modern knight of chivalry, not recollecting any similitude just in point. As he walked along he meditated, and determined to tell Miss Marianne, that he thought her the prettiest creature in the world; and that if she did not pity him, death must be the inevitable consequence: when, lo! as he turned round a corner to enter the court gate, she burst upon his view—not sitting alone in a shady bower—not gracefully reclined upon the turf, with a book in her hand, the emblem of elegant science; not awakening the echoes with her melodious voice; but pale, agitated, disordered in her look and appearance. She had just alighted from a carriage which stood

---

1 This is another reference to Greek mythology and to Helen of Troy, who was said to have been abducted by Paris, an act that brought about the Trojan War.

2 Paduasoy is a rich, strong silk fabric, popular in the eighteenth and nineteenth centuries.

3 Instead of a soldier, Mr. Alsop is dressed like a dandy. His hair is powdered white, and he is wearing what may be a large scarf or a wig tie. "To cut a dash" meant to make a showy appearance, and this may be what West means to signify with her description of the scarf or tie as a "beau dash." Beau is French for beautiful or pretty.

at the gate, and by the assistance of two gentlemen, who seemed absorbed in their attention to their fair charge, slowly entered the house. Mr. Alsop's alarm banished from his mind his intended heroicks, and he hastily enquired of a servant the cause of this incident.—He was informed, that Miss Marianne had ridden out that morning, and narrowly escaped a dreadful accident. Her horse had taken fright at a carriage which she met upon the road, and run away with her. She had sufficient presence of mind to keep her seat, till a young gentleman who followed the carriage, with equal agility and dexterity stopped the terrified animal, and extricated her from her perilous situation. The alarm however had overpowered her spirits, and she repeatedly fainted. Her preserver placed her in the chaise with his father, and both of them humanely accompanied her home.[1] Mr. Alsop judging his suit could not commence that morning, left his compliments, and after a great deal of sorrow for the accident, and joy that she was not hurt, promised to call again the next day.

Miss Dudley met her sister with tender anxiety, and assisted her to her chamber. As soon as she was assured that she had received no real injury, she left her to calm her agitated spirits, and returned to thank the gentlemen, for having preserved a life so truly valuable. The elder of the two, who seemed near sixty, had a keen, sensible aspect; the other did not appear to exceed twenty, and was remarkably handsome.

When Louisa had satisfied their concern, by informing them, that her sister was already much calmer, the elder of the gentlemen declared, that if the lady did not suffer from her alarm, he should almost be so selfish as to rejoice in a circumstance which had accelerated his introduction to a family, of whom he had conceived the highest opinion. He then said his name was Clermont, that he had lately arrived at a seat he had in the vicinity, and should be happy to be considered, by the Dudleys, in the light of a neighbour and a friend.

Louisa, who had heard Captain Target mention a Lord Clermont, with whom he was upon a most familiar footing, rightly concluded her present visitor to be that nobleman. She replied,

---

1 Compare to Jane Austen's *Sense and Sensibility*, Volume I, chapter IX.

that she felt assured her father (who was then from home) would be happy to cultivate an acquaintance so much to their honour. Mr. Clermont then requested permission to call and enquire after the lady's health next morning, which she readily granted, and the gentlemen withdrew, highly pleased with the exquisite beauty of Marianne, and the graceful politeness of her sister.

Miss Dudley now enquired of Marianne the circumstances of her late alarm, and was happy to see her recovered from every ill effect of it. She then told her what had passed in the drawing-room, the rank of the family, their wish to commence an acquaintance, the striking countenance of Lord Clermont, and the expressive beauty of his son. This latter circumstance Marianne denied, for possibly her fright prevented her from observing him; she also seemed to think there would be an impropriety in receiving a visit from him during her father's absence. Louisa laughed at her sister's prudery, till Marianne was rather displeased, and pettishly answered, that as she was determined upon a single life, her error was merely characteristick and of no consequence. She appeared, however, next morning dressed in an uncommonly elegant deshabille,[1] and her natural charms were improved by the advantage of well-adapted, but apparently unstudied ornament. I would not have my readers from thence conclude, that she was not really displeased at Miss Dudley's indiscreet permission; or that her resolution in favour of "blessed singleness" faultered; no young lady wishes to be seen a "mere figure," and a person may be very angry at their heart, and yet adorn their face with an enchanting smile.

Mr. Clermont was accompanied by his sister, a girl about fourteen, whom he presented to the ladies; as one zealously desirous to obtain their favourable opinion. He interrupted Marianne's thanks for the assistance he so fortunately gave her, by expressing the transport he felt at being able to render it. Miss Dudley directed her attention to Miss Clermont, who being

---

1 Although deshabille, from the French, indicates a state of being undressed or half-dressed, in this context the word means a casual morning dress. Probably, for the time, this would have been a thin white dress, drawn in under the chest, sometimes called a chemise dress.

too young and too timid to join much in conversation, it was principally supported by her brother and Marianne. Never was such a wonderful coincidence of opinion! Both were passionate admirers of the country; both loved moonlight walks, and the noise of distant waterfalls; both were enchanted by the sound of the sweet-toned harp, and the almost equally soft cadence of the pastoral and elegiack muse; in short, whatever was passionate, elegant, and sentimental in art; or beautiful, pensive, and enchanting in nature.[1]

When minds are in such happy unison, time flies unperceived. I cannot guess how long the morning call might have been protracted, had not the appearance of Mr. Alsop excited a different train of ideas. His dress and manner were equally calculated to caricature the part he meant to perform; and the hopes Mrs. Patty inspired had banished his natural timidity, without substituting any thing more valuable. His whole behaviour put the politeness of the party to a severe test. Marianne bit her lips to avoid laughing at his solemn enquiries respecting the consequences of her fright, and his assurances of the pain he felt at hearing of it. Mr. Clermont could only answer with a bow, when he assumed the office of Ciceroni, by offering to conduct him to all the *pretty places* in the garden.[2] Miss Dudley's embarrassment was encreased, by observing that Miss Clermont had by no means obtained a command over her risible muscles; but sat pinching her fingers to prevent a loud laugh. The Danbury Adonis determined when he left home, to *sit out* any company that might be at Stannadine; for to say truth he was tired of hot morning walks, and determined to carry off the prize before the return of her father.[3] The Clermonts, therefore, were compelled to order their carriage, and while the ladies accompanied them to the door, Miss Clermont expressed a hope that though her mother was not then in the country, Miss Dudleys would have the goodness to excuse her absence, and favour them with their

1 Compare to Jane Austen's *Sense and Sensibility*, Volume I, chapter X.

2 Ciceroni (from the Italian), a guide who conducts sightseers, or a mentor, a tutor.

3 Mr. Alsop (the Danbury Adonis, or handsome young man) intends to overstay his welcome and to outlast or "sit out" any other guests.

company at the park. Louisa, fearful of offending her sister's prudence, postponed the invitation till Mr. Dudley's return.

Mr. Alsop, who considered this visit as no good omen for him, felt his disagreeable prognosticks confirmed, by Louisa's returning to him with a slight apology for her sister's absence. He did not doubt that she was playing the part of a Duenna,[1] and despairing to elude such a watchful Argus,[2] at one time resolved boldly to demand a conference with his charmer. But recollecting that it would be as prudent to try to propitiate her keeper, he frankly owned that he was very deeply in love, mentioned his income, and earnestly implored her good opinion. He certainly knew which of the ladies he meant to address, but being much agitated, and not very clear in his expressions, he unhappily conveyed to her the arrogant hope that she was the object of his pursuit; she therefore thanked him for the honour he had done her, but intreated him to desist from an address which never could succeed. Mr. Alsop desired she would consult her sister, refusing to take a positive denial till Marianne was informed of his design. Miss Dudley thought this reference extraordinary, and told him her sister's sentiments could make no change in her determination. Mr. Alsop answered, she was then very barbarous, and said something about freedom, which Louisa mistaking, replied, she hoped freedom of opinion would be permitted to herself. At length the lover grew warm, and told her he saw her designs, and was determined to overthrow them, and to carry his point, in spight[3] of all the opposition she could make. Thus they separated, the gentleman in furious indignation; and the lady wondering what steps her resolute swain would take, to compel her to attend him to the altar.

---

1 Duenna here means chaperone.
2 A Greek mythological giant with one hundred eyes; thus, here, a very vigilant or observant person.
3 In the second edition, "spite."

CHAP. XVII.

A modern lover makes his exit, but not in a style of high heroism.

No sooner was Mr. Alsop gone, than Miss Dudley, impelled (I suppose) by the spirit of envy, flew to her sister, to inform her of the ardent passion she had inspired, in a heart which Marianne certainly accounted her own. I cannot say that the dispute between the ladies was carried on with as much acrimony as mirth; but certainly each heroically complimented the other with offers to resign the contested conquest. Poor Mr. Alsop's affair being soon dispatched, the conversation turned upon the Clermonts. Marianne commended the simplicity, propriety, and modest sweetness of the sister; and Louisa asked her, if she was not *now* a convert to the brother's uncommon beauty? Marianne was resolutely determined against love; but, since there was such a similarity of soul, intended to cultivate a platonick friendship with Mr. Clermont. I think in that heterogeneous composition beauty cannot be an essential quality. I rather suppose, since mind is the only object, it would subsist in its fullest perfection between old Blue Beard and Lady Medusa.[1] Marianne Dudley probably thought the same. She was shocked to hear her sister talk of Mr. Clermont as merely an handsome man; while she took no notice of that superior virtue, that inherent excellence, that sublime amiability which she already discovered was congenial to his soul. Indeed Louisa was apt to commend only what was apparent, and generally reserved her praise of those *latent* qualities, till their existence was confirmed by experience.

Marianne passed the remainder of the day in perusing pastorals, and playing upon her harp. At night, after having taken

---

1 Platonic friendship is heedless of beauty and could subsist between two unattractive people. Old Blue Beard was a character from popular mythology, said to have kept his murdered wives' corpses in a locked turret. Lady Medusa is the Greek mythological figure so ugly (with serpents for hair) she was said to turn onlookers to stone.

leave of her sister, Patty, with many apologies, many assurances that she would not do such a thing again for the world, many protestations that she met him quite by accident, and much pity bestowed upon the poor gentleman, put into her hand a billet-doux from Mr. Alsop.[1] Marianne at first declined reading it, till her sister was present; but being assured by Patty that Miss Dudley was not to know of it, ventured to break the seal. A love-letter is generally thought rather a difficult performance, and perhaps I shall be of service to the rising generation of sighing swains if I communicate a warranted original:

'MADAM,

'As I have certified by authentick testimony, that the party to whom I stated my case is biassed in judgment, and likely to hold back evidence, I have undertaken to plead my own cause; and though I will not be so bold as to ask a favourable verdict, depend upon receiving mercy. First, I premise, Madam, never was man more in love. Secondly, I could bring many witnesses to speak to my character. Thirdly, I possess the fee-simple[2] of an estate in the county of Westmoreland, of seven hundred pounds per annum, devised by my late father. Fourthly, I enjoy five thousand in the long annuities, by virtue of the will of my Aunt Margaret Alsop, spinster. Now, Madam, judge if I should be condemned unheard. Let the cause come speedily to issue, and believe me,

'Dearest of creatures,

'Yours till death,

'THOMAS ALSOP.

'N.B. Be pleased to avoid naming this subject to Miss Dudley.'

Though the humane Patty endeavoured to excite her lady's compassion for the miserable writer, she was too much diverted by the epistle to attend for some time to sentiments of pity. At length she enquired how she could assist him, since strictly prohibited from saying any thing about him to her sister, who

---

1 A billet-doux is a love letter. In French, it means "sweet note."
2 "Fee simple" means the estate is his absolute possession. The estate belongs to the owner (Alsop) and his heirs forever.

was the person whose favour he was solicitous to obtain. This question brought on an eclaircissement;[1] Patty vowing, that he protested he was in love with her lady, and Marianne as positively affirming that he had made proposals to Louisa that very day. There is no arguing against facts. Patty was forced to give him up as a base perjured lover, and deeply moralized upon the general infidelity of men, to exculpate herself from the charge of credulity, in having been imposed upon by Mr. Alsop's pretended passion. She received a positive injunction never to mention his name to her mistress again, and to return his letter, with an intimation that his impertinence would receive no other answer. Patty obeyed, and penned a furious epistle; in which she bitterly reproached him with having exposed her to her lady's resentment, and ruined his own hopes by his perfidious behaviour.

Nothing could exceed the astonishment of Mr. Alsop at this charge. Indeed the accusation of perfidy was extremely unjust, as ever since the first encouraging ray beamed upon his love, he had been invariably fixed to the object of his pursuit; I mean the lovely Marianne's fortune. It was the object of his daily thoughts and nightly dreams; he had proceeded so far as to plan the future method of expenditure. How then could he be false? Utterly ignorant of the name of the lady with whom he was charged with infidelity, he could only exclaim with Shakespear's Hero,

"That my accusers know who have condemn'd me."[2]

In this agony he flew to receive the soft lenitives[3] which friendship affords; but Captain Target thought proper to apply only corrosives to the wound. In pretty plain terms he called him a blundering fool, ornamenting his discourse with those flowers of rhetorick, which, though the repetition of them would be

---

1 An eclaircissement is a clearing up—a making clear of what is obscure or unknown.

2 Lady Hero, in Shakespeare's comedy *Much Ado About Nothing*, exclaims, "They know that do accuse me; I know none." It is amusing that the greedy dandy Alsop compares himself to Hero, a maiden defending her modesty against false charges of infidelity.

3 A lenitive is something that softens or soothes.

judged *disgraceful* to a female pen, are certainly esteemed by the gentlemen who use them as the very quintessence of wit, and the criterion of manly sense. He at length reluctantly consented to go to Stannadine, and endeavour to discover what this heinous offence was. Indeed he was not in reality sorry at his friend's miscarriage, having only made use of him as a skilful general does his raw, undisciplined troops, to discover the strength of the enemy previous to his arranging the grand attack; firmly persuaded that by a few of those skilful manœuvres allowable in love as well as war, he could at any time divert the laurel from Alsop's brows to his own.

But if that hope had ever been well founded, "the golden glorious opportunity" was lost. Miss Marianne, dazzled by the attractive beams of friendship, not only refused to look at love, but considered it as a false fire, and the source of all female wretchedness.

Captain Target had the penetration to perceive this, and after joining in a hearty laugh at his friend's mistake, prudently avoided discovering his own attachment; which would indeed have banished him from the enjoyment of Mr. Dudley's hospitality, for which he entertained a most *profound* regard.

CHAP. XVIII.

Variety, an antidote to satiety.

Louisa informed her father of the events which had happened in his absence, and soon received from him the following answer:

'TO MISS DUDLEY.

'The playful vivacity with which my dear girl relates Alsop's odd adventure, would lighten my bosom of many of its cares, were I not assured that your filial delicacy would induce you to conceal the affliction that rived your heart, and pretend to chearfulness[1] in the moment of agony; lest you should reproach a

---

1 In the second edition, "cheerfulness."

conscience deeply wounded. I will not however increase my real sorrows by imaginary ones, but will suppose that I have not made my Louisa wretched.

'I rejoice from my very soul at Marianne's escape: I will certainly wait upon Lord Clermont, to express my gratitude to him and his son, immediately upon my return. The intimacy he requests will, I fear, be incompatible with the plans we must too probably adopt. You tell me, unless a sister's partiality deceives you, Mr. Clermont looks on Marianne with more than admiration. I scarce wish her to make a conquest of so *young* a lover.

'You express a desire to hear of my own affairs. The only pleasant circumstances which have happened to me, have been owing to an accidental meeting with Mr. Pelham. As my connexions with Tonnereau *must* be divulged, I did not conceal from him the unpleasant motive of my journey. I am unable, Louisa, to express the manner in which this most excellent young man has endeavoured to console me. He positively insisted that I should remove from the lodgings I had taken, and accept of an apartment in his house. He behaves to me with yet superior esteem and respect, than when he was at Stannadine soliciting your sister's hand. Oh, that she had view'd[1] him with approbation! we then should have enjoyed the comforts of protection, without feeling the miseries of dependance. But let us not repine: the events of life are guided by a wise director, who often extracts real good out of seeming evil.

'Mr. Pelham has frequently mentioned you. He tells me Sir William Milton's attachment to you is more violent than ever, and that he is as wretched as pride, disappointment, and self-reproach can make him. I find he has not been quite so criminal as we conceived. The Mortons, my love, are artful women: the daughter, who is uncommonly beautiful, was educated for the infamous purpose of attracting the notice of some man of fortune. She lost her character before she went to India, where, Mr. Pelham says, she laid such snares, as his cousin's prudence was unable to resist. You will be astonished, but during the three years she lived with him, she made his lofty spirit submit to

---

1 In the second edition, "viewed."

what she pleased to propose. Mr. Pelham owns that she was at length left without any provision, but this was not wholly her paramour's fault, as at their quarreling she stubbornly refused to accept of any. Nothing was done for the children: this Mr. Pelham severely reprobates; and I find has at length persuaded Sir William to settle one hundred a-year upon each of them.

'Lady Milton's health is rapidly declining. From the high character she had heard of you, she persuaded herself you would soften those asperities in her son's manner, which even a partial mother could not avoid perceiving. Mr. Pelham is so persuaded that you are necessary to Sir William's happiness, that he wished me to say whether I thought it possible you could forgive the past, if his future conduct should appear to deserve your esteem. I would not encourage such a distant expectation, or bind my Louisa to an improbable contingence.

'It is a pleasure to see my amiable host in his own family: the regularity of his household, the chearful[1] respect of his servants. He mingles in the world, but is not fascinated by its pleasures. His father's sister lives with him; she does not seem remarkable either for her virtues or abilities; and I can perceive her temper is somewhat injured by the infirmities of age: yet Mr. Pelham contrives to make every one as attentive to her as himself, and thus gives her an importance she would not otherwise possess. His behaviour proceeds from gratitude; for she nursed him when an infant in a very dangerous illness; and it is principally owing to her care that his life was prolonged. I live, my dear, in times when I hear much about publick virtue. Those actions of a man's life which are exhibited upon the theatre of the world are always of doubtful origin. Ambition and avarice may in reality claim what appears to proceed from patriotism and benevolence; but the retired virtues of domestick life are sure indications of that excellence of heart, and rectitude of intention, which the author of all good promises to reward.

'Mr. Pelham never names your sister: in this he is equally generous and delicate. He knows how much my heart seconded his wishes, and kindly avoids a subject which could only give me

---

1 In the second edition, "cheerful."

pain. His active friendship has discovered a gleam of hope, which perhaps like many former ones will only end in deeper disappointment. An uncle of Mr. Tonnereau's, who died in Holland, bequeathed him an immense estate. This was supposed to be placed beyond the reach of our English laws; but an eminent counsellor, whose opinion, unknown to me, Mr. Pelham has obtained, states, that he conceives it may be amenable to his debts; and I am advised, as being the principal creditor, to attempt the recovery of it. My generous friend offers me every assistance, and I shall stay some time longer in London to hear further particulars.

'I will write to Marianne by this post. She is a truly amiable child, and my affections are equally divided between my daughters; but the peculiar circumstances of my present situation forbid me to disclose to her my *whole* heart. My Louisa has long had a prescriptive right to the confidence of her

'Affectionate father,
'RICHARD DUDLEY.'

Such an epistle could not but give delight to a heart in which the flame of filial piety glowed with purest lustre: but perhaps it was not wholly ascribable to that amiable quality, that Louisa, after pressing the letter to her lips, deposited it in her bosom, repeating at the same time her father's words, "that the author of all good would certainly reward the virtues of Mr. Pelham."

As Mr. Dudley's letter to Marianne is not essential to my design, I shall omit it. That young lady's apprehensions respecting her father's embarrassments had been considerably relieved, by the evasive answers of her sister; whose uniform chearfulness,[1] joined to the observation that the family arrangement was conducted in its usual liberal way, at length entirely removed the suspicion. Mrs. Patty too, who to serve a particular purpose had been the cause of exciting her alarm, perceiving that it did not take the right effect, took care to make Thomas unsay every hint, to the disadvantage of his master's fortune.

Marianne was now therefore *tolerably* easy; she never per-

---

1 In the second edition, "cheerfulness."

mitted herself to be more. Always dissatisfied with the present, regretting the past, and anticipating the future, she became peculiarly ingenious in the art of self-tormenting.[1] Her friendship for Mr. Clermont (though only friendship) was of such an apprehensive kind, that it could not promote the tranquillity of the bosom in which it was cherished. It was so peculiarly susceptible, that, notwithstanding his frequent visits and marked attentions, it continually suggested the idea that she was not so amiable in his eye, as he was in her's. These reflections did not excite any alarm respecting the state of her heart; was it not fortified by resolutions against love? Besides, she recollected that in the beginning of their attachment she felt the same doubts respecting the sincerity of her dear Eliza Milton.

The bar which had subsisted to prevent her confidential correspondence with that lady, during the period of Mr. Pelham's visits, being removed, Miss Milton had written her a most affectionate epistle; in which, though she lamented that the ill success of her brother and cousin had prevented the family connection so much desired from taking place, she observed a bond still subsisted, more sacred, more indissoluble than any other. She flourished a little upon the word friendship, and then desired her dearest Marianne to remember its hallowed claims. This produced a very diffuse reply, in which such reasons were given for Mr. Pelham's dismission, as entirely satisfied the fair confident, who declared that her friend had acted with her usual greatness of soul, in rejecting a man whom (however unexceptionable) she could not love.

Marianne had now an additional employment, besides playing upon her harp, reading pastoral poetry, walking in the woods by moonlight, and listening to distant waterfalls. She kept a journal of the events of the day, and every morning dispatched two sheets of paper, closely written, to her beloved Eliza. If any skeptical critick should censure this as a violation of probability, observing that a lady leading a retired country life could not find

---

1 This is a play on the title of a spoof instruction manual by Jane Collier, *An Essay on the Art of Ingeniously Tormenting* (1753), the ironic subtitle of which promises to teach readers how to plague all of their acquaintance.

matter for such voluminous details, I shall pity his ignorance, and refer him to the productions of many of my contemporaries; where he may be convinced, that sentiment is to the full as ductile as gold, and when beaten thin will cover as incalculable an extent of surface.

END OF THE FIRST VOLUME.

A

GOSSIP'S STORY,

AND

A LEGENDARY TALE.

IN TWO VOLUMES.

BY THE AUTHOR OF

ADVANTAGES OF EDUCATION.

" With calm severity unpassion'd age
    " Detect the specious fallacies of youth,
" Reviews the motives which no more engage,
    " And weighs each action in the scale of truth."

MRS. CARTER'S POEMS.

VOL. II.

LONDON:
PRINTED FOR T. N. LONGMAN, PATER-NOSTER-ROW.
1796.

CONTENTS

OF THE

SECOND VOLUME.

CHAPTER XIX.

An important incident, announced in pretty language.

But while the fair Nymph thus continued to hang her virgin offerings on the shrine of friendship, Mr. Clermont acknowledged himself subdued by the irresistible force of a superior divinity. His heart was naturally susceptible of the power of beauty, and his youthful imagination, unrestrained by experience, and unsubdued by time, annexed to the lovely form of Marianne Dudley, every idea of 'perfect, fair, and good;' all the images of excellence that

> "Fable ever feign'd,
> Or youthful poets fancy when they love."[1]

He perceived through the clear transparency of her exquisite complexion, a mind unclouded by any shade of error, and radiated by all the splendor of grace and virtue: and in the swimming lustre of her azure eyes he not inaccurately read the soft emotions of a melting soul. Did ten thousand worlds present equal attractions to that of calling such an angel his? I am confident every lover under twenty will answer—no.

To accelerate the conquest of his heart, love was increased by difficulty. Her rejection of Mr. Pelham was a convincing proof that she was not easily won; and though the smile which beamed in her lovely face at his approach, might have told him he was a welcome guest, he had too high an idea of her perfections, to suppose they would be the reward of his vows. But should the goddess be propitious, might not parental authority interfere? This, though a probable, was only a secondary terror; for supposing himself blessed with her favour, he felt disposed to brave the frowns of fortune and of fate.

---

1 From Nicholas Rowe's tragic play *The Fair Penitent* (1703). The line is, "Is she not more than Painting can express, / Or youthful Poets fancy, when they love?"

Miss Dudley had declined any family intercourse till her father's return; but Mr. Clermont always found excuses for another call. Sometimes he apprehended one of the ladies had a slight cold, and then civility required that he should make enquiries after her health. Again, Marianne expressed a wish that she could get a Canary-bird, and the attentive lover had it in his power to present her with a charming little songster; another day, she was hardly mistress of a favourite piece of musick, and Mr. Clermont was so happy in his manner of teaching, that she learnt much more from his instructions than the lessons of her master. Then on starting a literary topick, she had not read an author which he commended, and fortunately having the book at home, he insisted upon bringing it next day. Thus ever restless but when in her company, he repeated his visits, gazed upon her charms, magnified her perfections, and drained, even to its dregs, the intoxicating cup of love.

Such an admirer, or to speak with more precision an adorer, was too much adapted to Marianne's taste to be viewed with real indifference. But the passion, which in Mr. Clermont's heart flamed with ardour, and spoke with animation; in the softer character of Marianne assumed the form of gentle melancholy. Louisa perceived with pain the change in her sister's manner, and easily divined the cause. The behaviour of Mr. Clermont was too marked to allow her to doubt of his sentiments; yet she prudently wished that her sister might not bestow her *whole* heart, till certain that *no* obstacles would arise to make her regret its loss.

The frequent visits of Mr. Clermont during her father's absence, gave Miss Dudley the more concern, as she knew not how to decline them. She endeavoured to engage her sister in society, but Marianne's reluctance to quit her beloved solitude was invincible. At last, she succeeded so far as to prevail upon her to take a tour, for a few days, amongst the beautiful scenery with which they were surrounded; but hardly had they proceeded to the end of the first stage, when Mr. Clermont and his sister overtook them, who, as he thought, very fortunately, had just set out upon exactly the same route. How was Louisa to escape this new embarrassment? Even the *prudent* Marianne thought they could not decline his proposal of joining their party, without evident rudeness.

As no vigilance could now guard against repeated interviews, Miss Dudley felt herself obliged to commit her sister to the guard of her own circumspection. Frequent conversations amongst the delightful objects which nature presented to their view, so forcibly increased Mr. Clermont's enthusiasm, that he no longer brooked the restraint of silence. He seized an opportunity of addressing his charmer, as he was conducting her along a woodland dell, at a little distance from the rest of the party. With all the glowing colouring of romantick tenderness, with all the impassioned eloquence of youthful impetuosity, he communicated the secret of his heart. His blushing mistress listened in silent confusion, her complacency at seeing her own idea of a lover realized, was abated only by recollecting, that she "was sworn never to think of love." Being pressed for an answer, she with some hesitation mentioned her determined preference of a single life; but intermixed this declaration with so much esteem for Mr. Clermont, and so much pity for his misery, that though she doubtless intended to blast all his hopes, she did not actually reduce him to despair. He implored her forgiveness: it was readily granted; he then intreated he might preserve the tender regard, the enchanting confidence with which he had been favoured. To this the lady assented, on condition of his never naming the word love; he in reply promised to confine his unhappy passion *if possible* to his own bosom, and thus the quondam[1] lovers became ostensible friends.

The rest of the tour was extremely agreeable to both parties. Marianne's spirits, which probably had suffered by too close confinement, received considerable benefit from the excursion. The change was so visible to Louisa, that she could not avoid rallying her sister upon the cause of this sudden alteration. Marianne's heart was formed for confidence, and she readily informed Louisa of the circumstance of Mr. Clermont's addresses, and her total rejection. Miss Dudley did not appear to think the denial *quite* so peremptory as Marianne intended it should prove; and

---

1 Here, quondam signifies "one-time" or "former" lovers.

that opinion seemed confirmed by the vivacity of the rejected lover. Perplexed at this suggestion, Marianne determined to appeal to her Eliza Milton, who was an excellent casuist in all points of love and honour. On the evening she returned home, she retired early from supper, in order to write down the whole particulars. But the affecting sight which she saw on entering her dressing room, incapacitated her for using her pen. It was no other than the little canary-bird, her favourite pet, lifeless at the bottom of its cage, and insensible to the caresses of its weeping mistress. I do not insinuate that Marianne's regret was increased by any association of ideas; she was passionately fond of all kinds of birds, and certainly did not prize this the more, from having been the present of a *rejected* lover. The accident however afforded Mr. Clermont a fresh opportunity of urging his suit, for assuming the character of the dead warbler, he presented Marianne with the verses following:

SONNET,
ON THE DEATH OF A CANARY-BIRD.

Far from the sunny isle, and vine-hung grove,
   My native soil, to Britain's temp'rate sky
I came, to learn the tale of hopeless love,
   To chaunt[1] its woes to Delia,[2] and to die.
Oft shall the pensive maid those notes recall,
   Whose varied melody did once engage,
And oft the tear of kind regret shall fall,
   As sad she gazes on my vacant cage.
Yet, gentle mourner, not thy tears or sighs,
   Can life's extinguish'd taper re-illume;
And when for thee despairing Strephon dies,
   Thy angel pity cannot break his tomb:
Yet now such pow'r is lodg'd in thy soft eyes,
   One tender glance would clear the morbid gloom.

Marianne discovered in this composition a charm infinitely

---

1 Chaunt, a variation of chant.
2 Delia was an ancient literary female name—an idealized pastoral figure. The name was popularized in English by the pastoral poet Samuel Daniel's cycle of sonnets to Delia (1592) and used in similar contexts thereafter.

superior to that of a mere well-turned compliment, and censured Louisa's commendation of the poetry, as by no means sufficiently animated. Mrs. Patty, who happened to be present when the subject was discussed between the sisters, joined in the conversation, and did not, by any means, "damn with faint praise." She had now commenced as warm an advocate for Mr. Clermont, as she had been for his predecessors Pelham and Alsop, not from the mercenary motives which induced her to plead for the latter gentleman, but from the natural affection which she bore to handsome people. Though her lady seldom interrupted her when Mr. Clermont was her theme; still she so constantly persisted in her determination of "withering upon the virgin thorn," that Patty began to apprehend some serious disaster must befal her, as a judgment upon her obstinacy: either that she would be metamorphosed into a rock of marble, or fetched away by the ghost of some lover, who had died in despair. Resolved therefore, by giving fair warning, to discharge her own duty, she constantly entertained her lady during her hours of attendance, with the dreadful consequences of female disdain, beginning with Bateman hanging himself for love, and ending with the cruelty of Barbara Allen.[1]

CHAP. XX.

An example of polished benevolence furnishes a strong argument against melancholy discontent.

While the wavering balance of female resolution continued suspended, before Mrs. Patty's eloquence, or some weightier motive made the nodding scale preponderate in Mr. Clermont's

---

1 "Bateman's Tragedy," a narrative ballad dating from the seventeenth century, told the story of a woman who was not true to her lover, caused his suicide, was taken away by his ghost, and was never heard from thereafter. "Barbara Allen" is a folk song dating from the same period about a man's unrequited love and his object of affection Barbara's unwillingness to say encouraging things to him on his deathbed. Once he dies, however, Barbara is grief-stricken and also dies.

favour, Mr. Dudley returned home. His arrival relieved Louisa from much anxiety for his health, and peace of mind, and many apprehensions for her sister's future tranquillity, as she was now certain of the assistance of an able adviser. Mr. Dudley's account of his own affairs was more and more distressing. The limitations under which the estate had been bequeathed to Mr. Tonnereau, did not upon further examination appear to be surmountable; and even government had given up all hopes of the safety of the Leeward Island fleet: the underwriter too, who had ensured the ship in which Mr. Dudley's property was embarked, declared himself reduced by repeated losses, to a state of insolvency. Yet though exposed to the pressure of so many various misfortunes, Louisa with delight perceived that her father's mind had lost much of that gloomy despondency, which depressed it when he left Stannadine, and which had appeared to his excellent daughter a severer misfortune, than the loss of that wealth she had been accustomed to enjoy.

Mr. Dudley accounted for the change. "Perhaps, my love," said he, "of all the evils attendant on poverty, none are more to be lamented than the querulous humour it excites, even in liberal and benevolent minds. People in unhappy circumstances are not only apt to view the comforts they are forced to relinquish, with repining regret, almost approaching to envy; they too often consider the sons of affluence, as enjoying their calamities, making them the subject of illiberal mirth, and looking down with contempt upon the children of adversity. The real afflictions incident to penury, are less harassing to our fortitude, than the supposition of our being insulted by

> "The proud man's contumely,
> The insolence of office, and the spurns,
> Which patient merit of th' unworthy takes.[1]

"Bad as the world is, I believe this happens less frequently than the unhappy suppose; and doubtless it is their duty to avoid

---

[1] This is a selective and reordered quotation from William Shakespeare's *Hamlet*, spoken by the title character in his "To be or not to be" soliloquy. Contumely means insolence or rudeness resulting from arrogance.

indulging these painful sensibilities; but they are so congenial to a reflecting independent mind struggling with distress, and are so strengthened by the general opinion of mankind, and the opinions not only of poets, but of moral writers and divines; that it is almost impossible for a person to feel pecuniary difficulties, without supposing themselves to be ill-used and forsaken. It was with these sentiments I left you, and though not insensible to neglect myself, I anticipated it with greater terror, as I imagined it would fall with ten-fold violence upon you; who have been accustomed to be welcomed with delight, heard with attention, and answered with respect. Mr. Pelham, my dear, has made me open my eyes to a brighter prospect; and though few, like this excellent young man, measure their conduct to the unfortunate by that divine benevolence, which regards the keen susceptibility of misery, instead of the cold rules of civility,—though few, I say, like him divert by their kind attentions the recollection of that distress, which the yet unsubdued spirit of independence will not permit their fortune to relieve; yet still, Louisa, there are many generous minds in the world; and much of the neglect of which affliction complains is casual and accidental. May you, my dear, consider it as such! or rather may you meet with a Pelham, to raise you above the torment of these reflections!"

Mr. Dudley's conclusion was more affecting to Louisa than he intended. She would have repeated his energetick wish, but recollecting herself, determined to think of this most amiable man, only as the friend and comforter of her father.

Mr. Dudley's intention of paying a respectful visit of thanks to Lord Clermont, was prevented by that nobleman's assiduous politeness; for he waited upon him the morning after his return, and presented his son to him, as one whose highest ambition was to obtain his approbation. Lord Clermont expressed his wish for an intimacy between the families, with a warmth which neither admitted of denial nor evasion; and plainly shewed that more than a *neighbourly* intercourse was desired. Mr. Clermont's behaviour afforded a further explanation, and though the delicacy inseparable from female attachment prevented Marianne from making any intentional discovery of her sentiments; yet the blush of pleasure which lighted up her face at her lover's approach, and the pensive absence of mind which followed his departure, intimated a preference which the discerning father hardly felt inclined to limit to the name of friendship.

Lord Clermont did not long permit Mr. Dudley to found his opinion upon suspicion only; he avowed his son's attachment, and his warm approbation of his choice, in terms which seemed to indicate an apprehension that difficulties would be started on Mr. Dudley's side. What then was his astonishment when that gentleman declared, that his daughter was an absolute mistress of her person and fortune, and that if she inclined to favour Mr. Clermont, the paternal sanction would be chearfully bestowed? But in order to account for his Lordship's surprise, I must state some circumstances in his history and character.

Lord Clermont then, was one of those who imagine they are thoroughly acquainted with human life, from having contemplated it on the dark side. Disappointed in his expectations of preferment at court, he retired into the country, with somewhat of a saturnine cast of character; the asperity of which was not softened by the enjoyment of domestick happiness. His union with Lady Clermont was effected by interested motives,[1] and as the badness of her temper, and the inferiority of her whole character, was a perpetual source of disquiet, he attributed his infelicity to his own folly, in marrying a woman whom he beheld with indifference; erroneously supposing that if he had really loved her, her failings would have given him less pain. This predilection in favour of love-matches, strongly warring with his ruling passion, avarice, induced him to look forward with apprehension, to the period of his children arriving at maturity; for he supposed it improbable, that Cupid and Plutus[2] could agree in their choice, and each of these deities seemed in his eye of equal importance. To prevent his children therefore from falling in love, he educated them with strict severity, and railed at the

---

1 Here "interest" means monetary interest. The Clermonts' marriage was for money.

2 By invoking the ancient mythological figures of Cupid (the god of erotic love) and Plutus (the personification of wealth), Clermont means to say that love and money could agree in the choice of a spouse.

passion with increasing violence, till his accidental interview with Marianne Dudley, and his son's visible attachment to her, relieved his painful apprehensions, and changed his invectives into encomiums. Habitual severity prevented him from owning to Mr. Clermont the satisfaction he felt, but the young lover's impatience to lead his charmer to the altar, was hardly more violent than his father's desire effectually to secure him from the possibility of being attached to some beautiful beggar, or of sacrificing his future comforts at the shrine of unamiable riches.

The unfounded rumour respecting Mr. Dudley's intentions of restraining Marianne from marrying, had reached the Park; and Lord Clermont considered it as too probable to want authenticity. He esteemed it a very fortunate circumstance, that his son's acquaintance with the ladies had commenced during the father's absence; and instead of restraining, encouraged his frequent visits to Stannadine, in order that he might secure the affections of Marianne, before any opposition could be started. His observations on her behaviour convinced him that his plan had so far succeeded, and he considered the compliment he paid her father in asking his assent, to be merely a step to bring the affair to a crisis. That assent, given with no other restriction than what his child's happiness seemed to demand, astonished his Lordship; but an adept in *the ways of the world* will not ascribe any action to the principle of disinterested virtue, which is capable of being referred to consummate hypocrisy.

Lord Clermont, on his return to the Park, sent for his son to his closet.[1] The polished urbanity of manners, which distinguished this nobleman in company, did not enter into his domestick arrangements, and Mr. Clermont with reluctant steps obeyed the summons of a father, who, except in permitting his visits to Stannadine, had always appeared to combat his wishes; and who never called him to a private conference, but only to give him a pointed reproof. Even now that he had the most transporting tidings to communicate, he could not resolve to do it in a gracious manner. "Edward," said he, in a stern voice, "I wish to know if you have so far forgotten your duty as to engage your af-

---

1 A closet was, in eighteenth-century terms, a small, private room.

fections to Miss Marianne Dudley, without previously obtaining *my* permission." Conscious of the error, which he knew not how to vindicate, and could not disown, Mr. Clermont was silent. "I perceive," resumed his Lordship, "that my suspicions are just. I suppose, Sir, I have not deserved your confidence. I am an unnatural father, am I not?" The poor youth, supposing the next sentence would contain a peremptory mandate to banish him from one on whom his life depended, and against whom no reasonable objection could be urged, could not give a negative reply to his father's interrogatories, and remained dumb with terror and confusion. After his Lordship had thus gratified himself by the indulgence of parental power; he thought proper graciously to forgive him, and after slightly mentioning Marianne's inferiour[1] rank, expressed his willingness to overlook *that* objection in consequence of her merit, and his desire to ensure his son's happiness. He then related what had passed between him and Mr. Dudley, and claimed the acknowledgment which duty and gratitude must excite, in return for such considerate goodness. Mr. Clermont in a transport of joy flung himself at his father's feet, and acknowledged that he had made him the happiest of men; and his Lordship, while he raised him and held him to his heart, experienced for perhaps the *first* time in his life the real blessing of being a father.

Nothing now remained but to gain the approbation of Lady Clermont, and to prevail upon the lovely maid to sanction their hopes. The former, my Lord was too much of a fashionable husband to consider as of much importance; and the latter he was inclined to hope would not prove an Herculean labour.[2]

---

1 In the second edition, "inferior."
2 In ancient mythology, Hercules was a hero of superhuman strength and courage. He was the son of Zeus by a mortal woman. Herculean labor signifies something imagined as a nearly impossible act or feat.

CHAP. XXI.

A fair Platonist is compelled to marry, as a less hazardous expedient, than refining the opinions of an illiberal age.

The lover's task of propitiating his Goddess was rendered less difficult by Mr. Dudley; who, immediately upon the departure of Lord Clermont, informed his daughter of the purport of that nobleman's visit, and requested her decision.

Marianne, with blushes as animated and as beautiful as those of the morning, expressed a lively sense of Mr. Clermont's merits; but though she felt for him a tender friendship and a warm esteem, she scarce supposed her regard amounted to love, a passion of which she believed her heart never would be susceptible.

Mr. Dudley, who thought otherwise, replied, "Where, my dear, did you learn your opinion of love? If neither warm esteem nor tender friendship expresses the sentiments it inspires, by what other words can you define them?"

Marianne, a little piqued at having her knowledge of a science, in which she believed herself an adept, called in question, answered, that if she was convinced it would promote Mr. Clermont's happiness, she could chearfully resign him to another.

"You only tell me, my dear, that you are not selfish, mean, and illiberal; qualities of which I never supposed you capable."

The young lady perceiving that she had considerably the disadvantage in the argument, begged her father to give her *his* opinion of her lover.

Tenderly pressing her hand, "I am certain," said he, "my dear child is not one of those who discover irresistible attractions in the splendor of a coronet, or the possession of immense wealth. I therefore will not consider that Mr. Clermont's pretensions are by those advantages rendered irresistible. He appears to be an intelligent, agreeable young man, of a frank, candid disposition; and I am informed is irreproachable in his morals. As a lover, I presume, he must be as much of an Amadis de Gaul,[1] as modern manners will permit, and therefore certainly adapted to your taste in that particular."

Marianne smiled. "You are severe upon me, Sir, but is this all you have observed of him?"

"I could say," resumed Mr. Dudley, "that his character is not yet compleatly[2] formed. He has been educated in retirement, under the eye of (if the world says right) a stern father. Such a situation, so secure from every temptation to do wrong, and precluded from the possibility of acting and judging for himself, obliges me to consider Mr. Clermont's future conduct to be rather a matter of opinion, than admitting of a positive conclusion. He is extremely young, lively, and possessed of strong passions; for such an one the world will spread many snares, from which I sincerely hope his attachment to you may preserve him. Our sex, my dear, is formed to fill an ampler space in the world than yours, and the sphere of an English nobleman's actions is an extensive one. It is always fortunate for a woman, when she marries a man whose character can in some degree be ascertained, by his having been for some time under his own guidance. You who are formed to fulfil the retired, but not less important duties of life, can always be properly estimated while under the paternal wing; the attentive, submissive daughter, will make a tender, obliging wife; the retired, amiable maid, will form the prudent, domestick matron. But the manners of the man cannot be so well determined by the virtues of the youth; particularly if his father, like Lord Clermont, assumes that method of behaviour, which indeed tries his patience and good humour, but does not eradicate any wrong propensity, or call forth the latent qualities of his soul, by confidence and generous friendship. I must therefore upon the whole consider Mr. Clermont as a less eligible husband than Mr. Pelham."

---

1 *Amadis of Gaul* was a Spanish tale of knight errantry that was first published in the early sixteenth century, although its story had much earlier origins. It is a story of star-crossed love, travel, disguised identity, and damsels in distress. Amadis, the knight, is a sensitive man who might shed tears over a woman but was also a great warrior.

2 In the second edition, "completely."

Marianne entreated her father never to mention a name which she never heard without feeling dislike, bordering upon aversion. She then asked her father if patience and good humour were the only virtues he discovered in Mr. Clermont.

The fretful impatience with which she interdicted Mr. Dudley from mentioning *his* friend, and the tacit reproof her question conveyed, determined the observant father to suppress further observations; and endeavouring to give the conversation a lively turn, he told Marianne that patience and good humour were very good *connubial* virtues.

Still Marianne could not think of marriage, and wished that Mr. Clermont's sentiments coincided with her's, in preferring (for at least some years) the gentle tie of friendship.

"Will you tell me, my dear," said Mr. Dudley, "what the married state is, if it is not friendship in its most lively, extensive, and exalted sense? Is it not an union of interests and affections, sanctioned by an indissoluble tie? Does it not call for mutual esteem, confidence, forbearance, and tenderness? Contemplate it, my dear, in the light of a connection at first designed by divine wisdom, for the mutual advantage of two fallible creatures, and not as a fairy region of ecstasy and perfect happiness, inhabited by perfect beings, whose every wish, sentiment, and action flows in unison. I would not shock your delicacy, Marianne; but I must tell you, that the world is exceedingly apt to call in question the existence of that Platonick affection you seem to entertain; and I will apprize you, that it is necessary, either to receive Mr. Clermont's visits in the acknowledged character of your lover, or to request him to discontinue them."

Marianne was exceedingly displeased at the world's want of candour, sentiment, and refinement; but as more expert reformers than herself had often in vain tried to correct its prejudices, she did not feel sufficient courage to dare its censures, and to despise its frowns. The compassion inseparable from her disposition, prevented her from adopting the last alternative proposed by her father; as its effects would inevitably prove fatal to poor Clermont. But while she hesitated, perplexed and unresolved, the lover arrived to plead his own cause. His arguments, confirmed by a thousand vows of eternal gratitude, unremitting at-

tention, unalterable, tender, inviolable love, were successful: and
Marianne consented to accompany him to the altar.

CHAP. XXII.

*The Author's predilection for declamation, induces her to make no
use of a fine opportunity for introducing elegant description.*

No sooner had the lady's consent been obtained, than the Clermonts, as if fearful that she would retract it, urged on their suit
with the additional request of a speedy union. My Lord, with
the pettish impatience common to discontented people, would
not believe that an event so agreeable to his wishes would take
place, without the intervention of some mortifying circumstance
to abate his satisfaction. His fears of Mr. Dudley's opposition
being removed, by that gentleman's chearful acquiescence, he
adopted another set of apprehensions; and as he had discovered
the perplexed state of the father's affairs, began to fear a marriage with the daughter might entail upon his son the protection
and support of two beggars; and to this he calculated Marianne's
fortune was unequal.

A little time previous to his being certainly assured of Mr.
Dudley's misfortunes, his Lordship in conversation gave a hint,
which at least proved him to be a man of forecast, as it is generally termed. The purport of it was, that though Mrs. Alderson
had thought proper to distinguish Marianne as her favourite,
he hoped Mr. Dudley would still remember she was *his* daughter. Mr. Dudley not entering into the force of this suggestion,
answered it by declarations of the affection he felt for such an
amiable child; and in the warmth of paternal transport, repeated
many instances of the tender attachment she had shewn to his
person, and attention to his interests; adding, that he could
hardly have expected such regard, considering that he had been
separated from her in her early years, when the heart receives the
most lively impressions. The deep discernment of Lord Clermont, reflecting afterwards upon these words, and comparing

them with the state of Mr. Dudley's circumstances, led him to suspect that they conveyed more of design than of paternal tenderness; in other words, that he intended to take advantage of the filial virtue he commended; his Lordship therefore thought it right to take an opportunity of shewing him, that he would find some difficulties to impede his design.

The steady honour which was an inmate of Mr. Dudley's breast in every situation, anticipated his Lordship's cold prudence. On recollecting the conversation, he perceived, that "more was meant than met the ear;" and to prevent the expectations of avarice from exceeding their probable gratification, he determined, not only to inform Lord Clermont, that Marianne's fortune had been limited to Mrs. Alderson's bounty, by express agreement, when she and her sister were infants, but that in fact he had now nothing to bequeath. Determined to conquer false shame, since unconscious of intentional error, he frankly stated his alarming situation. My Lord heard him with much *sang froid*,[1] his eyes fixed on a beautiful landscape of Claude's,[2] which hung at the other end of the saloon. When Mr. Dudley had finished, he expressed great concern, but intermixed his consolations with reproofs for his misplaced confidence, declaring that he very well knew the instability of Tonnereau's credit a twelvemonth ago. He did not stop to hear Mr. Dudley exculpate himself, as he attempted to do, by pleading, that they were old family friends, and that his long absence from England gave him less opportunity of knowing the state of mercantile credit than others: his Lordship went on in a very composed, careless manner, to ask how he meant to dispose of himself, and what were his future plans respecting his daughter.

"People of our age, my Lord," said Mr. Dudley, with a warmth he could not restrain, "may employ themselves better than in forming distant plans for the support of an existence they may almost hourly expect to resign. I felt misfortune at a time when I looked forward to many years, which hope had dressed in gay

---

1 Sang froid means coolness or indifference.
2 Claude Lorrain, a seventeenth-century French painter known for his landscapes.

alluring colours: if I *then* sustained my trials with firmness, much more may I now, when experience has taught me the insufficiency and instability of temporal blessings; and when nature reminds me of a speedy summons from all sublunary prospects. With respect to Louisa, I am happy in seeing her possess a dignity and composure of mind, which will in any circumstances prevent her from sinking into despair. Both of us my lord, have independent spirits. We can neither solicit nor accept the cold assistance of reluctant friendship. Fortunately for her, her grandfather's prudence placed the means of procuring her the necessaries of life beyond the power of my indiscretion: and in all my troubles, I have the consolation to reflect, that the child, whom my folly injured, has the ability, as well as the virtue, to offer me an humble but secure asylum."

"Your numerous friends, Mr. Dudley, will doubtless prevent you from putting the young lady's filial piety to an inconvenient trial. I should, for instance, think my son would be extremely happy; but really there is no answering for young men; and people of quality are often embarrassed to support what the world expects from them. But suppose we mention the affair to Edward."

"By no means, my Lord. My expectations from Mr. Clermont extend no further than to his making my Marianne happy. In so doing, he will confer upon me a lasting obligation; and my heart is too proud to be easy under the sense of multiplied favours. Could I have submitted to become a pensioner upon Marianne's bounty, I believe I could easily have taken advantage of the melting kindness of her temper; and by depriving her of the advantages she had a right to expect, have secured myself in affluence. But as I have taken no dishonourable step to secure myself from poverty, I trust I shall not want firmness to endure it."

Though Lord Clermont (practised in the ways of the world) was not inclined to place implicit confidence in declamatory integrity, the serene firmness which irradiated Mr. Dudley's countenance almost induced him to lament, that a man of such principles should be left the unassisted prey of misfortune. To do justice to his Lordship's benevolence, he really felt an inclination to stand forth as an active friend; a wish which like many of the desires human nature is apt to entertain, seemed to encrease with the improbability of its completion. Upon the whole, he considered this conversation to be *very* satisfactory: a connection with a ruined man was not indeed desirable, but when poverty was accompanied with the firm spirit of haughty independence, it was infinitely less troublesome to its acquaintance and friends. The humane might dare to express their sympathy; and the polite venture an offer of service, without any hazard of having appropriate services annexed to general expressions.

He therefore hurried on his son's nuptials with additional impatience, and Mr. Clermont seconding his solicitations with all the ardour of young romantick love. Marianne found her maidenly reluctance yield to the entreaties of such importunate suitors. Within a month from the time of Mr. Dudley's return, Mr. Clermont had the transport of hearing his blushing bride publickly confirm, with solemn vows, the tender assurances she had before given him of eternal love.

The younger part of my readers will doubtless expect a description of the nuptial ceremony, the bride's paraphernalia, and all the gay et cætera of a wedding; which often diverts the juvenile mind from reflecting upon the important duties this grand change in female life prescribes. I had proposed myself the pleasure of gratifying them in this particular; but when these affairs came to be discussed in a grand committee-meeting of our society, convened at Danbury, for the express purpose of judging whether every thing was properly managed; the whole proceedings appeared nothing but a chain of improprieties, and I therefore think it better to omit a description which could only excite the painful duty of unfavourable criticism. Why should I tell the publick that *we* determined that the marriage was too private; that the bride's clothes were ill fancied, and sat frightfully, or that the jewels laboured under the double disadvantage of being *horridly* extravagant, and *odiously* unbecoming?

But one circumstance as connected with the historical part of my present labours I must not omit. It was the extreme plainness of the dress, in which Miss Dudley accompanied her sister to the altar. Such meanness was so little consistent with the other circumstances of her character, that we found no difficulty in attributing it to the most malignant envy. The sagacity of this observation was confirmed by hearing, that instead of assisting at the ceremonial visitings, Louisa and her father set out for their estate in Lancashire a few days after the nuptial ceremony. Such a want of attention to even common decorum, excited all our philanthropy, and in proportion as we hated the partial father, and his darling daughter, we wished all imaginable happiness to the poor young people, thus left to themselves without any prudent friend to direct them in family management. Unsolicited, and prompted only by our natural generosity, we resolved to take upon ourselves the *kind* office of general inquisitors into the conduct of Mrs. Clermont's family, and we accordingly assumed the self-invested character.

CHAP. XXIII.

The nuptial present of a Father.

Amongst the arrangements preparatory to Mrs. Clermont's nuptials, it was determined that Mr. Dudley should immediately resign Stannadine to the young couple, for their residence; and Marianne acceded the more readily to her father's proposal, because she had lately heard him express an intention of accompanying Louisa to her Lancashire estate that autumn. It must be observed, that the train of thought in which the fair enthusiast had hitherto indulged, did not supply the most accurate ideas respecting real life. Though educated to enjoy all the elegant comforts of affluence, she did not know that competence was a blessing; and she would perhaps have declaimed against the narrow, illiberal mind that dared to reckon it amongst the prime ingredients in the cup of human happiness. She had too great a soul to enquire what the value and extent of her sister's estate was; she had heard there was a cottage upon it, and that name suggested every thing that was pastoral and charming. Nothing but the society of her adored Clermont could have prevented her from envying the elegant retirement her father and sister were going to enjoy. At parting, she repeated her injunctions to Louisa, not to be so captivated with rural beauty, as to forget her promise of spending Christmas at Stannadine, and in the interim she was to be a punctual and diffuse correspondent. The charming scenes of artless nature could not fail to afford ample materials to a skilful hand; the tender attachments of the nymphs and swains would throw living figures into the landscape; and who knows but some new Palemon might present himself, with taste to select, and virtue to reward the new Lavinia.[1]

Louisa, with a pensive smile, wished her sister a long continuance of her present happiness, while the starting tear seemed to indicate that she formed no very high idea of the rural felicity she herself was going to enjoy.

While Mr. Dudley, the evening previous to his departure, repeated the blessing he first pronounced on consigning his child to the protection of a husband; prudence suggested a few salutary precepts. "May I always, my dear Marianne, see in your countenance this delightful appearance of heartfelt satisfaction! But in order to preserve it, let me conjure you to banish from your heart that extreme sensibility you have hitherto cherished."

"My dear Sir," cried the astonished bride, "you advise me to dismiss the very faculty by which I know how to appreciate my present happiness. I owe to it the exquisite sense I have of Mr. Clermont's unremitting tenderness. To this lively sentiment I ascribe the ineffable delight his presence excites, and the refined transport which I feel at all his observant assiduous attentions. My dear father, do not think I can surrender a quality, which has taken the deepest root in my soul."

"I perceive," said Mr. Dudley, "that you are not yet a convert to my doctrines, that the lover and the husband are different characters; yet as my opinion is warranted by long observation, you will I am certain be convinced at last: I hope not painfully.

---

1 In an episode in James Thomson's poem *The Seasons* (1726-30), Palemon falls in love with Lavinia, an agricultural laborer or "gleaner." The poem's episode was based on the Biblical story of Ruth and Boaz.

Much of your future happiness, Marianne, depends upon yourself; do not at least err through principle. Many duties are interwoven with the sacred character which Mr. Clermont has lately assumed: he is no longer the enamoured youth, whom nothing unconnected with his fair Idol can interest; he is become the country gentleman, the neighbour, the landlord, the master of a family. With these obligations, though highly pleasing to an intelligent mind, many irksome duties are necessarily involved; and when his temper is ruffled by any exterior perplexity, those assiduous, observant attentions which you say are the source of your refined transports, must appear to him as a disagreeable restraint. There is no part of the female character dearer to us men, than the idea that you are the soothers of our inquietudes, the solacers of our sorrow, the sympathizing friends to whom we may at all times retire for comfort, in every distress. The enthusiasm of youth often mingles with the addresses of the lover, an overstrained submission which places your sex in an exalted, but let me add in a false point of view. The husband, when he reflects coolly upon every circumstance, will, if he judges right, consider it better to preserve the heart he has gained, by displaying the manly qualities of sense, philanthropy, integrity, and fortitude, than by the lover-like arts which his juvenile affection urged him to adopt; and the discreet wife will hasten to elevate her own character, by adding to the delicate tenderness of the bride, the dignified virtues of the matron."

"Exert the powers of your understanding, my dear child," continued he, tenderly pressing her hand. "Even during the first fond period of wedded love, strengthen the bonds by which you hold Mr. Clermont's heart, by displaying those mental excellencies which will be ever new, and valuable when your person, your conversation, and your many fine accomplishments, shall have lost the gloss of novelty. Providence, by placing you in an affluent situation, has imposed upon you a thousand motives for exercising a benevolent heart; and by making you as it were a mark of distinction, enjoins that nice propriety of conduct, by which if we cannot escape censure and sorrow, we are at least secure from the self-reproach of having deserved it. You are commanded to prepare yourself for a spiritual world, not to languish out life in luxurious softness. You may, like yonder glorious Orb now sinking in the West, spread comfort and delight all around you, and become a noble spectacle both to men and angels. And will you give up all these privileges, to place your whole of happiness in the unremitting tenderness of a sincere, amiable, well-intentioned, but undoubtedly of a fallible being? No, my child, summon your resolution, and ere he changes the mode of behaviour his fondness has imposed, do you imperceptibly release him from the restraint. With pain I have heard you both declare, that you wish to shut out all the rest of the world, and to live only to yourselves. I must tell you that if this opinion was circulated, you would subject yourselves to much opprobrium, not to say disagreeable ridicule: but I will predict that your opinions will be changed before you are three months older."

Mrs. Clermont here interrupted her father. "You have formed your judgment, Sir, upon common attachments, and common marriages, and seem inclined to think that there are no exceptions from a general rule."

"I have formed my judgment," resumed Mr. Dudley, "upon my thorough knowledge of your character, and all I have seen of Mr. Clermont's; but I perceive my lecture wearies instead of convincing you. I will therefore conclude with two requests. I would wish to give them the efficacy of commands. In the first place, do not appear to avoid mixing in the society of your neighbours, and endeavour to engage Mr. Clermont in amusements, which will occasion frequent little absences. He will return to you with additional satisfaction, and your relish of each other's society will be improved, by the occasional interruptions company will give. My second request is, that you will study your husband's temper and character, with the deepest attention; in order that you may discover the peculiar tendency of those errors and prejudices, from which the best of us are not free, that by familiarizing them to your mind, they may steal upon you in the diminished form of little imperfections. If you neglect to do this, you may perhaps first perceive them, at a moment when passion has encreased them beyond their usual magnitude; and your alarmed imagination may still further extend them, till they eclipse their neighbouring virtues. Besides, a wife's discretion may often guard her husband from an error, by knowing the peculiar temptation to which he is most liable. I have now done, and this, my child, is the only legacy I can bequeath you."

Reflections of the most poignant nature agitated Mr. Dudley, as he spoke the last words; Mrs. Clermont with disinterested affection thanked him for the valuable gift, and after assuring him it was all she wished for, she intreated him to consider Louisa as his *only* child in the disposal of his fortune. She then obliged him to repeat his promise of visiting Stannadine at Christmas. "You will then, my dear father," said she, "see how I am improved by your precepts, and how far I am a convert to your opinion."

CHAP. XXIV.

An attempt at local description. The Author sees something like an enchanted castle, in which she immures a fair Arcadian.

The asylum which filial piety prepared for Mr. Dudley, was little calculated to banish from his memory the glowing fertility of the tropical islands; or the convenient elegance, with which well-regulated art had embellished Stannadine. The most enthusiastick imagination could hardly associate pastoral ideas with the neglected wildness of Seatondell, could suppose it peopled by Naids and Dryads, or fancy that Pan ever awoke its echoes with his tabor and pipe, while Cynthia and her maids of honour danced cotillions.[1]

Little did Mr. Alderson think when he bequeathed this estate to his grand-daughter, as a supply for pin-money, that it would soon become her *only* permanent possession. Much more im-

---

1 Naids (or Naiads) and Dryads were water and wood nymphs respectively. Pan (depicted with the horns, legs, and hoofs of a goat) was the god of woods, fields, shepherds, and flocks. Cynthia here is a reference to the Greek goddess Artemis (Diana in Roman mythology), born at Mount Cynthus, on the beautiful island of Delos. In other words, Seatondell (a fictional place) was in no way the rural ideal.

probable would it have appeared to his widow, could she have foreseen, when on her death-bed she requested that her old dairy-maid, Mary Arby, might be permitted to end her days in the farm-house, which she had for many years inhabited; that she was providing a companion for the intelligent, accomplished Louisa. But the vicissitudes of fortune have often afforded copious themes for declamatory astonishment.

Though Mrs. Arby had answered Miss Dudley's intimation of her design of coming to reside upon the farm, with an assurance, that she should be proud to entertain young madam; she certainly did not feel any *real* satisfaction in the idea, that she was to be interrupted in the possession of a place, over which she had long reigned with paramount authority. Few young women, accustomed to the elegance of refined life, would have been inclined to disturb her. The house was built at a period when the substantial and gloomy style of architecture was preferred to the convenient and cheerful plan. Before the front was placed a little square garden, surrounded by a cut hedge, and subdivided at right angles, by an ornamented fence of yew. Behind the house was an orchard, terminated by a rookery, the trees of which appeared at least contemporary antiques with the dwelling they belonged to.[1] On the left hand lay the farm-yard and out-houses; and on the right the decayed village of Seatondell, many of whose inhabitants, allured by the superior comforts which a large manufacturing town in the neighbourhood afforded, had deserted their parental abodes. There now remained only a few opulent farmers, their labourers, and the curate of the parish; the latter of whom, after enjoying the mental luxury of literary conversation, in college society, during the early part of his life, had been confined for many years, to the dry discussions of haughty, illiberal ignorance; and the painful reflections of disappointed hope. A pitiable, but not uncommon situation![2]

---

1 A rookery is a collection of nests of rooks (black crows) found in a clump of trees.

2 The description here is reminiscent of George Crabbe's *The Village* (1782), a poem that described the ugly realities of rural life of the period. It was written in response to Oliver Goldsmith's far more idealized picture in *The Deserted Village* (1770).

The arrival of the Dudleys in a post-chaise, was such a novelty, that every inhabitant of Seatondell ran out of doors to gaze at the strangers. Mrs. Arby, trembling alike with infirmity and apprehension, unbarred the massy porch door, and led them into an antique stone hall. Anxious properly to perform the honours of the house, she attempted to place Mr. Dudley in the wicker arm chair, but unhappily in the hurry of politeness flung down a large flower-pot that decorated the open chimney, upon Louisa's cloaths[1]. That amiable girl, possessed of the true benevolence which can exert itself in trifling affairs, as well as upon important occasions, diverted the good woman's concern for the accident, by kind enquiries after her health, and recollections of the early kindnesses she had received from her, when she visited at her grandmamma's in her childhood. By mentioning some articles of rural cookery, in which Mrs. Arby used to excel, she in a great degree reassured her trembling diffidence, and sent her

> "With dispatchful looks in haste,
> As one on hospitable thoughts intent,"[2]

to make trial of her skill.

Miss Dudley now addressed her father, who sunk in the arm chair with his head resting upon his hand, his listless, unobservant eyes fixed on the immense stone window-frames, which seemed rather to exclude than to admit the day. The deepening shades of evening added to the gloomy appearance, and encreased the dejection of his too conscious heart. "My dear sir," said Louisa, "I find this place infinitely preferable to what I expected: a little paint and paper will enliven the house exceedingly, and when the yew ornaments are removed, I shall be delighted with gratifying my taste for flowers in that neat little garden. We shall find both health and amusement in improving our farm in summer, and in winter books and musick will afford a never-failing resource

---

1 In the second edition, "clothes."

2 From John Milton's *Paradise Lost*, Book V, in which Eve prepares food. The eighteenth-century periodical *The Spectator* (no. 327, by Joseph Addison) quoted these lines as evidence of Eve's domestic employments and skills as a housewife.

from chagrin. My dear father, do resume your wonted cheerfulness; you have often taught me resignation, let not the preceptor need instruction from the pupil."

Mr. Dudley, after gazing upon his daughter for a few moments with a look of delighted affection, excused his want of spirits as arising from the fatigue he felt from their long journey. Louisa hoped the depression which she also felt might be ascribable to the same cause;—they separated at an early hour.

Awakened by the clamour of the domestick poultry, Miss Dudley rose with the sun, and opened the casement of her chamber window, to take a view of the adjacent country. Her apartment fronted the orchard, a thick autumnal mist hung upon the horizon, but had the morning been more favourable, the trees would have effectually impeded her design; for they were crowded together with a profusion which entirely obstructed the sight of any other object. She sat down, listening to the murmur of a distant rivulet, which by a natural association of ideas, recalled to her memory a beautiful cascade at Stannadine; near which she first beheld Mr. Pelham, when introduced by her father in the character of Marianne's lover. There are moments in which the firmest spirits yield to the pressure of calamity; and while Miss Dudley recollected the happy hours she had passed in the society of that amiable man, a tear of involuntary regret, and a spontaneous sigh, expressed how much she felt the contrast of her present situation.

She was roused from this reverie by the sound of footsteps under her window, and looking out perceived her father. Mr. Dudley, after passing a restless night, had left his apartment, with the hope of diverting the reflections he knew not how to endure. His amiable daughter immediately banished from her thoughts the indulgence of her own peculiar sorrow, and lifting her beautiful eyes to heaven, with meek solicitude implored the beneficent Author of Creation to assist her endeavours to restore tranquillity and self-satisfaction to one of the worthiest of human hearts.

To give efficacy to her prayers, and to confirm her exalted principles by calling them into action, she immediately joined her father, and with the winning sweetness of which she was absolute mistress, imperceptibly detached his thoughts from brooding upon irremediable misfortunes. She persuaded him to walk round her little demesne, and, with unfeigned transport, at length succeeded in reviving in his mind that passion for agricultural improvement to which he was naturally inclined. A party of labourers were soon set to work, to prepare the ground for plantations, which were to be so disposed, that ornament might unite with utility. Others were employed in clearing some waste land, which could usefully be converted into arable. A third set were occupied in cleaning a large fish-pond, which through neglect had been nearly filled with earth, by which effort of industry Mr. Dudley proposed the double advantage of draining a morass and furnishing his table with an agreeable luxury. The orchard and garden underwent a complete metamorphosis, about two thirds of the trees in the former were felled, and thus the chearful rays of the sun were permitted to break in upon the green mouldering walls of the old mansion. The clipt hedge was in part removed, and a neat green paling substituted in its place, and the ornamental yew pillars were completely annihilated, to make room for a plantation of odoriferous shrubs. These alterations involved the Dudleys in some serious disputes with Mrs. Arby, who feeling all the local attachments age is apt to indulge, considered every object with which she had long been familiar, with a sort of sacred regard. Even the gloom and damp which had hung for many years upon her residence, seemed in her eyes a perfection, the loss of which nothing *new* could supply.

Doubtless all the antiquated Dryads of Seatondell, if any such there were, joined with Mrs. Arby in her regret, but amidst the general devastation, a large White Rose, which entirely overshadowed the dairy-window, was preserved with most religious care. A tender sentiment was united to the uncommon beauty and fertility of the plant, to preserve it from destruction, for it had been set by Mrs. Dudley in her childhood. Her affectionate and grateful daughter, while she cleared it of its decaying branches, and with pious assiduity decorated the sod from whence it grew with

"The rathe[1] Primrose that forsaken dies,
    The glowing Violet,
With Cowslips wan, that hang the pensive head,
And ev'ry flower that sad embroidery wears;

MILTON'S LYCIDAS

indulged the pleasing melancholy which a departed friend im-
presses upon the memory, when time has softened the agonies
of grief into mild regret and pious resignation. The approach
of winter had already begun to strip the branches of the Rose-
bush of their verdant honours; and Miss Dudley's thoughts were
naturally led from the ravages of the season, to recollect the more
terrible devastations of death. Her melancholy muse expressed
this idea in the following elegiack sonnet:

TO A

ROSE BUSH,

PLANTED BY A DECEASED FRIEND.

Rob'd in the mantle of luxuriant spring,
    To thee the village-nymphs for chaplets[2] sue,
O'er thee the Bee extends his filmy wing,
    Inhales thy sweets, and drinks thy nectar'd dew:
From his high throne the flaming lord of day
    Pours on thy bursting germs his fervid pow'r,
While zephyr,[3] pleas'd amongst thy leaves to play,
    Casts thy soft fragrance on each meaner flow'r;
Thy foliage shall again salute the skies,
    Thou shalt not languish long in winter's gloom;
But lifeless still thy honour'd planter lies,
    The beams of summer cannot pierce the tomb:
Man, lord of all, beneath the reign of time,
    Awaits perfection in a nobler clime.

---

1 Blossoming early in the season.

2 A chaplet is a wreath of flowers or leaves, worn on the head.

3 Zephyr in classical mythology is the god of the west wind. It also refers to
a soft, gentle breeze.

CHAP. XXV.

*Proving, that the creative power of the imagination may be
employed in producing pleasure, as well as pain.*

The superior excellence with which Miss Dudley adorned retirement, was not wholly confined to the duties of a daughter;
her heart glowed with the purest flame of benevolence, nor could
disappointment obscure, nor distress absorb the sacred radiance.
The inhabitants of Seatondell certainly presented no very alluring qualities to a polished mind; but my heroine considering
them in the light of fellow-creatures, discovered in the common
nature she shared with them, an unalienable claim upon her to
discharge all the social and charitable offices, which dependent
and accountable man from "brother man requires." She was
not restrained by observing that prejudice, malevolence, and
calumny prevailed even in this obscure retreat. She considered
these hateful passions as the natural characteristicks of an ignorant mind and an unbridled temper, and she even conceived
it possible to counteract their baleful effects, by exhibiting the
contrary virtues in the most amiable point of view. This hope
was too romantick to be the *chief* motive which regulated her
conduct, for she principally looked forward to the approbation
of her own conscience, whose silent voice can best appreciate the
effects of external circumstances.

By the most engaging affability of look and manner, Louisa
conquered the dislike her wealthy neighbours had conceived
against her, and induced them to visit the "fine lady," who was at
first equally the object of their ridicule and abhorrence. My poor
heroine soon perceived, that it would be a vain attempt, to discuss
any of the topicks of conversation of which she was mistress, and
prudently assuming the learner, permitted her visitants to lead
the discourse, and endeavoured to improve herself in the knowledge of local politicks, and rural œconomy. The matrons were
all charmed by this modest humility; and the fair rustick belles

perceiving nothing intimidating or haughty in her manner, endeavoured to acquire some hints respecting dress and behaviour, from the graceful stranger; and almost forgot their first idea, that she was come on purpose to ridicule and eclipse them.

Though Miss Dudley, instead of succeeding in her well-meaning design, of healing the village animosities, was forced to listen to many a dull detail of wrongs and insults; yet she derived considerable advantages from the occasional sacrifice of an afternoon. She more clearly knew the value of candour and placability, by perceiving how necessary they were to tranquillity and self-satisfaction. From a tedious uninteresting conversation she returned with double avidity to her favourite amusements; her books, her needle, her musick, her garden, the society of her beloved father, and those active exertions of charity from which her limited purse could not wholly restrain her. Accustomed to œconomick attentions, she knew how to husband her bounty, and by adding to it her personal services, to render a trifle valuable. She visited the sick, consoled the afflicted, instructed the ignorant, and reproved the idle. She founded a village-school, inspected its management, and distributed its rewards. She was not discouraged by the murmurs of caprice, mistake, or ingratitude, though they often interrupted her benevolent plans; for while her heart bore testimony to the rectitude of her intentions, it taught her to look for her reward in an approbation transcendently superior to the changeful plaudits of variable man.

No part of her conduct appeared more deserving of imitation than her behaviour to Mr. Walden, the unfortunate Clergyman whom I before mentioned. He had long been exposed to the supercilious neglect of ostentatious wealth, or the rude insults of conceited ignorance. Depressed by poverty, perplexed by the care of providing for a numerous family, and harassed by the unpleasant temper of his wife; his mind sunk under the pressure of these accumulated evils, which his education had taught him to feel; and though he continued faithfully to discharge his ministerial duties, he performed them with the mortified air of a self-denying anchorite,[1] instead of the cheerful satisfaction of the Christian pastor.

---

[1] A recluse who has withdrawn from the world for religious reasons.

The Dudleys at their first arrival at Seatondell, conceived for him all the respect his character and sacred function deserved, and treated him with the most marked civility. Flattered by an attention to which he had been so little used, he endeavoured to revive his dejected spirits, and to recollect those agreeable talents which had lain buried in oblivion. His attachment to those who had recalled him to the sense of pleasure was extreme, and his eager enjoyment of the long denied luxury of literary conversation led him frequently to their house; where, solicitous to exhibit his mental acquirements, he anxiously sought to engage Mr. Dudley or his daughter upon some ingenious topick of discourse. They were too candid to call this conduct by the harsh terms of intrusion, or pedantry. Louisa felt happy at being able to give him a moment's respite from chagrin. Far from indulging a jest at the expence of his quaint rusticity, or scholastick expressions; they excused his failings, pitied his misfortunes, and esteemed his virtues.

Nor was Mrs. Arby exempt from the mild influence of Louisa's excellencies. Happily blending the mistress with the friend, and kindly allowing for the petulance and prejudice of age, she soon taught the old woman to consider the once dreaded arrival of her young lady as the greatest blessing she had known; and to join in the general applause, which in spite of a few malevolent detracters was bestowed upon such exemplary conduct.

Thus increasing the happiness of all around her, was it possible for Miss Dudley to be wretched? Could a liberal, reflecting mind avoid partaking of the felicity it imparted; or at least, enjoying the pure satisfaction arising from the consciousness of having acted right? Yet sometimes, when alone, a tear would steal down her cheek. It was *not* called forth by recollecting the splendid establishment Sir William Milton had once offered, for that she had resigned without the least reluctance; but alas! Mr. Pelham was not quite forgotten, and his agreeable character appeared to greater advantage, when contrasted with the society in which she now supposed herself destined to spend her future life. Filial piety, fortitude, and female delicacy united to restrain the unavailing regret, and she never met her father but with a smile indicative of the most heartfelt satisfaction.

Mr. Dudley was *almost* persuaded that the ruin of his daughter's fortune had not materially affected her happiness, and the thought was a cordial to his depressed spirits. He looked forward indeed to Christmas with anxiety, because he intended, while Louisa was with her sister, to take a journey to London, and endeavour to collect the scattered remains of his fortune. In the mean time the hours did not pass uncomfortably away. The unusual mildness and serenity of the weather proved favourable to their rural occupations. The mornings were generally spent in the field, and the evenings enlivened by the perusal of some approved author. Our immortal Shakspeare held a distinguished place amongst them, and it is probable it was his animated description of a winter, similarly beautiful, which suggested to Miss Dudley the following address to the one she spent at Seatondell.

SONNET TO WINTER.

Be crown'd with flow'rs, gay winter. From thy wing
    Shake the round-moulded hail and flaky snow,
    Bid from Aquarius' urn soft streamlets flow,
And Pisces wanton in the warmth of spring:
Say to the shiv'ring Twins, no longer bring
    Your tulips copy'd from th' aerial bow,
    Or paint the Roseate[1] bud. Let tempests blow,
And o'er the wond'ring world my mantle fling:
    For still with Oberon Titania jars,
    And still the sullen Queen indignant flies,
While Elfin squadrons who before these wars
    Led the successive seasons down the skies,
Their charge deserting, supplicate the stars
To heal the ills that from contention rise.

---

1 In the second edition, "Roseat."

CHAP. XXVI.

The dawn of Connubial Felicity, with a word or two on the pleasure of tormenting.

My two preceding chapters were peculiarly adapted for those who feel the inconveniencies arising from depressed circumstances, a disagreeable situation, or an unpleasant neighbourhood. It seemed a humane office to point out to them independent amusements, and comforts absolutely beyond the power of fortune. I now address to the favourites of the fickle Goddess a few intimations, that they should receive her bounty with gratitude, and use it with moderation; frequently comparing their situation with that of their neighbours, in order to induce them to meet with fortitude the little evils from which even the happiest human beings cannot be exempt. With fortitude, did I say? I want a term implying the most cheerful acquiescence; for considering the calamities to which our nature is subject, the trivial vexations of life are beneath our regard.

It may be remembered, that Mrs. Clermont was left in the full possession of all the blessings the most flattering imagination can conceive. No sooner had her father and sister left Stannadine, than the happy pair agreed to devote one fortnight to the uninterrupted pleasure of each other's society. The congratulatory cards were therefore answered, with a hint that they did not at present receive company, and an invitation to go and spend a week at the Park was respectfully deferred.

For the honour of wedded love it shall be mentioned, that they persevered in this resolution, though candour compells[1] me to acknowledge, that before the expiration of *that* time, the hours moved upon leaden pinions. As every adventitious aid to conversation was rejected by mutual agreement, the invincible power and eternal durability of Love, though illustrated by their own

---

1 In the second edition, "compels."

example, seemed after frequent repetition but a vapid topick. Mr. Clermont with some degree of pleasure recollected the amusement his pencil afforded, and his fair bride was more than once tempted to look over her nuptial ornaments, and to appropriate her several dresses to different occasions of grand display.

Meanwhile Lady Clermont, who had *reluctantly* left a very "high-lived party" at Brighthelmstone[1] to be present at her son's nuptial, was dreadfully chagrined to be detained with her Lord for a longer period than she at first proposed, and since decorum would not permit her to leave the country till the intended visit was over, she determined that her new daughter should deeply feel the mortification of which she had been the cause. It was not difficult for her Ladyship to endeavour to persuade herself to dislike a young woman, possessed of beauty, sweetness, and elegance; it was a character to which she could form no pretension, and naturally hated, because it eclipsed her own. She received the bride with the hauteur of affected superiority; her plebeian rank was considered by the high-born Lady Clermont as an indelible disgrace; and her ignorance of the fastidious niceties of etiquette which the great world requires, afforded an inexhaustible fund of raillery, for one who had long considered *such* knowledge to be the compendium of valuable science.

Mrs. Clermont had been accustomed from her earliest infancy to unremitting tenderness, and she was by nature peculiarly susceptible of unkind treatment; it therefore cannot be wonderful that the dislike between the mother and daughter was reciprocal. But her Ladyship's temper was too violent to permit her to confine her's to her own bosom. She nursed the detestable design of rendering her less amiable in the eyes of her impassioned husband; and unrestrained by the strong impatience visible in his countenance, whenever the idol of his soul was spoken of in terms short of admiration, she continued to point the most mortifying sarcasms against romantick attachments and first impressions, mixing her observations with those faint commendations of Marianne's beauty and simplicity, which might almost be termed implied censures.

---

1 An old name for Brighton, a resort town on the south coast of England.

Mr. Clermont's behaviour to his mother had always been distinguished by respectful attention, in part arising from gratitude for the marked preference she had shewn to him, and in part from pity at witnessing the unkind neglect she experienced from his father, and which had greatly contributed to sour a temper naturally unamiable. But his deference as a son was now put to a severe trial, and could scarcely resist the stronger feelings of offended love.

One day, after having been particularly piqued by his mother's invidious observations, he hastily retired to his wife's apartments, to lose the painful recollection in her engaging sweetness. He found her in tears. The tears of beauty are interesting; its distresses inspire the heart with the warmest resentment; and Mr. Clermont had infinitely more of the knight-errant in his character than generally falls to the lot of an husband.[1] He conjured her to disclose the cause; his tender solicitude, while it gave her heart the liveliest pleasure, considerably increased her tears; for Mrs. Clermont had not yet adopted her father's advice, of aspiring to that more exalted part of our sex's character, which teaches us to share in the sorrows of our husbands with magnanimity, and to teach them fortitude by our unobtrusive patience. She was the "feeble vine," always clinging for support to "her wedded elm."

Sobbing with distress, which seemed rather to proceed from weakness than from any real affliction, she at length answered his importunities, by confessing that her tears proceeded from Lady Clermont's unkind behaviour. But when she found that she had excited a tempest which all her skill could not allay, she deeply regretted the imprudent discovery. Mr. Clermont burst from her in a rage, and hastened to his mother. A most violent altercation ensued between them, in which they mutually seemed to forget what was due to the sacred ties of blood. Lord Clermont's authority, and the gentle mediation of his daughter, produced an *apparent* reconciliation; but the seeds of disgust were deeply sown, and in their final effect were ruinous to Mr. Clermont's peace.

During the remainder of the visit, her Ladyship behaved to

---

1 In the second edition, "a husband."

the bride with ceremonious coolness and affected respect. This behaviour, though less reprehensible than the former, was equally painful to a candid ingenuous mind. Marianne deeply reflected upon the preceding events, and though there was nothing in her husband's behaviour which could be construed into an implied censure upon her conduct; her conscious heart told her it had not been worthy his esteem. She had been apprized of Lady Clermont's bad temper, and the little influence she possessed in her family was publickly known. It was absurd to expect to be exempt from the general influence of constitutional ill-humour, and cruel to degrade and expose an unhappy woman, who already laboured under the severe affliction of a husband's contempt.

On discovering her past indiscretion, Mrs. Clermont fell into an error not uncommon to a generous susceptible heart. Prompted by a keen sense of her fault, she determined to apply to Lady Clermont for forgiveness; and had the application been made with prudence, or had the person to whom it was addressed, possessed but half the generosity of herself, the most happy effects might have been produced. But in the letter she wrote, (for she had not courage to name her offence in conversation,) she proportioned her concessions rather to the acuteness of her own feelings, than to the enormity of the fault, which was in reality nothing more than an irritable sense of undeserved provocations. This letter afforded the malevolent Lady Clermont the liveliest satisfaction. It convinced her of her power to distress a placable susceptible mind, and she preserved it with care, to be produced as an incontrovertible evidence against her daughter, on any future occasion. Her reply was dictated by great apparent kindness and ostentatious urbanity.

CHAP. XXVII.

A fête champêtre.[1] *Excessive tenderness is sometimes troublesome.*

Soon after the Clermonts returned to Stannadine, the con-

---

1 An elaborate garden party, popular in the eighteenth century.

gratulatory visitings commenced. Our society was unusually animated, by the exhilarating entertainment of anecdote and observation which this circumstance supplied. As I have already anticipated the general conclusions, and hate repetitions, I shall hasten to the description of a grand fête, given by Mr. Clermont, to the inhabitants of Danbury; for in compliance with his father's wishes, he had formed a parliamentary design upon our ancient respectable borough.[1]

The entertainment consisted of a ball, and supper, given in the gardens; in which such of the company who chose might appear in an assumed character. The bride arranged the plan of the entertainment, and perhaps felt a secret pleasure, that the superior elegance of her taste had now an opportunity of publickly displaying itself. Every ornament was perfectly rural, and the whole proceedings were adjusted with pastoral simplicity. In the attire of Calypso she presided as mistress of the feast, and welcomed her guests to her bower with an air of inimitable sweetness. Her Ulysses hung with enamoured eyes upon his fair enchantress, and forgot his father's senatorial projects: unlike his old archetype, who only remembered Ithaca, even when first infatuated by the Queen of Ogygia.[2]

The company afforded a great display of character, but not all strictly classical. Captain Target, with his head dressed à la Pigeon,[3] a chapeau under his arm, and a sword, exhibited a tolerable *modern* Mars. Miss Cardamum happily returned from Scarborough in time for this festivity; rich in polite anecdote, and gayly decorated by fashion. She treated us with a very lively Diana, in a pink sarsenet jacket: while Miss Dolly Medium displayed as happy an imitation of Venus, in a white frock altered into a Grecian symar for the occasion. For my own part, I was

---

1 Mr. Clermont intends to enter politics and hopes to become an MP (Member of Parliament) in the House of Commons.

2 Mrs. Clermont was costumed as a sea nymph. In Greek myth, the nymph Calypso, who lived on the island of Ogygia, imprisoned the shipwrecked Ulysses with her for seven years. Her name means "she who conceals."

3 A pigeon's wig was a type of men's headwear, popular in the mid-eighteenth century. See Helena Chalmers, *Clothes On and Off the Stage*, New York: Appleton and Company, 1928, p. 214.

contented with the simple, unambitious character of a shep-
herdess, and put myself to no further expence than a few blue
ribbands, with which I metamorphosed my walking cane into a
crook.

I thought the evening extremely agreeable, and returned
home perfectly satisfied; but my unfortunate facility in being
pleased, exposes me to many inconveniencies, and frequently
obliges me to retract the applause which is controverted by better
judges. It was determined in full consistory, that the lights were
ill disposed, the ornaments childish, the refreshments parsimo-
niously supplied, and the bride and bridegroom visibly too much
attached to each other, to pay proper attention to their friends.
But what was most lamentable, so little regard had been paid
to proper arrangement, with respect to the dancers, that the
Captain and Miss Dolly were placed below Mr. Inkle and Miss
Allbut, the common brewer's daughter. This might indeed be
the effect of chance, but such misfortunes must be expected from
the heterogeneous mixture jumbled together on this occasion. It
was undoubtedly an insult to the Danbury patricians, to invite
them on the same evening with their plebeian neighbours, and
a breach of the etiquette their present member, Lord Grimbly,
always observed. As the Clermonts were *young* people, it certainly proceeded from ignorance, but then a friendly hint should
be given, that such improprieties may be avoided in future.

As these observations were not whispered in closets, they
were detailed to Mrs. Patty, when she paid an *extraordinary* visit
to Miss Lappel's in order to learn what was said of the entertainment. As in the opinion of the sanguine Abigail, it had been
a compleat[1] piece of perfection, she had anticipated the high
encomiums which would be passed upon her lady; and by im-
plication upon herself, as a most able assistant in producing the
happy effect. Judge then of her astonishment to find it had been
voted an absolute *bore*. Mrs. Patty's tongue was not deficient in
the grace of volubility, and she certainly poured upon the calum-
niators a torrent of what might be termed retributive abuse; but
when we expect a panegyrick upon *ourselves*, to meet only an

---

1 In the second edition, "compleat."

opportunity of abusing *others*, is certainly a mortification. I can compare it to nothing but what a Roman general must feel, who was only permitted an ovation, when he expected a triumph.

Patty's anger was too violent to evaporate in defamation at Miss Lappel's, and she seized the first opportunity to inform her lady what her enemies said of her. Whenever my fair readers are threatened with a similar communication, I will entreat them, for the sake of their future peace of mind, to repress the imprudence of rising curiosity, and to silence the injudicious or perhaps malevolent informer. Mrs. Clermont did not exert this useful self-command, and Patty was too fond of using the acid in her mental stimulants, to adhere rigidly to truth. She *aggravated* therefore the *aggravations* which Miss Lappel, through her indignation at the ill usage of so good a customer, had already supplied; and thus the Danbury critique upon Mrs. Clermont's fête champêtre became at last a most highly coloured lampoon; capable of agitating a firmer mind than the fair entertainer possessed. How extremely hard it was to be disappointed, in her first attempt at gaining popularity! To be so *unexpectedly* disappointed too, rendered it still more provoking; for every one of her guests had declared themselves quite enchanted during the whole evening. One satisfaction still remained,—the sympathy of an affectionate husband. She had made the entertainment on purpose to oblige him, and doubtless he would warmly espouse her cause against a malevolent *world*. Her quarrel indeed was only with a very small part of the universe; but injured people are fond of using indefinite terms.

It was at an inauspicious moment that Marianne flew to impart to her dear protector the cruel injuries she had received. Mr. Clermont had employed the whole morning in attempting to sketch a likeness of the sweet Calypso, who had so enchanted him a few evenings before. After many unsuccessful attempts, he at last executed a very promising outline; but whilst he was bending over it, with the mingled exultation of an artist and a lover, a favourite spaniel rushed into the room, and in its ecstasy at the sight of his master, leaped upon the pallet, and entirely obliterated the unfortunate performance.

Mr. Clermont had ever borne his father's peremptory behavior and his mother's caprice with submission and deference. But the mandates of his Lordship issued in the compulsatory tone of a despotick monarch, and received with silent awe, were not calculated to eradicate any evil propensity, nor to inculcate any generous virtue. Fortunately his son had received from nature an amiable, affectionate disposition; and his uncorrupted mind, elevated by a fertile imagination, and the strong enthusiasm of early youth, gave a romantick, but engaging turn to his character. From nature *too* he received as foils to his virtues, impetuous passions, and vehemence of temper; and these errors no paternal *precept* taught him to subdue; nor did the yet surer rule of paternal *example* inculcate the important duty of self command. The restraint which the presence of his parents imposed was temporary, and his violence was still more apparent when that curb was removed.

On opening the door of the library, Mrs. Clermont surprized her husband in the first paroxysms of anger; correcting the trembling dog. Though her presence had always used to harmonize his soul, it rather added to his vexation on this occasion. He wished to have concealed from his Marianne every defect in his own disposition. He felt the resentment which rises in the mind of persons conscious of error; a resentment at first extremely apt to fall upon those who happen to witness the fault, instead of pointing the reproof to their own bosoms. To her terrified enquiries as to the cause of his violence, he remained for some time silent, and at last *complained* that she had interrupted him, when he was most particularly engaged. Mrs. Clermont immediately withdrew. Her spirits had been previously agitated by Patty's gossiping communications; this was the first time she had ever seen the "God of her Idolatry" in a light that obscured his supposed divinity. What a discovery for one who measured the virtues and the vices by a gigantick standard! She reached her dressing-room, and sinking into a chair, fell into strong hystericks.

Her screams instantly alarmed her family, and Mr. Clermont was the first to fly to her assistance. His heart was candid and affectionate, and soon penetrated by remorse. He had corrected his dog for obliterating the portrait; but he had himself cruelly discomposed the charming original. In the lively pangs of compunction, he flung himself at her feet; terrified at the apprehension of her danger, he implored her forgiveness, and styled himself the basest of villains. No pungent aromatick could boast the reviving power which his voice possessed; his gentle bride, with sobbing tenderness, assured him of her forgiveness; but her delicate frame had been too much affected by the acuteness of her sensibility, immediately to recover from the shock it had received. Mr. Clermont attended her with the most watchful solicitude; intreaties for pardon, and assurances that it had been long ago granted, were repeated every minute; and if this unlucky incident could be termed the quarrel of lovers, it certainly confirmed the proverb, by proving the "renewal of love."

The lady's indisposition necessarily obliged some of the servants to be present during the eclaircissement; and as uneducated minds are ever apt to suspect more than they know, and to exaggerate what they really see, the circumstance was soon published, in a manner not very favourable to the wedded pair. My sagacious neighbours entered deeply into the dispute, and seemed willing to allow Mr. Clermont entire possession of the epithet of "basest of villains," which he had been pleased to affix to his own character. Indeed, general report brought no instance to confirm this *unqualified* abuse; but will candour permit us to question the veracity of voluntary confession? Our inquisitors-general, after bitterly inveighing against the guilt of hypocrisy in a young person, resolved upon a *permanent sitting* to discover the latent depravity, which they were certain must exist. And they executed this task with a degree of watchfulness, that would have done honour to Argus himself; who perhaps was the mythological emblem of our sisterhood.

CHAP. XXVIII.

In wedlock, characters may be too similar to produce harmony. This axiom is proved by a well-fought battle between female weakness, and male folly.

While pity sang the plaintive dirge over the misfortunes of "poor Mrs. Clermont," that lady had entirely recovered from her indisposition; and fully confiding in her husband's assurance, that she should never behold the *smallest* error in his temper and conduct again, she yielded to the transporting reflections which the expected arrival of her dear Eliza Milton had excited. Several months had elapsed since the friends had enjoyed the gratification of a personal intercourse, and though the important events which had taken place in that period had been described by a very diffuse pen; yet, many circumstances would admit of further amplification, in which art both ladies were adepts.

As I cannot conceive that it could be from the want of a proper relish for the beauties of female conversation, that Mr. Clermont was not constantly of the party, I will ascribe his absence to his commendable wish to gratify the fair friends with opportunities of indulging the confidence they so highly relished. Delicacies are apt to satiate the appetite, and to produce such a whimsical craving after novelty, as to render the coarsest food palatable. The most luxurious Epicures sometimes prescribe to themselves abstinence, in order to excite the greater relish for an expected dainty. Judging by these rules, Mr. Clermont invited a party of young friends to Stannadine, very soon after Miss Milton's arrival. They had all been his companions at school as well as at College, and their society had been productive of a thousand pleasures, before despotick love became the "master passion in his breast," and "swallowed up" every competitor.

The foils who were thus introduced as a contrast to female *softness* were men of fortune, animated by youth and lively spirits, and exceedingly disposed to enjoy themselves with their old friend. They beheld his happiness with that sort of good-humoured envy, which warm admiration is apt to inspire, and which, though it desires as fortunate a lot for itself, has no malev-olent wish to lessen the felicity of another. "Where did you meet with such an angel, Clermont?" was the general exclamation; and the epithets "Lucky dog!" and "Happy fellow!" were interrupted[1] by many hearty shakes of the hand, and wishes of long life and uninterrupted harmony. I could here moralize upon the instabil-ity of human wishes.

The young gentlemen were all passionately fond of field sports; it was the season for enjoying them, and the surround-ing country was favourable to their desires. The restless humour of their sex soon made them weary of sedentary amusements, one proposed hunting, another shooting, a third coursing;[2] but Mrs. Clermont's tender disposition supplied her with very strong objections to all the three diversions, and she looked with so much horror upon the cruel nature of these sports, as almost to detest those who practised them. She defended the cause of the dumb creation, with all the irresistible graces of plaintive oratory; and as her insinuating countenance, no less than her words, was peculiarly adapted to soften the hearts of her op-ponents, the majority seemed more than half convinced, and inclined to give up their darling pursuit. But one of the young Acteons,[3] (by name Aubrey,) possessing more humour than im-plicit deference, encountered the fair pleader with a great share of agreeable vivacity, at the moment that her triumph was going to be acknowledged. He gayly ascribed the commiseration the ladies generally expressed for the sufferings of animals of chase, to sympathy, arising from the recollection of their own terrors, while exposed to the persecutions of the grand *pursuer* Man. He cautioned them against the dangerous, though generous design,

---

1 In the first edition, "interpreted."

2 Coursing is a type of hunting using dogs that have been trained to chase game using sight, rather than scent. Rabbits were a commonly used game.

3 Actaeon, in Greek mythology, was a hunter who accidentally saw the god-dess Artemis bathing. She changed him into a stag, and he was killed by his own dogs.

of diverting the *whole* attention of that mischievous creature from other objects of prey, to themselves; and he illustrated his argument with so many whimsical ideas, that a loud laugh announced his victory. Neither Mrs. Clermont, nor her echo Miss Milton, dared to oppose their lively antagonist, and a shooting party was fixed for the next morning, to which Mr. Clermont was prevailed on to accede, though he had in reality no relish for the sport.

The company had no sooner retired than Mrs. Clermont began to exert her influence to detach her husband from what she termed an *inhuman* diversion. Certainly shooting could appear no better, when her lively imagination had embellished the terror of the poor birds which had escaped, the misery of such as were wounded, the anguish of the dying, and the grief of the survivors. Mr. Clermont heartily wished he could have retracted his promise; but as it had been given, thought he must adhere to it. His lady had now a new cause for dissuasion. Accidents often happened with guns, and as nothing but his staying at home would pacify her, he at length acquiesced; but so unwillingly, that he spent the remainder of the night in anticipating the awkward appearance he should make to his expecting friends in the morning. This apprehension was not ill-founded; the apologies he had framed were too jejune to be admitted; the real cause of his absenting himself was instantly guessed, and a loud laugh excited; which Mr. Clermont affected to parry with great bravery.

A jest upon the subject of female usurpation is dreadfully grating to lordly man, and it is peculiarly so when (as in the present instance) it happens to apply. Mr. Clermont declined his lady's invitation to breakfast, and as soon as his friends had set off, retired to his library, and there continued to pace the room with desultory steps; frequently imagining he had caught a glimpse of the chains which Hymen is *suspected* to wear under his long saffron mantle.[1]

Respecting the real existence of these said chains, I, as an old

---

1 The "chains" of marriage is what is meant here—that marriage is fettering to a man.

maid, must not be allowed to give any decided opinion; but as the very apprehension of them has been known to drive many of the "Lords of the creation" frantick, I constantly advise my newly-married friends to endeavour as much as possible to divert their husbands' attention from this terrible bugbear. I intreat them to hold the reins of government (if by great chance committed to their hands) with circumspect propriety, and to surrender them the moment that the possession of them becomes disputed.[1]

Dinner summoned the party again together. The young sportsmen, delighted with the pleasures they had enjoyed, were in most excellent spirits; but the fretful vexation which appeared in Mr. Clermont's look and manner effectually suppressed the indulgence of genuine mirth. A forced conversation was faintly supported, and the ladies soon withdrew. The bottle then began more freely to circulate, and Mr. Clermont's chagrin was not proof to the general hilarity it inspired. Old school exploits were then recollected with infinite satisfaction, and the classical enjoyments which College had produced lost none of their attick zest by repetition.[2] In short, mirth and good-humour were completely re-established in the dining-room.

Mrs. Clermont was in the mean time indulging in a luxury, of which I would prescribe a most temperate use to all young wives: I mean the dangerous pleasure of unreserved confidence, with what is termed a *bosom* friend. The ruin of wedded peace may often be ascribed to such injudicious communications. To what purpose is it to talk over an husband's errors, or the little vexations which may be casually endured from him, unless to quicken our sensibility, to keep our minds and our tempers in a painful irritable state, and to prevent that happy forgetfulness which is in many instances the greatest blessing we can enjoy?

Mr. Clermont's ill-humour was too apparent to escape Miss

---

1 This is a moment in which West's ideas about women and marriage can be directly contrasted to Wollstonecraft's. West would have wives, if they are unusual enough to have any power in their marriages, to exercise it lightly or surreptitiously and always to give it over once it is suspected to be in their hands.

2 Attick (or "Attic") meant of Athens, Greek, or classical. In this instance, it refers to the reputation for elegance and wit.

Milton's observation, and Marianne's streaming tears evinced her painful sense of it. Encouraged by the pleasing sympathy of her friend, she indiscreetly related every little incident which had before occurred of a disagreeable nature; and the adventure in the library was largely discussed, together with Mr. Clermont's anxiety at her illness, and his solemn promises of never again giving way to ill-humour. Instead of considering a breach of that engagement as a constitutional defect, or a transient forgetfulness, and therefore but a venial error, Miss Milton aggravated it into wanton perjury and consummate cruelty. She had no malevolent design in so doing, but she had never made any observations upon real life; and Mr. Clermont's present behaviour was certainly very opposite to the perfect excellence and perfect felicity which exists in the land of Hymen;—as described in the Utopian geography of many modern novelists.[1]

"Ah, my dearest Marianne," cried the affectionate but imprudent Miss Milton, "are you indeed united to a lordly spirit, insensible of the value of your lovely tenderness, your charming sensibility? I observed you at table, and felt astonished that Mr. Clermont could resist the soft complaining anguish that appeared in your countenance. Hark!—No I am not mistaken, the gentlemen are extremely lively now. They can enjoy themselves as soon as the restraint which we imposed is removed. Good Heaven! and have I lived to see my Marianne an impediment to her husband's happiness?"[2]

"My father's cautions," resumed Mrs. Clermont, "pointed out to me all these evils; but I did hope that Mr. Clermont would prove an exception to the general rule. Too plainly do I discover that my society has lost its wonted fascination. Alas! my heart

---

1 This is an instance of West implicitly declaring the difference of her fiction from that of her contemporaries. Eliza Milton, too, is painted as a female Quixote, having internalized misleading ideas about love from modern romance fiction.

2 Miss Milton echoes the purple prose of modern romance. ("Hark!" etc.) Her speech suggests that she has mistaken the utopian ideals in fiction for the workings of actual modern marriages. She imagines Marianne as a female victim who has been wronged by a villainous husband, such as would have been found in the period's Gothic novels. In her subsequent response to Miss Milton, Marianne plays the Gothic heroine part to perfection.

will ever be unalterably his, even if he continues to treat me injuriously."

Here a sudden interruption prevented her from proceeding, and gives me an opportunity of closing my chapter.

CHAP. XXIX.

The consequences of a confident's interference when unrestrained by discretion.

Mr. Clermont and his friends rose from table in high spirits, and proceeded to the drawing-room in the gay hope of spending a pleasant evening. The first object they beheld was Mrs. Clermont rising from the sopha, and loosening her hands from Miss Milton's; her eyes red and swoln[1], and her cheek wet with tears.

Confused, surprised, and perhaps secretly ashamed of a weakness she had not time to conceal, she could only answer the general enquiry of what was the matter, with a complaint of indisposition; and seizing her friend's arm, hurried to her apartment. Mr. Clermont followed, full of real anxiety, but when he tenderly enquired into the nature of her complaint, she only answered him with a soft sigh, and a request that he would not distress her.

Lady G. (in Sir Charles Grandison)[2] complains, that mediators and mediatrixes had extended her whimsical disputes with her lord, and given them a more serious aspect than she designed. There can be no doubt that the present fracas between our young people would have terminated as easily as the last, if Miss Milton had not been seized with the warm Knight-errantry of friendship. Conceiving that the timid Marianne wanted an orator to open her cause, she informed Mr. Clermont that his wife's uneasiness had proceeded from his evident ill humour, and she

---

1 In the second edition, "swollen."
2 Samuel Richardson's *The History of Sir Charles Grandison* (1753-54) was an immensely influential epistolary novel about a perfect hero in search of a perfect wife.

requested him to consider what kind of treatment gentleness and sensibility required.

To borrow a phrase from the vocabulary of Bacchus, Mr. Clermont was a little elevated,[1] and consequently felt the high dignity of man too warmly to submit to reproof. "Does Mrs. Clermont, Madam," said he, "appoint you the judge of my be-haviour?" Then turning to his lady, he desired her for her *own* sake to behave with more propriety, and then humming a favou-rite tune, he rejoined his companions.

Neither my hero nor my heroine were models of prudence. Mr. Clermont's renewed vexation was strongly written in his face, and he was too much agitated to evade his friends' enquiries. They were quite in a disposition to enjoy *fun*, without retaining sufficient judgment to distinguish humour from mischief. A grand rebellion against female influence was resolved upon, and as such projects always succeed best when reason is entirely ban-ished, they all determined to spend the evening in high jollity; and to call in Champaign and Burgundy as glorious auxiliaries, for the supporting of male authority, and for humbling a wife's spirit.

As Mr. Clermont's heart, in spite of his resentment, could not be wholly alienated from his Marianne, he was the first to quicken the circulation of the glass, in order to silence the re-proaches which he could not endure. The hours of night flew rapidly away, enlivened by what the gentlemen called Anacre-ontick[2] sallies. About twelve o'clock, Mrs. Clermont dispatched a request to speak with her husband; but the general voice cho-rused his answer, that he was particularly engaged, and could not leave his party till the morning.

If the gay Bacchanalians perceived the "broad pinions of time swifter than the wind;" to poor Mrs. Clermont he appeared "to creep decrepid with old age."[3] Unkindness must ever fall with

---

1 Bacchus was the Roman god of wine and fertility. Those who followed him were called Bacchanalians. In other words, Clermont was drunk.

2 Anacreaon (c. 570-476 BCE) was a Greek lyric poet. Although just a handful of his verses survive, poems about love and wine have become known as "anacreontic" verse.

3 "Broad pinions swifter than the wind" and "creep decrepit with his age"

severest weight on those who have ever been accustomed to extreme indulgence. Miss Milton's interposition had indeed been able to aggravate a trivial vexation into a real sorrow, but it was utterly incapable of healing the anguish a tender mind endured, while labouring under the *known* displeasure of a beloved husband.

Mrs. Clermont flung herself upon the bed, pretending sleepiness, but in reality to escape from the impertinence of consolation; which administered no relief to her agonized heart. Her anxious friend insisted upon watching her slumbers, and positively refused to quit her chamber. This fond attention, contrasted with Mr. Clermont's cruel neglect, rendered the latter but more apparent, and fixed another dagger in Marianne's breast. Besides, her faithful Patty believing her lady to be asleep, began a conversation in audible whispers with Miss Milton, of which the following was the prefatory speech.

"Pray, Madam, what can be the matter between my master and my lady? though I always thought they would soon fall out, for Miss Lappel has told me, that all the people in Danbury say, Mr. Clermont is the greatest villain in the world."

"Hush!" said Miss Milton, "so I am afraid; but don't let your lady hear you for the world."

"O," replied Patty, "she is fast asleep. 'Tis a shocking thing, Madam, that she should be *so* married. The sweetest, best tempered creature in the world."

"It is indeed a fatal engagement," said Mrs. Clermont to herself, but her desire to hear more kept her silent.

"Pray, Mrs. Patty, do you know how this match was brought about?" enquired Miss Milton.

"It was my old Lord's doings, Madam. To be sure there must be a fate in these things. Perhaps they wanted money at the Park; but I think it was not so neither. Mr. Clermont never let my lady have any rest; teaze, teaze; but such hot love is generally soon cold, as the saying is."

---

are both lines describing Time personified in Edward Young's famous long poem *Night Thoughts* (1742-46). It begins with a quasi-autobiographical speaker lamenting the death of his child and moves on to consider issues of Christian faith.

"Not always so," returned Miss Milton, "but only with such ungrateful wretches as he."

"Wretches indeed, Madam. Well, to be sure, you only say what all the world does of him."

Here Mrs. Clermont's agony could no longer be suppressed. She fell into violent fits, and it was at this period that the message was sent to Mr. Clermont, and the answer returned, which I have before stated. The footman was again dispatched to say that his lady was extremely ill; but he judging his master's presence, in the state he then was, could afford no consolation, brought for answer that Mr. Clermont was extremely sorry, but really was unable to attend her.

CHAP. XXX.

Human passions, like the sea, vary from tempests to sullen calms.

The night passed in scenes of distraction; I shall now usher in the morning.

Mrs. Clermont, exhausted by her strong emotions, sunk into a slumber, in which she had continued a few hours, when Mr. Clermont and his friends awoke. A confused recollection of what had passed, mingled with much secret compunction; for the delights of intemperance will never stand the test of returning reason.

The visitants, on being informed that Mrs. Clermont was exceedingly indisposed, judged that their remaining longer at Stannadine would be a great impropriety; and desirous to remedy as far as possible the evil they had caused, at taking leave of Mr. Clermont, strongly urged him to an immediate reconciliation with his lady. Shocked at the idea that the world should know that he and his beloved Marianne were at variance, he sat agitated by the most sensible regret, which his friends strove to diminish, by softening his offence into a *venial* failing.

The moment their carriages drove off, Mr. Clermont went into his wife's apartment; but not with that lively transport which is expressive of the happy husband. She had just risen from her bed, and did I indulge myself in the use of similes, I might now justly apply the trite one, of a broken lily wet with rain. Her pale, dejected aspect heightened in Mr. Clermont's mind the tender sensibility which resentment and inebriety had obscured: he folded her in his arms, and with impassioned agony besought her to forgive him. Mrs. Clermont assured him that she did, but her averted eye, and half-stifled sobs, gave no pleasing confirmation to her words.

Mr. Clermont walked to the window mortified and dejected. Undoubtedly he was too arrogant in expecting his recent provocations could be immediately forgotten, and himself received with a complacent smile. I am, however, afraid that the generality of husbands, from the high idea they entertain of their own superiority, would be apt to think a wife very capricious who should retain her resentment after they have made the *slightest* concession. Men are remarkably tenacious of their opinions, and since protracting a domestick[1] quarrel must always be at the hazard of future happiness, I must advise my sex to be "easily entreated." I can assure them that a placid smile will convey a very forcible reproof to a generous heart conscious of error, and that forgiveness is not the *less* valuable because it is cheerfully bestowed.

After a moment's hesitation, Mr. Clermont determined upon another effort;[2] "You have been ill, my dear," said he, "I hope you are better." A faint affirmative was the only reply. "I conjure you, Marianne, by all our former happiness, do not treat me with indifference. I feel more compunction than I can express when I recollect the past; but let this acknowledgment suffice. Banish the events of yesterday from your remembrance. Give me your hand, and promise to think of them no more." She coldly gave her hand, and with a forced smile uttered the desired promise.

Though it would be very entertaining to a professed gossip, to follow our young couple's proceedings in a journal-like narrative, the apprehension of not meeting with the congenial soul

---

1 In the second edition, "domestic."
2 In the second edition, "effect."

of a sister-gossip in my readers, imposes brevity. The Clermonts continued to behave to each other for some weeks with civility instead of tenderness, and with attention instead of confidence and harmony. The conversation she had overheard between Miss Milton and Patty, cruelly agitated *her* mind, and induced her to view all her husband's actions with the askance eye of suspicion; while her knowledge of the violence of his temper imposed a sort of terrified compliance. Mr. Clermont, on the contrary, attributed his Marianne's melancholy reserve to an implacable disposition, and feeling unwilling to gratify her pride by any further submission, he permitted his attachment for his once adored idol insensibly to decline.

After having for some time silently endured the agonizing terror, which the fear of an husband's unworthiness must excite in an ingenuous heart, Mrs. Clermont unfortunately resolved to disburthen her mind, by confessing to Miss Milton that she had overheard the conversation between her and Patty. That lady candidly acknowledged, that the violent epithets she had used against Mr. Clermont, proceeded from her lively interest in her friend's sufferings, and not from her knowledge of any secret depravity. "But," added she, "I am afraid your maid can give you further information."

"Will my enquiries[1] be justifiable, and to what purpose will they tend?" resumed Mrs. Clermont.

"They will at least relieve the anguish of suspense, and if he appears innocent, your harmony will be in some degree restored; if the contrary, you will have the comfort of knowing the worst, and the sooner you are separated from a depraved husband—"

"Separated!"—exclaimed Mrs. Clermont, turning pale with terror; "for Heaven's sake, Eliza, how could you suggest such an horrid idea? you little know with what passionate attachment my heart is irrevocably his. But let us change the subject, for I will make no inquiries that may lead to such a horrid catastrophe."

"Act as you judge best," returned Miss Milton; "I have only mentioned what an attachment like that you express would urge *me* to do. I confess, uncertainty seems to me the most dreadful of

---

1 In the second edition, "inquiries."

all conditions; and recollect, my dear, that the event you shudder at, is at all times optionable, and not the certain consequence of your endeavouring to re-assure your mind."

To this fallacious reasoning, Mrs. Clermont weakly yielded her "better judgment," and Patty was applied to for further information. Mr. Clermont's behaviour had been so truly inoffensive in every respect, but in the instances I have detailed, that Patty had nothing new to communicate; but out of her great zeal to make her lady *easy*, she undertook the office of spy upon her master's conduct, and opened an indirect communication with the Danbury inspectors.

Nothing however could be procured but petty detractions and general invective; so evidently the result of malice, as to be even in *Patty's* opinion undeserving of repetition. During the course of these inquiries, Miss Milton terminated her visit; Mr. Clermont's mind was still so little in unison with his Marianne's, that he rejoiced at the departure of a person, who he perceived was honoured with that confidence and those marks of affection which he believed to be exclusively his right, while she bitterly regretted the absence of her dear companion.

The happiness of the Clermonts soon assumed a more favourable appearance. The indefatigable Patty could hear nothing that was of sufficient importance to disturb it, and her lady indulged the hope that the expressions which had so deeply disturbed her mind, were only "unweighed words," or thoughtless repetitions of the vague calumnies of envy and malevolence. She and Mr. Clermont equally felt the pain of discord, and they began insensibly to re-assume the tender affectionate behaviour which had endeared the early hours of their union; when this fair promise of felicity was interrupted by an unfortunate incident.

CHAP. XXXI.

Very palatable to the Lords of the Creation, as it exhibits them in the possession of plenitude of Power.

In compliance with her friend's parting request, Mrs. Clermont had given a solemn promise of continuing her journal; and as it was to be truly circumstantial, it necessarily employed great part of her time. While thus engaged, she generally locked her door to prevent interruption; but one day having unfortunately forgotten that precaution, Mr. Clermont suddenly appeared. Three sheets of paper had been filled ready to dispatch; to say the truth, they were as innocent a composition as ever issued from a female pen: but as they contained a repetition of what had passed in conversation between herself and husband, with comments on the happy change in his behaviour, she anxiously wished to conceal them from him; and on his playfully attempting to take them from her, she threw them into the fire, and watched them till consumed, with serious solicitude.

Mr. Clermont's mind was not wholly free from the meanness of suspicion, and he felt deeply mortified at the idea of a wife's concealing secrets from him, which she implicitly confided to another. He suppressed his chagrine[1] at the moment; but since his curiosity to penetrate into this interdicted correspondence was irresistible, he determined to use *any* means to develope the mystery.

He soon procured a letter of Miss Milton's, and upon breaking the seal, realized the proverb respecting the fate of suspicious people, for certainly the first paragraph was not very complimental to himself: it follows,—

"Do not, my dearest Marianne, think me insensible of the pleasure you express, at your husband's appearing conscious of his cruel injurious treatment of you; I rejoice that your meek

---

1 In the second edition, "chagrin."

sensibility at last seems to touch his heart with remorse, may the compunction be lasting! But oh, my sweet friend, guard against the amiable susceptibility of your temper, nor any longer fix your happiness in the frail promises of weak irritable man. Recollect your father's admirable precepts, and contract your fond affection for one who never deserved, and does not return it."

If Mr. Clermont had possessed sufficient patience to peruse the whole letter, he would have found the asperity of this paragraph softened by several concessions in his favour, and would have perceived the epithets "weak" and "irritable," which had most piqued him, were in reality intended as a censure upon his whole sex. But his passion entirely overcame him, and flying to his lady's apartment, he peremptorily charged her immediately to break off all connection with an artful, base calumniator, who under the specious mask of friendship, dared to interfere in the sacred concerns of wedlock, and to traduce a husband's character even to his wife. He concluded with a *threat*, that if she refused immediate compliance, she should never see him more; and after thus justifying Miss Milton's sentiments by his conduct, he tore the letter into a hundred pieces, and rushed out of the room.

Mrs. Clermont remained for some moments stupified with surprise, and gazing upon the fragments, in which she recognized the writing of her dear Eliza. Tears, her usual resource, at length came to her relief, and she was indulging in a very plentiful flow, when a servant entering the room, announced the arrival of Mr. and Miss Dudley: Marianne flew to meet them, and for a moment forgot her sorrow in their embraces.

I must now account for their sudden arrival. Mr. Dudley was hastened to London by letters from his agent, informing him that a clear discovery had been made of the long suspected villany of the elder Tonnereau, and that in consequence he was taken into custody; Louisa's ardent desire to see a sister, whose letters had for some time betrayed an expression of tender melancholy, induced her to expedite her intended visit to Stannadine.

Mrs. Clermont did not wait for their inquiries to explain the reason for the tears which still swam in her radiant eyes; she frankly owned that her father had formed the justest estimate of the married state, but added, that perhaps even *he* would not have expected that Mr. Clermont's love should already have so far evaporated, as to permit him to insist upon her abandoning a friend, who had been the chief blessing of her life. She sobbed out her resolution never to renounce her Eliza, and then asked if her lot was not that of peculiar misery?

"No, my child," said Mr. Dudley, "you only participate in the ills common to humanity; and I have a satisfaction in reflecting, that the troubles arising from contrariety of temper and opinion, may be remedied by prudence and concession. Mr. Clermont has doubtless reasons to urge for this peremptory style. Where is he? I must see him, and bring about an immediate explanation."

A servant being summoned, informed them, that his master was gone out on horseback, and had refused any attendance. Mrs. Clermont's distress now assumed the appearance of phrenzy, from apprehensions respecting the safety of the person, whom she a few moments before considered as a relentless tyrant. Every domestick was dispatched in search of the dear fugitive, and scarcely could the efforts of her father and sister restrain her from joining them.

Intelligence at length arrived, that he had been seen on the road to the park; Mrs. Clermont now earnestly pressed her father to follow him, and to conjure him immediately to return home. Nothing else could alleviate her anxiety, and having obtained this promise from Mr. Dudley, she became tolerably calm.

Louisa's heart not only melted with pity for her sister's wild distress, but for the silent anguish which oppressed her dejected father. She knew his mind had lately received an additional weight of anguish, from the apprehension that he must either engage in a criminal prosecution, against a man with whom he had formerly lived in the strictest bond of friendship, or else suffer a nefarious villain to escape punishment; "My dear father," said Louisa to herself, while her sister was in the extremest paroxysms of grief, "with what calm dignity do you support sorrow?"

Having persuaded Marianne to recline on the sopha[1] for a few minutes, she followed her father to the door, to breathe her ardent

---

1 In the second edition, "sofa."

wishes for the success of his embassy; "I do not fear," replied Mr. Dudley, "but that I shall persuade Mr. Clermont to return; do you exercise your influence over your sister, and conjure her to abandon a friend, who I suspect has acted a most indefensible part; if she yields, her husband will probably be ashamed of his unmanly violence. My fears, Louisa, were but too just. They have good hearts, and a real affection for each other; but Marianne is married to a man as enthusiastical and imprudent as herself. How disgraceful are these baby quarrels! how ridiculous these high theatrical passions, which subject them to the laugh of the neighbourhood! nay, worse, which point out to artful villany, a means whereby it may *effectually* undermine domestick happiness."

Miss Dudley exerted all her eloquence, to persuade Mrs. Clermont to consent to any terms of reconciliation her husband should impose; her arguments were answered by declamatory flourishes on the inviolable sanctity of friendship, and the justice of defending one whose zeal, if allowed to be imprudent, was yet the result of pure affection.

Mr. Dudley was not more successful in his mediation; Mr. Clermont, after an exaggerated detail of his provocation, urged the fond *idolatry* with which he had loved his Marianne, and her *ingratitude*, in hesitating to sacrifice to his *just* resentment her blind partiality for a dangerous woman, who assumed the pretext of friendship, to further her execrable designs against his peace. Lord Clermont, though less violent than his son, was *firmly* of opinion, that the intimacy with Miss Milton must be immediately terminated; and Lady Clermont, who happened unfortunately to be at the park, took this opportunity to vent her sarcastick malignity. She termed Marianne a well-meaning young creature, but to her *certain* knowledge, too deficient in her ideas of propriety, to be entirely intrusted with her own conduct.

Mr. Dudley checked the resentment of wounded paternal affection, by recollecting his character of mediator. He gave up Miss Milton's conduct as wholly indefensible; and in general condemned confidents as dangerous to matrimonial peace. But he urged the propriety of gently loosening those ties, which though absolutely fantastick, had a real influence over his daughter's mind. The very word Mr. Clermont had used (sacrifice) implied reluctance, and he pointed out how much more desirable it was that her reason should be convinced respecting the impropriety of her friend's conduct, and consequently the necessity of dissolving the connection; than, that a sudden breach should be imposed upon her, as an act of obedience. In the former case, Mr. Clermont might expect his wife would soon look *up* to him with grateful deference, for having rescued her from a dangerous error; in the latter, a recollection of the violent measures which had been taken, would induce her to honour her severed friend with a regret of which she was unworthy. In conclusion, he urged his son-in-law to a generous unconditional return, by the consideration how powerfully such a concession would affect his daughter's heart.

Lady Clermont here interfered, and prevented these arguments from determining the yielding husband. She produced the letter in which the incautious but well-intentioned Marianne had confessed, that weakness and precipitate confidence were her constitutional failings. Her Ladyship prevented all the impression the unquestionable ingenuousness of this acknowledgement might have made, by observing that she had long ago entirely forgiven the little offence which this letter was meant to palliate, and only produced it as a proof of the indisputable necessity of her son's supplying the firm decision, which the dear creature confessedly wanted, and of his rescuing his amiable wife from such a dangerous friend as Miss Milton was. This opinion met with general approbation, and Mr. Dudley on his return to his daughter, recommended unconditional submission, as the only terms on which Mr. Clermont would consent to return home.

"I do not," said he to Mrs. Clermont, "now urge your determination by common *motives*. Every thing which ought to be most dear and sacred to you, is at stake. It is not four months since the world saw you enter into marriage, under the happiest auspices of mutual love. Your disagreements cannot be concealed, and the most candid will hardly be able to persuade themselves that they could have proceeded to this length, without somewhat criminal on one side at least. Let your story, my dear girl, be told even by a partial friend, believe me the prudent part of the world will severely reprobate an attachment (though to a female) to which you can resolve to sacrifice the higher duties you have recently bound yourself, by the most solemn and inviolable oaths, to fulfil."

"Are then the names of wife and friend incompatible?" exclaimed Mrs. Clermont.

"I will give you my opinion on that subject hereafter, at present the *known* duty of a wife calls upon you for immediate performance. Risk not your future happiness by any further delay. Take your pen and dictate an adieu to Miss Milton. It may be affectionate, but let it be determined; and then recal your husband whilst it is yet in your power to recal him."

Mrs. Clermont reluctantly complied. Her letter to her Eliza was blotted with tears, and incoherent through distress. After *one* gentle reproof, it was filled with copious complaints against the hard necessity which imposed a separation, and with protestations of inviolable regard. To these fond ebullitions of love, Miss Dudley subjoined a softened narrative of the events which had led to the prohibition; and she urged Miss Milton, by all her regard for her Marianne's future peace, not to attempt to dispute its validity.

I will insert Mrs. Clermont's letter to her husband—

"I have complied with your injunctions, and have given up for *you* the friend whose affection constituted my chief felicity for fourteen years: a friend whose only fault was indiscreet partiality for me! In doing this, I have torn from my heart its dearest object, yourself *alone* excepted. My regret cannot be disguised, nor will it yield to time. Your renewed and uniform tenderness can alone recompence me, for the sacrifice *you* have enjoined. Return, my Edward, immediately, and save your once beloved Marianne from sinking under the weight of her sorrows."

Mr. Dudley did not disapprove the pathetick sincerity expressed in this letter. It had the desired effect. Mr. Clermont immediately returned to Stannadine; again intreated his lady to forget the past, and encouraged her to look forward to future golden days, by the *gracious* assurance that he would always remember her meritorious compliance.

CHAP. XXXII.

The author's opinion of the politicks of Hymen seems to be in favour of a limited monarchy.

Though the quarrels of the Clermonts might in their violence, frequency, and speedy termination, be justly compared to the disputes of children, they did not end in *quite* so cordial a reconciliation. It is perhaps impossible to "pluck memory from her seat," or to "erase a written trouble from the brain," when the mind has passed the first stage of adolescence. Mrs. Clermont recollected that every disagreement had been adjusted with increased difficulty, her experience of the past gave her but a melancholy anticipation of the future, and the renunciation of so dear a connection was too painful, and imposed in too authoritative a manner, to be cheerfully submitted to. The fear of offending taught her to *try* to conceal her grief, but her pallid cheek and swoln eyes the next morning, plainly proved the night had been spent in tears.

Conscious of past severity, Mr. Clermont endeavoured to conciliate his wife's affections, by more marked attentions to her father. He earnestly pressed him to postpone his intended journey to town, to give up all endeavours to recover his fortune, and to depend entirely upon the steady friendship with which he would cheerfully use every effort to alleviate his sorrows. Mr. Dudley's conduct in influencing his daughter's submission, had banished from her husband's mind a suspicion which an expression in Miss Milton's fatal letter excited, and Mr. Clermont now felt gratefully inclined to promote the wishes of a man, who had gratified his.

"Make my child happy," said Mr. Dudley, "and you will impose upon me the highest obligation."

Mr. Clermont threw his eyes upon the ground, and with a remorseful air said, it should in future be his study to prove how highly he rated her compliance.

"I do not, Sir, mean to reproach you, or wholly to vindicate my daughter; but I wish strictly to caution you against two errors. Avoid calling in any person to witness your little domestick disputes; a mediator in matrimonial quarrels is more likely to widen than to heal the breach. Rather chuse to keep every disagreement a profound secret, for if they are at all exposed, curious impertinents will publish them with *added* circumstances, and however painful these circumstances are to yourselves, the world will find in them matter for entertainment and ridicule.

"Let me also, my dear Sir, intreat you to look upon your wife's errors with the tenderest indulgence. If an action can be referred to two motives, kindly affix that which is least reprehensible. You used an expression at the park, Mr. Clermont; it was inconsiderately uttered, yet it struck me to the heart. You called my child ungrateful. Her heart is devotedly yours, you may break it by unkindness, but you cannot estrange it. She is young, inexperienced, and romantick, but she is not, cannot be ungrateful. Ingratitude is the vice of a narrow or depraved soul, it never exists in a warm impassioned disposition. Oh, Sir, pardon my agitation, but the daughter of the exalted woman I have long lamented, and speedily hope to rejoin, never could disgrace her mother's memory by ingratitude to an affectionate husband."

"Proceed," said Mr. Clermont. "Your words sink into my soul; have you more to urge?"—"Nothing!" replied Mr. Dudley emphatically, and grasping him by the hand; "except that you will never suffer my Louisa to want a protector, or an asylum."

The ladies here entered, and Mr. Clermont turned aside to conceal the emotion Mr. Dudley's solemn reproof had excited. The fond father took this opportunity to slip a letter into Marianne's hand. "I had much to say to you, my dear child," said he, "and it is of too important a nature to be intrusted to the vague impression conversation imprints upon the mind. Your worthy husband has urged me to reside with you; his request is the more pleasing, as it evidently proceeds from his affection for you. If I live, I shall be often with you; if not, consult that paper, I shall speak in it when dead."

At these words his daughters burst into tears. "I must go with you to London, Sir," said Louisa. "You shall not leave me while you indulge these afflicting forebodings."

"My mind is uncommonly tranquil and serene, my dear girls, this morning. I wonder, Louisa, you do not perceive my artifice. I wished to make a deep impression upon Marianne's mind, and see I have succeeded. Dry your eyes, my darlings, and bid a cheerful adieu to that father whose only remaining wish is, to see his children happy."

While Mrs. Clermont threw herself into her father's arms in an agony of affection, the dignified Louisa raising her meek eyes to Heaven in a silent ejaculation, implored its beneficent attention to that interesting object, a good man in affliction. The air of forced gayety[1] which Mr. Dudley assumed at parting, could not banish the dejection the solemnity of his expressions had inspired. His daughters followed him with their eyes as long as possible, and then silently withdrew to their respective apartments.

I shall conclude this chapter with a copy of his letter to Mrs. Clermont.

'Before I leave my Marianne, happy, I trust, in the recovered affections of her husband, I will give her my promised opinion, respecting a subject to which I thought her yesterday too much agitated to attend.

'You asked me if the name of wife and friend are incompatible: certainly not. They are titles which mutually reflect lustre upon each other; and I have ever considered *that* young woman as particularly fortunate, who had secured the esteem of some discreet matron, and regulated her conduct by the dictates of experience. I must, however, repeat that a wife should *retain* no connections which her husband decidedly disapproves. A prudent woman indeed will never *form* any which can give pain to a reasonable man. She will chuse her friends with judgment, confide in them with caution, and love them with sincerity, yet

---

1 In the second edition, "gaiety."

still with moderation. You may think these limitations cold and narrow, they are such as you ought always to regard.

'Female friendship, my child, is often disgraced by a ridiculous imitation. Two romantick girls select each other from the general mass of their acquaintance as fancy dictates. They relinquish the practice of acknowledged virtues, to indulge in a frivolous intimacy, and while they gratify a propensity for mere gossip, capricious expectations, and fantastick desires, suppose that they exhibit a model of one of those angelick perfections which *dignify* our natures.

'You say you have been accustomed to communicate every sentiment of your soul to your dear Eliza, and you think while so doing, you were at least *innocently* employed. Time was not given us to be idled away; has any moral or mental improvement resulted from this correspondence? Your heart is good, your understanding not contemptible; yet could you without confusion see those sentiments publickly divulged, of which you have made her the unreserved depository. Has not the desire of having somewhat to communicate, induced you to form a precipitate judgment, and to utter opinions which you afterwards wished to retract? Have not the commendations and tender expressions you have been used to re-echo to each other, vitiated your affections, and rendered you less sensible of the tempered but uniform attachment of your other connections?

'But supposing this perversion of time pardonable in early youth, it can no *longer* be excusable; and had not Mr. Clermont's disapprobation suddenly obliged you to terminate your connection with Miss Milton, I should have thought that your sense of the higher duties to which you are called, would have convinced you of the necessity of appropriating less time to multiplied expressions of unmeaning tenderness. You are a wife, my love; you will, I hope, soon be a mother; you are the mistress of a family; you are a person of fortune; you have had a liberal education. What an extensive scope of action do these characters imply! Go, Marianne, and thank that Providence, who has placed you in a capacity to employ every portion of your time in important occupations, and to exercise the noblest feelings of the human heart.

'Do not droop with vain regret, because Mr. Clermont appears less faultless than your enthusiastick imagination once supposed. Do not arraign the dispensations of Heaven, because you are not wholly exempt from the common ills incident to humanity. Instead of indulging a foolish curiosity respecting your husband's conduct, fix your attention upon your own. Do not regard what the idle and malevolent say of you, or him: you will both be impleaded at a different audit. Go, and comfort those who drain the dregs of that cup of sorrow, of which you have but slightly tasted. Go, and relieve the wants of poverty, smooth the bed of sickness, alleviate the anguish of incurable grief, dissipate the gloom of ignorance, and if possible limit the ravages of vice. Rise to the noble task for which you were called into existence. You cannot want employment when you have to prepare yourself for eternity. You cannot be wretched while you can make your fellow-creatures happy.

'Adieu, my Marianne, respect your husband's virtues, and divert your attention from his failings. Love your sister, she deserves your confidence and esteem. Her trials have been singular, but they have rendered her merit more conspicuous. Once more farewell, my child; if I should not again see you in this world, give yourself to my arms, and to the arms of your sainted mother, as an angel of light, in a purer state of existence.

'RICHARD DUDLEY.'

CHAP. XXXIII.

The discerning Reader may discover symptoms of approaching events, of the painful kind.

For some time Mr. and Mrs. Clermont appeared to have derived considerable advantage from the precepts they had received, and their whole behaviour promised a perfect renewal of harmony and happiness. *He* divided his time judiciously between the claims of social life, and the elegant amusements to which he was attached; and *she* turning her attention to the active engagements of benevolence and domestick management, soon made a considerable proficiency, being assisted in her progress by her sister, who was an adept in the practice of the retired virtues.

Christmas is a season peculiarly adapted to the purposes of hospitality, and whilst the Clermonts liberally supplied the wants of their indigent neighbours, they did not neglect those inferiour but not unimportant claims, which the laws of society require. Notwithstanding their disappointment on a former occasion, the surrounding country were invited to an elegant entertainment; and as the hope of the inviters, respecting giving pleasure and acquiring popularity, was not so sanguine as before, their humble views were more fully gratified. Indeed they seemed to conciliate the affections of their neighbours, by not attempting any extraordinary degree of splendour or novelty; for we always reluctantly pay the applause *demanded* of us by that merit which is avowedly superiour, or that excellence which is conscious of its own desert.

This flattering prospect was interrupted by the illness of Lord Clermont. He had been for some weeks at Bath, indisposed by an hereditary gout; and at length grew so alarmingly ill, as to render his son's presence necessary. It was Mr. Clermont's wish, that his Marianne should accompany him, but she, unused to publick scenes, fond of retirement, disgusted with society, and attached to the habits she had lately adopted, preferred remaining at Stannadine; till her sister strongly urged the danger of risking her newly-recovered happiness, by appearing indifferent to her husband's desire of her society.

Another motive influenced Louisa to give this advice. Though Mr. Dudley had prudently concealed his observations from Marianne, he had imparted to his elder daughter his apprehension of some latent malignity in Lady Clermont; and intreated her occasionally to guard her sister against the machinations of envy and revenge. Miss Dudley, confiding in the rectitude of Marianne's heart, and the innocence of her conduct, supposed her presence would most effectually silence calumny, and defeat cunning. This opinion was theoretically right, but it argued little knowledge of the world, or, to use a more appropriate and less hackneyed phrase, of extreme human depravity; for I am persuaded that real malevolence is not so common, as mistake, prejudice, and a censorious habit. This last, the busy daughter of Idleness and Vanity, does an infinitude of mischief, with no worse design than amusing itself, and shewing its own importance. It is the "fool who tosses about firebrands in sport."[1]

The motive that hurried the Clermonts to Bath, precluding Miss Dudley from accompanying them; she returned to Seaton-dell, and there had leisure to moralize upon the incidents of her sister's history. From it she deduced another proof to illustrate these important truths, that happiness is distributed with a much evener hand than a cursory observer would suppose; and that its true seat is in the soul, which, when well disposed, can humbly imitate its great Author, and create a Paradise in a desert.

Recollecting the high expectations her sister had formed, and her father's unregarded predictions that they would be disappointed, the Trojan prophetess[2] came into her mind, and she composed the following

SONNET.

Her hair dishevel'd, and her robe unty'd,
    Cassandra rush'd amongst the festal train,
    What time young Paris sang his nuptial strain,
And led to Priam's roof the Spartan bride:
Of certain woes that must that crime betide
    The holy virgin prophesied in vain;
    Her warning voice could no attention gain
'Till Pyrrhus levell'd Ilium's tow'ring pride.
Ah! in the horrors of that night aghast,
    What shrieks, prophetick maid, thy truth declar'd!
And thus when youth beholds Misfortune's blast
    O'erturn the fairy bow'rs by Fancy rear'd,
Too late it muses on the precepts sage
Of cool experience, and predictive age.

---

1 This seeming quotation actually reworks several phrases from the Bible's Proverbs 26.

2 The Trojan prophetess was Cassandra, a princess who was the daughter of King Priam. As a result of a curse, Cassandra's prophecies, though true, were disbelieved. Her warning that the Greeks would capture Troy was ignored.

The letters Miss Dudley received from London informed her, that Mr. Tonnereau had dissipated his whole fortune, previous to his being taken into custody; the creditors, therefore, could propose no other end in prosecuting him for having concealed part of his effects, than that of bringing a villain to punishment. Mr. Dudley started another hope, which appeared more than a phantom. The particular ship in which his property was embarked, instead of having been captured with the rest of the fleet, had escaped into a neutral port in Spanish America; the Government of which had ordered the cargo to be confiscated, under the pretence of its being designed for contraband trade; but in reality, from the suspicious spirit with which the Spaniards conduct their colonial affairs, and their jealousy of the commercial importance of England. Here Mr. Pelham's friendship promised a most fortunate interposition; he was luckily very intimate with the Spanish ambassador, and through his means a strong memorial was forwarded to the council of the Indies, stating the injustice of the transaction, and demanding restitution. Little doubt was entertained of that illustrious synod's deciding with equity, and the only disagreeable circumstance would be, the obliging Mr. Dudley to take a voyage to Spain. The fond father concluded, exulting in the hope, that he should at last be able to reward the exemplary virtue of his child.

Louisa's heart experienced a sensation very different from pleasure, at the apprehension of what her father's declining health might suffer from a sea voyage. In her answer she begged him to abandon a project which she knew he formed principally with a view to her emolument. Her desire, she informed him, centred[1] in her dear little farm, which, even at that early period of spring, wore a promising appearance. The crops looked vigorous, the plantations were healthy, and the house was so considerably improved by the little sums which had been expended upon it, as to appear quite a chearful habitation. "My garden," said she, "is now decorated with a profusion of vernal flowers, the germs of the lilack are bursting; and my morning walks are enlivened with the carol of birds, and the busy hum of bees. I look forward to the

---

1 In the second edition, "centered."

approach of May with lover-like expectations, and have indeed solicited the agreeable goddess to hasten her approach, in the following address:

SONNET TO MAY.

Come, May, attir'd in splendor all thy own;
    Enchantress, come! reanimate the grove,
Hang on the buoyant breeze, thy floating throne,
    And wake the song of universal love:
The sprouting herbage for thy mandate stays,
    Long nipp'd and shrivel'd by protracted cold;
And the swoln corn still fearfully delays,
    'Till thou shalt bid the tender blade unfold.
The shiv'ring Naids, who despairing fled,
    When rude Aquarius rear'd his icy pale,
Led[1] back their fountains to their wonted bed,
    Prepar'd to murmur through the grassy vale:
The fair-hair'd graces, and Idalian boy,
Await thy call to lead the dance of rural joy.

"Your presence, my dear father, will add to all the beauties which the season promises, a charm in which they are deficient: I mean that of society. Poor Waldon regrets your absence almost as much as myself; he visits me very frequently. I believe we entertain our neighbours; but in defiance of scandal, I always tell him that I am glad to see him; and have just persuaded him to teach me backgammon. Sometimes I divert him by musick and singing; yet I will own our tête-a-têtes have a sameness in them, which I believe proceeds from the recollection of more agreeable trios. Dear Sir, return to Seatondell, I need no Spanish dollars to make me happy.

"If your resolution is too far fixed to yield to my intreaties, you must allow me to be equally tenacious of my determination of accompanying you. My fear of the sea cannot deter me from fulfilling the duty which I owe you. Do not contest this point with me, I claim it as a right due to the affection of your ever-grateful daughter,

"LOUISA DUDLEY."

---

1 In the second edition, "lead."

CHAP. XXXIV.

Mrs. Prudentia further developes a character of extreme malevolence, but without copying the likeness from her own sisterhood.[1]

The order of my narrative conducts me back to Marianne's history.

Mr. Clermont, on his arrival at Bath, found his father considerably recovered from his alarming indisposition, to the extreme mortification of Lady Clermont, who flattered herself that she should be speedily released from the hateful yoke of unhappy marriage. The natural disagreeableness of her temper, completely soured by contemptuous treatment, and now galled by *disappointment*, in spite of the assumed suavity of politeness, impressed upon her peevish countenance the wretchedness of her heart. The youth, beauty, and sweetness of Marianne, had at first excited in her mind the baleful passion of envy. Her tender affections had never been poured into the bosom of her family; she was still in the prime of life, and unwilling to renounce the false satisfaction she received from listening to the Syren song of adulation. Mrs. Clermont must now of necessity be introduced into that part of the great world, which the season had convened at Bath. Her Ladyship expected to find her a powerful rival; but when Marianne first visited the rooms,[2] her beauty excited an attention far exceeding *those* expectations. Unfortunately the lovely recluse became quite the fashion; her simplicity and *naïveté* encreased[3] her elegance; and her modesty and diffidence had all the charm of novelty, in the circle to which she was introduced. The town rung with, "did you ever see so lovely a creature? How

---

1 The sisterhood she invokes is other old maids. One of the stereotypes of old maids from the period is their alleged peevishness.
2 The "rooms" means assembly rooms, which were gathering places for members of the elite of both sexes. Late eighteenth-century Bath was known for its balls, concerts, and conversational parties in its assembly rooms.
3 In the second edition, "increased."

astonishing she did not come out sooner." The compliments and attention paid to Lady Clermont's rank were cold and faint, and rendered the admiration which youth and beauty attracted still more apparent.

There was besides another motive to excite envy and hatred in her Ladyship's breast; Marianne appeared to have recovered the heart of her husband; their behaviour to each other, though not distinguished by the unremitting assiduity of fond lovers, was indicative of complacence and mutual affection. Sometimes a soft melancholy appeared in her countenance, but it was so tempered with sweetness, that instead of offending it seemed to charm Mr. Clermont, and to engage him to a more studiously tender attention, in hopes of dispelling the meek, placid dejection.

Lady Clermont was both wretched and disagreeable herself, and every person who appeared amiable and happy, was to her an object of disgust. The mild lustre of wedded love, which she now every day beheld, increased, by the power of contrast, the gloom of her own misery. She determined to endeavour to interrupt the happiness she could not share, and reconciled herself to the diabolical design, by overlooking Marianne's merits, and aggravating her faults. She *resolved* to think her a weak, yet cunning girl; she termed her refinement and sensibility, affectation; her tenderness, hypocrisy; and she pretended to pity her son, for having been duped by such an inferior character.

Meanwhile Mrs. Clermont's conduct, though not free from indiscretion, was amiable and intentionally right. Instead of being captivated by the noise and glare of fashionable life, she seemed disgusted and confounded. The voice of admiration which every where pursued her, did not excite even a momentary satisfaction. Instead of being enchanted with the attention of the fine gentlemen who followed her, she attached criminality to what others termed innocent gallantry; and by the rustick morality of her notions soon offended all her Cecisbeos.[1] In her opinion, every deviation from the strict rules of virtue and delicacy sunk a character into the lowest pit of infamy; had she

---

1 A cicisbeo was an escort or a lover of a married woman. The word is of Italian origin.

confined this sentiment to her own breast, it would only have had the salutary effect of regulating her own conduct; but Mrs. Clermont was one of those who think aloud, and she was remarkably injudicious in the choice of those persons to whom she imparted her opinions. If their behaviour was decent, and she had never heard any harm of them, she candidly concluded that their hearts were as innocent and undesigning as her own; and that their sentiments must correspond. She had seen too little of the world to know that propriety of manner is often assumed by profligacy, and that many characters are infamous which have not been exposed to publick notoriety. Indeed she was unacquainted with the private history and connections of the great world; and one day in the pump-room exclaimed against the folly and wickedness of using cosmeticks, to a faded ghost of beauty, who was just arrived from the Hot-Wells, where she had been endeavouring to repair the ravages which paint had made in her constitution.[1] Another time, Mrs. Clermont left off dancing, to protest against the shameful effrontery with which a married Lady who stood near her, encouraged the advances of her partner. Her indignation was proper, but the person to whom she vented it was a celebrated demirep, who had been separated from her husband for more than *doubtful* gallantry: though, as she was a woman of high rank, the world *chose* to be charitable, and still admitted her into society.[2] But Mrs. Clermont committed a still more pointed error, upon being invited to play at gold

---

1 The Pump Room was a famous gathering place in Bath, in which the town's famed and supposedly curative waters could be drunk. It was notorious for its people-watching and gossip. Hot-Wells was also a spa and a resort town, though it was seen as second to Bath. Hot Wells got its name from the hot springs found in its location, near Bristol. In this sentence, we see Marianne's naiveté in telling a "painted" (or excessively made up) old woman that cosmetics are foolish and wicked. Marianne doesn't realize that the woman is wearing make up or that she has been in Hot-Wells and then Bath because the make-up has damaged her health. In the eighteenth century, cosmetics included white lead as a paling agent, and mercury was used to cover blemishes. It was not well understood that these substances could poison users.

2 A demirep was a woman with a half-reputable character. She was someone whose chastity was suspected but, as this sentence makes clear, continued to circulate in polite society.

Loo, when she positively assured a peeress who had just ruined her lord at Pharo, that nothing should ever induce her to engage in the infamous habit of gaming, which she thought not only foolish and extravagant, but indelicate and immoral.[1]

Lady Clermont beheld her daughter-in-law's mistakes with pleasure, hoping that they would have the effect of terminating her popularity. Nor was she disappointed. Some hated the fair reprover, from the idea that she intended to affront them. Others despised her as a fool, because she was ignorant of what every body else knew. The most candid considered her as an impertinent moralist, and every body was ready, at least, to *hear* tales to her disadvantage.

I shall hazard a bold conjecture, yet I am inclined to affirm, that the genius of gossiping has as many worshippers in the refined circles of high life, as even in the environs of Danbury. They indeed assume a more polished appearance, and speak out of a courtly vocabulary; but their idol is still the offspring of vanity and idleness, and their pursuits and pleasures are eventually the same.

Amongst the company which the season had summoned to Bath, Mr. Clermont had the pleasure to recognize his friend Aubrey. That young gentleman *really* possessed a good heart, joined to an agreeable originality of manner. He was delighted to find that the thoughtless impropriety of his behaviour at Stannadine, had not essentially injured his friend's happiness, and he was impatient to obtain Mrs. Clermont's *full* forgiveness; for he sincerely admired both her person and character. Marianne was placable in her disposition, she felt a predilection for her husband's most intimate friend, which might be esteemed an implied compliment to his taste, and she found Mr. Aubrey a man of good sense and information, qualities not always discernable in modern men of the world. Nothing could be purer than her heart, or more innocent than her conduct; but even discretion will not always preserve us from calumny. An invidious

---

1 Pharo (or faro) and Loo were card games that involved gambling. Although many women played these games, there were those who (like Marianne) found female participation in such activities to be a sign of immorality.

whisper, first invented by the watchful malice of Lady Clermont, was rapidly circulated by that pestiferous humour of detraction, against which I will ever dart my lance with true Quixote fervour, until I have banished it from society. The success of my warfare is at best but problematical; yet surely the laudable design merits approbation. I am convinced its accomplishment would prove a greater blessing to society, than most of the projects of reform suggested by *modern* patriots and philosophers.

To return from my digression; detraction was not the only engine employed by Lady Clermont against her daughter's peace: the reader will remember that I some time ago left Mrs. Patty busily employed in an unsuccessful endeavour to discover her master's faults. She had been lately thrown into the shade; for Miss Dudley, during her visit at Stannadine, had argued so forcibly against the folly and danger of low confidents, that a visible alteration took place in Mrs. Clermont's behaviour. Our redoubted Abigail was piqued at the change, and determined to recover her mistress's favour; even if it was at the expence of her repose.

Chance promoted her design by a common incident. A violent fracas took place between herself and Mrs. Bonjou, Lady Clermont's waiting-woman; on precedency, beauty, and consequence. On the last head Patty urged, that her lady had never treated her like a common servant; that she told her all her secrets, and whenever a quarrel took place between her master and her lady, she was the first person informed of it. She added, that she could say a great deal more if she chose it; but that her lady *knew* her prudence, or she never would have given her the commissions she had done.

Highly as Patty thought of her own understanding, she had to encounter people of superior art. Mrs. Bonjou flew to her lady, whose saturnine features relaxed with pleasure at the intelligence. Recovering from a hearty laugh, a luxury she did not often enjoy, "Well, Bonjou," said she, "I desire you will henceforth honour Mrs. Patty's consequence with proper treatment, or, as she is her mistress's particular friend, I may chance to be implicated in your quarrels. But seriously I cannot think Mrs. Clermont quite so great a fool; suppose you try. Get acquainted with this prodigy of prudence, and bore her with some story, no matter what. We shall see if it circulates, and if it does, I will make it a means to deter *my* son's wife from disgracing herself by such respectable attachments."

Mrs. Bonjou understood her office. She made a conciliatory apology to Patty, and they became sworn friends. In the course of their intimacy, the latter divulged every family secret which she either knew or suspected; and Mrs. Bonjou was extremely sorry for the pretty young creature, for she knew her young Lord never deserved her. "Vat you think," said she, "he go to Monsieur Aubrey for love, so often. Oh no, all sham. He do not go to see Monsieur Aubrey, but one sad diable[1] woman, little way off: and then says he goes there."

Patty hastened to communicate this terrible intelligence. She found her mistress in her dressing room, waiting for Lady Clermont's summons to attend her to the rooms. There was an unusual degree of sprightliness in her manner, and a placid smile upon her countenance, which few people would have chosen to disturb. Patty's prefatory assurance that she had something very important to say, interrupted this happy calm; and ere her tale was finished, a death-like paleness stole over every feature. At this instant Lady Clermont entered; "The carriage, my dear, waits," said she, and without appearing to perceive that Marianne's trembling limbs could scarce support her, hurried her into the chariot with officious attention.

CHAP. XXXV.

Innocence and simplicity are insufficient guards against malignity and detraction, unless accompanied by discretion.

Lady Clermont, though not naturally of a communicative disposition, happened this evening to be unusually conversible.

---

1 Diable is French for the devil. In other words, she is suggesting he sees a prostitute or a courtesan.

She indulged herself in a number of bright sallies, and finding them not honoured with proper attention, descanted in praise of cheerfulness, which she defined to be an infallible sign of a good heart, and a contented mind.

During her Ladyship's harangue, the afflicted Marianne sat almost devoid of utterance or recollection. Thought followed thought, in agonizing succession, but none of them tended to organize the chaos in her soul. The carriage at length stopped, and they proceeded to the ball room, where Mrs. Clermont declining every invitation to dancing or cards, retired into an obscure corner, and absorbed in her own distress, remained insensible to the gay scene around her.

Roused from this reverie by the voice of Mr. Aubrey, she started, looked round with apprehension, and felt in his unexpected appearance the confirmation of all her fears: for Mr. Clermont had declined accompanying her that evening, on the pretext of a pre-engagement to dine with his friend. She enquired after her husband, with an eagerness for which Aubrey could as little account, as for the melancholy position in which she was sitting when he first accosted her. He attempted to relieve her distress, by assuring her, that his friend was perfectly well but two hours ago. "Where is he now?" enquired Mrs. Clermont with redoubled agitation. Aubrey vowed he could not tell. The party had broken up sooner than was intended, and he knew not how Clermont had disposed of himself, he believed to the play, and offered to go and look for him. "Have the humanity," said she, "first to order my carriage; I will return home immediately." He begged she would let him go and call Lady Clermont, who was engaged in a party at cards. "Oh no!" exclaimed Marianne; "her presence will only be a restraint upon me, and my heart is too full to consult propriety." He offered her his arm, it was a support which her extreme agitation rendered necessary, and she hurried out of the room, either unconscious that her behaviour had excited general attention, or too much disordered to regard it. The rival beauties whom her superior charms had mortified, and the specious hypocrites whom her unguarded remarks had tacitly reproved, now joined in exclaiming against "the detected moralist," as they termed her. Her declining Lady Clermont's attendance had been overheard; the words she used were capable of an invidious construction, and they readily gave them that tendency; but when it was observed that Mr. Aubrey was not afterwards seen in the assembly rooms that evening, they all declared that candour itself could suppose no other than that Mrs. Clermont was criminal; sarcastically adding, that it was doubtless the first affair she had ever engaged in, or she would have managed her assignation less publickly.[1]

I will however vindicate Mrs. Clermont to my readers, and *assure* them that she returned home *alone*, that she retired to her chamber, declined Patty's attendance, and judiciously entered upon the task of calm recollection. She remembered her father's invaluable letter, and again perused it, with a design to see if any thing he said, would apply to the present emergency. His precepts against suspiciously watching her husband's conduct, and believing (or indeed listening to) every idle tale were in point, and she began to think that she had yielded to her old infirmity of afflicting herself upon slight grounds, and suffering her passions to obscure her judgment. She determined to dismiss the officious Patty, who she perceived sedulously employed herself in agitating her mind, and while she was in this temper, she heard Mr. Clermont's voice upon the stairs. She flew to meet him; he anxiously enquired respecting the indisposition of which Mr. Aubrey had just given him a confused and alarming account. He told her that he had hurried out of the theatre the moment his friend brought him this intelligence, and the candour and solicitude of his manner confirmed this assurance.

It generally happens when a suspected person clears himself in one instance from a fault of which he was accused, that a generous mind immediately forgets its former doubts, and invests the acquitted person in the white robe of unsullied innocence. It proved so in the present instance. The towering edifice of tragedy sorrow which Mrs. Clermont had been for some hours erecting,

---

1 Adultery was also known as "criminal conversation," hence the label "criminal" to describe Marianne's supposedly leaving the party with Aubrey, with a "full heart" that would not "consult propriety."

fell to the ground. *He* was no longer treacherous, false, ungrateful, but every thing that was kind and good; nor was she a miserable forsaken woman, but a credulous creature who had behaved very ridiculously, for a reason which she was ashamed to own. Candid and generous, she confessed herself exceedingly to blame, in giving way to her feelings from slight mistakes and misrepresentations; she intreated Mr. Clermont would not require an explanation of the past, and promised greater self-command in future. No husband would like to be summoned in an alarming manner, from a favourite diversion, to attend upon a wife's whims. He felt disposed to give a gentle lecture, which she was receiving with meek contrition, when Lady Clermont appeared full of anxiety for the dear creature's health, having but that moment heard of her illness. Her apprehensions on that head being removed, she very *tenderly* blamed Marianne for not requiring her attendance. "It was very *odd*, my dear, in you, particularly in *your* situation, to take Mr. Aubrey home with you; you ought to have had a female friend." "Aubrey, Madam!" exclaimed Mr. Clermont. "Aubrey could not go home with her. He saw her to the chariot, and then came in search of me." "Indeed!" replied her Ladyship; "then I beg, Edward, that you will make that circumstance known. It is highly important that it should, I assure you. I will take care to tell Lady Richly *myself*, that the world is mistaken. Mr. Aubrey did not go home with Mrs. Clermont."

So innocent was Marianne's heart, that she did not even understand the *point* of this insinuation, and the next morning, when Mr. Aubrey called to enquire after her health, she did not consider her being alone in her dressing room, a sufficient reason to prevent her from receiving a visit from her husband's friend. She even met him with a smile of gratitude, and after assuring him that she was perfectly recovered, and thanking him for his attention the preceding evening; "I have," said she, "two requests to make. Endeavour to forget how absurdly I behaved last night; and when you hear me censured for it, try if possible to invent an excuse for me."

"I must first *see* your absurdities," replied Aubrey, "before I can forget them; and as for the censures of the idle and the envious, it is the tax which merit must always pay. I assure you I should never have wished for the honour of your acquaintance, if I had not been told by every body, that you was the strangest of all strange beings."

At this instant Mr. Clermont entered the room. He was just returned from a publick breakfast, where he had heard his wife's conduct canvassed in an audible whisper. The ladies affirmed that she must be very seriously indisposed; for it was evident she knew not what she was about. The gentlemen affected to envy Aubrey as a lucky fellow, in having the honour to escort the divine creature home. Though these witticisms afforded mirth to *them*, they were death to Mr. Clermont's peace. He construed every enquiry after his lady, which politeness dictated, into an oblique affront, and unable to command himself, he returned home in very ill humour; and surprised Mr. Aubrey and Mrs. Clermont engaged in very lively conversation, which the gloom in his manner suddenly terminated. His Aubrey was never before unwelcome, nor did his Marianne's smiles ever give torture to his heart till that moment. He restrained his feelings, but they made an indelible impression upon his mind; and Mrs. Clermont might certainly refer the misery of her future life to these apparently trivial incidents.

I have described these circumstances with some degree of minuteness, for though the effect of them did not immediately appear, or only in a small degree of sullen reserve, they sunk deep into Mr. Clermont's soul and gradually produced a *total* change of character. I will not minutely detail this alteration, but will confine my garrulous humour to a general account of its causes and consequence.

The spirit that took possession of Mr. Clermont's mind, though not strictly jealousy, bore a near affinity to that "green-eyed monster." He was not so credulous as to believe the calumnies of detraction, nor so undiscerning as not to perceive his mother's malice: nor did he doubt his Marianne's innocence, or even *once* suspect that her gentle heart had strayed from its acknowledged possessor. He knew the purity of her soul, and the constancy of her temper, but this did not acquit her of levity and indiscretion; upon which basis he judged it possible that slander and calumny had erected their fabrick of falshood.[1] She was herself conscious of impropriety, and ashamed to disclose the motives of her behaviour. She had owned herself to have acted very wrong, and this confession carried with it the force of a thousand witnesses. His thoughts ran in the same strain of fastidious delicacy with the great Roman conqueror. "My wife must not only be free from guilt, but also from suspicion."[2]

Early in life, before his character was formed, or his opinions methodized, Mr. Clermont entered into marriage; with vague, floating ideas of angelick goodness, and consummate bliss. In proportion as his romantick enthusiasm had raised the mortal nymph into a goddess, his cooler, but not more accurate judgment, as the infatuation of love subsided, magnified her errors into indelible offences. He saw her weakness, timidity, irresolution, and imprudence: he forgot her gentleness, sweetness, candour, and generosity. Vanity had ever been intermingled with his love. He fancied that when he produced his idol to the world, every heart would acknowledge its perfection, every tongue confess his happiness, and applaud his judgment. His Marianne had been produced to the world. The transient admiration which she had at first excited had rather been a tribute paid to her beauty than to her intellectual endowments; it soon subsided, and now her conduct was ridiculed and her character defamed. He had not courage to withstand "the world's dread laugh, which scarce the firm philosopher can scorn."[3] His temper was not naturally gentle, it had only acquired an occasional suavity from love; and as love expired, it resumed its usual tendency. The polished manners of the gentleman decorated his behaviour with the faint gilding of civility, and softened surly contempt into polite

---

1 In the second edition, "falsehood."

2 This is a reference to Julius Caesar's second wife, Pompeia. A patrician named Clodius (disguised as a woman) gained admission to Pompeia, allegedly with the intent to seduce her. Clodius was caught and prosecuted, but no evidence was given against him, and he was acquitted. Still, Caesar divorced Pompeia. This gave rise to the proverb, "Caesar's wife must be above suspicion."

3 A line from James Thomson's *The Seasons*, "Autumn."

indifference: but affection was extinct, esteem did not supply its place, and pride alone prompted him to give some degree of consequence to the woman whom he had honoured with his name; when he treated her with occasional complacency, and rescued her from his mother's virulent malice.

Mrs. Clermont had adhered to her resolution of dismissing Patty, and she, like most confidential servants, ungratefully revenged herself upon her lady's supposed unkindness, by disclosing all the secrets with which she had been intrusted. Miss Milton's highly indiscreet advice, and the irresolute Marianne's weak compliance, were now known by every servant in the family; and Lady Clermont took care that her son should *not* be ignorant that his wife had employed a spy upon his conduct. The breach now became irreparable. Lord Clermont's urgent desire of having a grandson to inherit his estate, could scarce impose a temporary civility upon the enraged husband; or prevent him from breaking forth into the most violent expostulations: while the insidious mother, by appearing to plead for the poor, inexperienced, well-meaning, misled young creature, effectually undermined every sentiment of confidence and regard; and sunk the unhappy Marianne into an object of pity, and perhaps contempt.

Mr. Clermont now determined to carry his wife back to Stannadine, where he resolved she should in future conceal her folly in obscurity. For himself, he intended soon to plunge into the bustle of publick life, and endeavour to forget both the expectations and disappointments of love. The state of Mrs. Clermont's mind upon discovering that she had lost her husband's heart, will not require explanation. It was wretchedness in the extreme. She tried to recal the dear unkind by tears, and soft complaints; but he always avoided the latter by leaving the room, and he had now too often seen the former to be affected by an April shower.

The history of Mrs. Clermont's married life, may teach ladies not to depend upon the durability of that evanescent affection which lovers feel. It may admonish their sanguine adorers not to expect too much, nor yet to reject and despise what is amiable, because it is not perfect. Perhaps I shall be censured for ascribing the destruction of married happiness to such light causes; but

I am willing to appeal to the experience of every wedded pair, whether *great* criminality on either side is necessary, in order to render the bonds of Hymen a galling yoke of misery. My mind is open to conviction, and if I have been wrong, I shall at least acquire a more consolatory prospect of the happiness of my fellow-creatures.

CHAP. XXXVI.

Integrity and duty are the cordials of affliction.

My thirty third chapter concluded with a letter from Miss Dudley to her father; I shall begin this with his reply.

'It is not upon slight grounds and capricious motives, that I reject the intreaties of my dear child, so affectionately and earnestly urged. I am influenced by a principle which I have venerated through the whole course of my life, and which I ought not to renounce in the closing scenes. I *know*, when I have explained myself, you will have the greatness of soul to approve my conduct.

But I must first inform you of an incident which has deeply afflicted me. Mr. Tonnereau yesterday disgracefully terminated his existence by his own hands. Unhappy man! He found that some of his creditors were resolutely bent to expose his conduct, and to push their discoveries to the utmost extremity. He knew that his guilt was so far developed, that no subterfuge could avail; and he dreaded the austerity of those laws which he had provoked. He trembled at the *vengeance* of man, but he did not fear to brave that of God!

'You know, Louisa, how much I once esteemed him. He was the friend of my early youth, and for many years I can *affirm* that his conduct was formed upon principles of honest industry. I am assured that latterly he considerably deviated from the auspicious commencement of his life. He has been dissipated and extravagant, and then to redeem his tottering credit, he has applied to the dangerous resources of the gaming-table.

'When I consider this man's last scenes of life, can I term my own situation unfortunate? Deserted by the licentious companions of his follies; justly execrated by those injured people, who (though once his friends) now consider their acquaintance with him as the most disastrous circumstance of their lives; his character held up by those who are strangers to his person, as a mark of abhorrence and infamy; alone in a prison, destitute of the comforts of life, though till then accustomed to its superfluities; no one near him, but a mercenary attendant, callous through familiarity with misery; no eye to pity his sorrows; no friendly bosom on which to repose his griefs; his own reflections his worst enemies; and even despairing of mercy from the fountain of goodness. Unhappy Tonnereau! I pity thee too much to hate thee.

'But let me recollect myself. Since I have been in London, I have taken an inventory of my effects, and find they will not be sufficient to discharge the debts which I contracted, with, as I thought, full ability of payment. Integrity is no less the character of an English merchant than enterprise; nor can I willingly renounce the glorious boast which I have hitherto enjoyed, of having never injured any one in person or property. I cannot retain it, if I neglect any probable opportunity of recovering enough of my fortune to satisfy every legal claim upon me. The infirmities of the body may interrupt the soul in the exertion of its sublime speculative functions; but they never ought to impede us in the performance of positive duties, unless by imposing total inability. I have not long to live, my dear, even according to the course of nature; and lately I have been frequently unwell. A sea-voyage may be of service to me, but supposing the worst, what is the loss of a few months of painful existence, to the pleasure of reflecting in my last hours, that by sacrificing it, no injured orphan or widow has cause to curse my ashes; and that I have prevented my children from being followed by the clamours of my defrauded creditors?

'Mr. Pelham has received intelligence by means of the Ambassador, that the Council of the Indies have admitted the legality of my claims, and as soon as I appear personally to identify them, the value of my part of the ship's cargo will be punctually paid. I am determined to take my passage on board of the first packet that sails for Corunna.[1] I shall not decline the kind offer of your company, for the complaint in my side is at times very troublesome; it often affects my breath, but when my dear nurse is with me I shall be better. Set out, my love, as soon as you receive this. I am still with my friend, nor can I offer to change my residence during the short stay we shall make in London, without offending him. His aunt, Mrs. Penelope Pelham, is desirous to be acquainted with you. She is a little singular, but upon the whole a worthy woman. I will promise you a most affectionate reception from Mr. Pelham. Let us know when you set out, and we will meet you at the last stage. Adieu, hasten to the arms of your

'Affectionate father,

'RICHARD DUDLEY.'

In little more than a week from the receipt of this letter Miss Dudley arranged her affairs at Seatondell, preparatory to an absence of some months, and finished a journey from Lancashire to London. It was part of her character to form her plans with propriety, and to execute them with dispatch. I therefore forbid any conjectures as to the effect the promised *affectionate* reception from Mr. Pelham might have upon her expedition. Desirous to surprise her father with her speed, she forbore to send any intelligence of her motions, but wished to be the agreeable herald of her own arrival. An accident which happened during the last day's journey, detained her upon the road, and she did not arrive at Portland-Place till near midnight. She sent in her name, and Mr. Pelham immediately appeared to conduct her from the carriage. Her heart throbbed with the liveliest transport, and a crimson blush irradiated her countenance; but he received her with a solemn embarrassed air, and led her almost without speaking to his aunt. My friend, Mrs. Penelope, might, both in person and manner, be termed a brief abstract of our sisterhood: she moved by rule, and spoke in a measured cadence. The cold formality of her welcome added to poor Louisa's chagrin, she

---

1 La Coruña, a port city in the northwestern corner of Spain.

ventured to turn her eyes upon Mr. Pelham, his were fixed upon the ground. Was this the promised reception? Did "that sun of benignity which shone in his countenance," to adopt an expression of her father's, shine on all but her? Was it possible for *her* to have displeased him, or had she by the pleasure she shewed at seeing him, unguardedly discovered the secret of her heart?

After a few faint efforts to support ceremonious conversation, Mr. Pelham with hesitation said, he would go and acquaint Mr. Dudley of his daughter's arrival. Louisa recollecting her father's early habits, to which since his indisposition he had strictly adhered, observed the lateness of the hour, and begged that he might not be informed till morning.

Mr. Pelham gravely replied, he was afraid his friend was not asleep. A thousand distracting fears rushed into Miss Dudley's mind. She recollected that her questions respecting her father's health had been evasively answered. She started from her chair, and with a look of inexpressible alarm, laid her hand involuntarily upon Mr. Pelham's, and conjured him not to deceive her; she knew her father was worse than usual.

"He is indeed," replied Mr. Pelham, holding her trembling hand. "I need not assure you that I take the most lively interest in his safety. We have called in Dr. L. You have probably heard of his medical reputation; but I hope most from your presence. Your father's anxiety to see you has considerably aggravated his disease. Be calm, dear Madam, I beseech you. We have by no means abandoned hope."

"When was he seized?"

"He has been evidently unwell ever since he has been with us; and I have sometimes drawn from him a reluctant complaint, that the disorder in his side was at times insupportably painful. I fear the uneasiness of his mind has encreased his disease; and the dreadful criminality of Tonnereau's death gave him a shock, which has hastened the crisis. He has been confined to his bed these three days. He is now extremely feverish. We fear an abscess is forming."

Unable to support the painful intelligence, Louisa sunk into her chair. "Nephew," said Mrs. Penelope, as she advanced, holding out her salts, "do not keep the lady in suspense. You ought to tell her the worst at first. Your papa, Madam, is quite given up by Dr. L. and I am very glad he has done with him, for *I* never liked his prescriptions, and I hope you will now persuade Mr. Dudley to try an invaluable medicine, which I have often administered, and never knew it fail of effect. Mr. Pelham knows that he owes his life to it."

Louisa could only reply by a flood of tears; a salutary relief to her big swoln heart. Her head dropped almost lifeless upon Mrs. Penelope's bosom, who, whilst busily employed in rubbing her temples, and administering pungent restoratives, alternately censured her want of fortitude, and commended her affection; aggravated Mr. Dudley's danger, and comforted her by the assurance, that while life remained, her recipe would prove infallible.

The natural firmness of Miss Dudley's mind was perhaps more conducive to her recovering her wonted calm, than my good friend's oratory. She dried her tears, and thanking her with an air of mild benignity for her attention, intreated that she might see her father immediately, "while my mind," added she emphatically, "can exert its recovered strength."

Mr. Pelham's generous heart melted with compassion. He withdrew to apprize his friend, that "the fond darling of his soul," as he styled her, was arrived. Mrs. Penelope had now a fair opportunity for describing the cures effected by her nostrum; but I am afraid she had not an attentive auditor, for at the most interesting period of her narrative, Louisa received the expected summons, and obeyed it as fast as her trembling limbs would permit. She drew aside the curtains with eager impatience. Her father, supported by Mr. Pelham, had raised himself upon his elbow; and he welcomed her with a penetrating smile. "My dear nurse is come to take care of me," said he. "I have been too impatient, love, for thy arrival. Come to my arms. Restoration hangs upon thy lips."

His emaciated countenance, and the laborious weakness of his voice, shook his daughter's fortitude. She hung over him in silence, and bathed his pallid cheek with tears.

"Do not alarm thyself so much," continued Mr. Dudley; "my danger is not so imminent. My worthy friends here are too anxiously solicitous, too apprehensive. Recollect yourself, my child. I expect consolation from your society. Your are to enable me to suffer."

"Oh!" the tortured Louisa was tempted to exclaim; "who will console, who will support me? In what asylum shall *I* hide my orphan-head? Gracious Heaven! deprive me not of my only friend and protector?" Her native piety recalled her thoughts from this melancholy excursion. She recollected the endearing titles of "friend of the friendless," and "father of the fatherless," which the great author of creation had deigned to assume; and her soul firmly anchored upon the rock of ages.

CHAP. XXXVII.

An instance of the strong interest which dignified distress can excite.

No sooner had Miss Dudley recovered sufficient strength to look beyond the gloom of a temporary parting, than a serene smile diffused itself over her countenance. She now fixed her eyes steadily upon her admirable father, and with awful plea- sure contemplated the undiminished glory of the never-dying intellectual power, which beamed forth with superior splendor from under the ruins of the tottering mortal fabrick. Though her countenance was not regularly beautiful, it generally attracted admiration from being an expressive index of the excellence of her heart. Her composed tenderness and dignified patience did not now escape the attention of an accurate judge of character and manners.

Mr. Dudley raised his eyes to the amiable youth, who still supported him. "Thank you, my dear Pelham," said he; "now lay me gently down upon my pillow. I hope to have a good night, and will dismiss you all."

"Miss Dudley," returned he, "must be fatigued with her jour- ney; but I must insist upon watching you to-night. To-morrow morning I will resign you to her cares."

"I am not sensible of the least fatigue," replied Louisa; "and you know we *professed* nurses always sleep best in our patient's apartment. I shall be able to repose myself in that arm-chair, and if my father appears easy, enjoy a very comfortable night."

"We must yield to her in this point," said Mr. Dudley. "The dear girl is very tenacious of her opinion, and will not consider my medicines to be efficacious, unless I receive them from her hands. Besides, we must settle the plan of our voyage. Good night, Pelham, do not fail to enquire when the next packet will be ready; for we must not expect to take our passage in that which is now under sailing orders."

Mr. Pelham withdrew in silence, with his heart divided between grief and admiration. Mr. Dudley's anguish not permitting him to lie composed, he affected a degree of sprightliness, and enquired after his plantations and improvements, with the interested curiosity of one who hoped to see them rise to perfection. At intervals he talked of their intended expedition; and described the natural advantages of Spain, and the austere manners of its haughty indolent inhabitants, from observations which he had made in a former journey to that kingdom. His discourse was merely intended to confirm his daughter's agitated spirits, for he felt *certain* that he should never set out for any other country, but that from which no traveller returns.

Thus passed the night;—in the morning Dr. L. came to make what he termed a friendly, instead of a professional visit. Mr. Dudley understood the distinction. He wished to ask some questions, but was interrupted by Mrs. Penelope, who came again to urge the propriety of administering her infallible medicine. Dr. L. on being consulted, owned the patient was in a state to admit of hazardous experiments, and withdrew, promising to call again in the evening.

Mrs. Penelope might now be said to enjoy her full importance. Every domestick was employed to procure or prepare the respective ingredients, which she mixed with her own hands, according to the prescribed rule. She at length approached Mr. Dudley's bedside with the celebrated compound, but whether like Circe with the poisonous chalice, or like Hygeia with the restorative cup, the event will determine.

The immediate effect certainly did not realize her sanguine expectations. Perhaps Mr. Dudley's strength was too far exhausted; or he might want *faith*, which I am told is a necessary auxiliary in this class of remedies; for they often lie *dormant*, unless quickened by a sort of reaction in the patient's mind; or the herbs might not be gathered at the right period of the moon, whose influence in pharmacy is unquestionable. I will not dare to arraign the infallibility of the recipe, but will only state, that Mr. Dudley appeared considerably worse after the operation, in the opinion of every body but Mrs. Penelope; who, having the same *faith* in her preparation as Don Quixote had in the balsam of Firebrass, perceived strong symptoms of immediate recovery. She retired exulting in her physical knowledge, to enjoy the pleasure of a pool at Tredrille, with two select friends.

Dr. L. did not confirm Mrs. Penelope's opinion at his evening visit. Mr. Dudley had previously requested to be left alone with his physician; "I perceive, Sir," said the exalted man, "that you are sensible I am much worse, and I thank you for your explicit behaviour. I *could* not be deceived by common professional forms, and you are too liberal to adopt them. I have seen enough of life to be willing to resign it; but we are not called into existence merely for ourselves, and there are circumstances which make me wish that I could at this time recover. Do you know of any experiment that has a chance of success?"

The Dr. replied that an operation might be performed upon his side, but that it was excruciating and highly dangerous.

"I will submit to it cheerfully," replied Mr. Dudley. "Let the surgeons attend me at five o'clock to-morrow morning. I do not wish for any of the family to be informed of it."

In pursuance of this resolution he answered every interrogatory with an assurance that he was much better, and disposed to slumber. He perceived by Louisa's eyes on her re-entering the room, that she had discovered his increased danger, and he endeavoured to confirm her sinking spirits by inspiring a degree of false hope. "Do not, my love, intirely[1] depend upon my physician's report; a sick man is the best judge of his own feelings. I

---

1 In the second edition, "entirely."

flatter myself that I shall have a comfortable night. Go early to bed, and you will be sufficiently refreshed to attend me in the morning. I shall compose myself with the thought that you are tranquil."

Miss Dudley did not controvert this opinion. She tenderly wished him a good night, and withdrew to her own apartment. Her breaking heart required some relief, and she now recollected that, at her express desire, she was lodged in a small room separated from her father's by a thin partition. She therefore hastily left it, and took two or three turns in an adjoining ante-chamber, undetermined how to dispose of herself for a few hours. If she joined Mrs. Penelope's party, it would only be to receive felicitations, and to hear prognosticks which her reason sadly disproved: or probably she might be pressed to take a hand at cards, as a sure specifick against melancholy. She had ever felt a tenderness for the prejudices and peculiarities of age; but at this time, her mind was in a state to render "solitude the best society."

She at length withdrew to the library, and endeavoured to relieve her dejection by applying to some of the treasures with which it was stored. But wit had lost its attick point, and elegance its forcible attraction. She could not follow an argument through its long train of deductions, and the best-told narrative failed to interest her attention. She returned the books to their places, and after a minute's pause sunk upon her knees. Grief has been termed the parent of eloquence;—it is peculiarly so in an informed well-regulated mind. She raised her eyes, the feelings of her agitated soul animated every impassioned feature. Her snowy hands remained clasped in anguish, and regardless of the tears which fell copiously upon them. In the warm flow of unstudied elocution her lips expressed the piety of a seraph, chastised by the humble awe of a weak, dependent mortal. She supplicated Heaven to spare her father, her only friend and comfort; but she asked with submission. She painted an orphan's sorrows; but not with the dark colourings of despair. Her mind appeared to gather strength from her divine employment; her tears ceased to flow; a serene sweetness beamed in her countenance, and when she rose from her knees to retire, her whole form seemed inspired with supernatural intelligence, and expressed the most lively resemblance of superior beings which the human imagination can form.

Mr. Pelham's apprehension for his friend having rendered him unfit for company, he had retired to spend his evening in a reading closet at the upper end of his library. His attention was drawn from his studies by the sound of a female voice. He stepped softly to the door, and became an unobserved spectator of the scene I have described. His sensations were in some respects similar to those expressed by Sir Eldred of the Bower;

> "My scorn has oft the dart repell'd
> Which guileful beauty threw;
> But goodness heard, and grace beheld,
> Must every heart subdue."[1]

After she had withdrawn he returned into his closet, but even his favourite authors were now tasteless. The pleadings of Demosthenes[2] were studied and artificial, when compared to the more lively oratory of a deeply-affected heart; nor did the morality of the divine Tully[3] strike the soul with such strong conviction in favour of the noblest virtues, as it received from the powerful example of youth and innocence.

He left his books, and walked to the table, against which Miss Dudley had lately knelt; it was still wet with her tears. There, bending over the marks of holy sorrow, he recalled her image to his recollection. Even when his heart was most infatuated by the superior brilliancy of Marianne's charms, it had done justice to Louisa's virtues. Time and absence had blunted the pain of disappointment, and gradually reconciled his mind to the loss of his first love; but his attachment had been too strong to permit him to form a second choice, though every hope had been excluded by her marriage. He had too strong sense to

---

1 From Hannah More's *Sir Eldred of the Bower: A Legendary Tale* (1776).

2 Demosthenes (384 BCE-322 BCE), Greek statesman and lawyer, renowned as one of the great orators of ancient Greece.

3 Marcus Tullius Cicero (106 BCE-43 BCE), Roman writer and philosopher.

yield to whining complaints, and he submitted to a *severe mortification* with manly firmness; but whenever Fancy recalled to his mind any pleasing ideas, the attracting image of Marianne Dudley rose to his view, and the charms of other fair ones faded at the comparison. Yet even that fascinating form seemed to yield to the superiour loveliness of intellectual beauty, and he determined if possible to rescue Louisa from an orphan's woes, and to solicit the affections of so invaluable a woman.

CHAP. XXXVIII.

A circumstance of awful solemnity prepares the way for a very desirable event.

Mr. Dudley spent the night in agony, but his fortitude seemed to increase with his pains; and his desire of not disturbing his daughter, who, he found, lay near him, repressed the groan of anguish. The powers of his mind continued unimpaired; he felt his danger, and considering it possible that he might not survive the intended operation, he desired that Mr. Pelham might be called at an early hour. The worthy man flew to his apartment, but shocked at the visible change in his friend's countenance, he burst into tears, which the dying hero thus reproved: "Check this unmanly sorrow, my good Sir; mine is no uncommon lot. I do but undergo the general law of nature, to which this world is subject; a world mortal and perishable like man its lord. I have many comforts, at times they predominate over my sufferings; my soul is tranquil; I look forward to futurity with hope. I have only *one* trouble."—"Confide it to me," said Mr. Pelham, endeavouring to stifle his grief.

"Blessed be Heaven for a little interval of ease," resumed Mr. Dudley; "I am persuaded that you will exert your kind endeavours to procure that satisfaction to my family from the Spanish government, which I could not in person demand. The peculiar circumstances of my story must move attention, but should you fail of success, I commend my character to your care. Defend it from opprobrium; say that I was not intentionally unjust; unforeseen incidents, a variety of misfortunes, all united to prevent the favourite wish of my heart. Those whom I have injured will complain; endeavour to soften the asperity of their complaints."

"Your memory," said Mr. Pelham, clasping the hand of Mr. Dudley, "shall be as irreproachable as your life. I do not doubt but that ample justice will be done you, yet if it should be withheld, I will make myself your *executor*. I know the amount of your debts; calm your worthy heart; were they double the sum, I would with pleasure discharge them."

"You are too good, too generous; I asked not this; I expected it not; your kindness pains me." Mr. Dudley sunk upon his pillow, and remained silent a few moments.

The surgeons now entered; he opened his eyes, and welcomed them with a slight motion of his hand: "I have some private business," said he; "go, dear Pelham, leave me a little while; if I am worse I will send for you."—"Gentlemen," resumed Mr. Dudley, when every thing was prepared, "I am afraid your intended assistance will not succeed; I am much weakened by a bad night; but act as you think best. I am ready, my mind is collected. Yet if you think I shall not survive the operation, I would first see my daughter."

On hearing these words, Miss Dudley rushed into the room; her anxiety had only permitted her to throw herself upon the bed, from which she had frequently risen during the night, and with laudable curiosity hastened to hear if any groans proceeded from her father's chamber. From the silence which prevailed there, she had composed herself with the thought that Mrs. Penelope's hopes were not entirely visionary. The sound of strange voices which she imperfectly heard, had cleared away her broken slumbers, and her father's words hurried her into the room in an agony.

The principal surgeon humanely endeavoured to console her. He persuaded her that opening the ulcer in the side might be attended with salutary consequences. "Let me stay then," said she, "while it is performed; I can rub his temples: I know I can be of service,"—"Retire my love," said Mr. Dudley: "Your presence would overpower me. If I faint you shall be summoned." Louisa clasped her pious hands in mental prayer, and withdrew.

The surgeons now examined their patient, and unanimously declared, that from *present* appearances the proposed incision must be declined. No good could possibly arise from it, a mortification having already taken place.

"I am sensible," said the heroick object of their care, "that nothing can *now* be done for me. I thank you for your humane attention;—yet if you can inform me how long I may continue to suffer"—

"Your sufferings, Sir," said one of them, "will very speedily terminate, but you may live several hours."

Mr. Dudley waved his hand, and they withdrew in tears.

He now resolved to prepare his soul by the most solemn christian duties for its expected journey. Previous to the clergyman's arrival, Mr. Pelham seated himself beside the bed of death, lost in sorrow, and insensible to the frequent sobs which proceeded from Louisa's apartment.

Mr. Dudley pressed his hand; "Comfort my child, dear amiable friend, comfort my forlorn Louisa: a singular attachment subsisted between us, it was more than the tie of blood. She was my adviser, my comforter, my companion, my friend; our tastes, our habits, our desires corresponded. I am not anxious *now* respecting her fortune. I know that she has sufficient greatness of soul to dignify narrow circumstances by cheerful patience; but my loss will sit heavy upon her heart, console her as a *friend*, and if the weakness of her sex should expose her to injury, be her *protector*."

"My heart," said Pelham, sinking upon his knees, "aspires to a more sacred title. Ever since I knew *you* it has panted to be allied to your virtues; disappointed in the object of my youthful love, I have with maturest judgment formed a second attachment. You once promised me your Marianne, I now ask for *your Louisa*."

"Gracious Heaven!" cried Mr. Dudley, raising himself up, and with an energetick voice which seemed to intimate recovered health and strength, "but did I understand you rightly? Do you indeed love my Louisa?"

"Even when I was her sister's adorer, I honoured her character, and esteemed her virtues; they now blaze upon me with invincible splendor. The delicacy of her sentiments may induce her to reject a man who confesses a prior attachment. Support my pretensions by your consent, and rest assured my present love is sincere and ardent. The exalted Louisa may be influenced in favour of a passion which *you* have approved."

"Son of my soul!" exclaimed Mr. Dudley, stretching out his arms, "come to my heart, and let it tell thee that all its *secret wishes* are *now* fulfilled." Go and call my darling to me. How blissful are my departing moments!" Mr. Pelham withdrew.

Miss Dudley hastily threw herself into her father's arms. "You seem," said she, bending over him in meek affliction, "to be somewhat revived."—"I am, my child. I thought my blood had stagnated, but joy has quickened the languid current. Why did I despair, or think thy merit could pass unnoticed? My Louisa, the worthy Pelham loves thee. Canst thou reward thy father's generous friend? He has asked me to bestow my only treasure upon him. I have not many moments to lose. Speak, my love, wilt thou be his? Away with that reserve which keeps thy *dying* father in suspense, on the only subject which interests him upon earth."

No language could do justice to Miss Dudley's feelings. Grief and surprise, gratitude and love, were elevated to a painful extreme. She was told that the passion which had long been an unobserved but pensive inmate of her bosom, at length had met a reciprocal return. She was even called upon to confess the affection which virgin modesty had concealed. But by whom, and in what circumstances was she urged to this disclosure?

Thrice she attempted to speak, and thrice the wild palpitations of her heart forbade her utterance. At length she faintly exclaimed, "I have long esteemed him—loved him I should say. But oh, my father, at what a moment do you claim this confession."

"At a blissful one, dear delight of my soul! It is a moment which sends a joyful pilgrim back to his native country, and seals the happiness of two kindred minds. Pelham, my humane, generous, noble son, where art thou? Come and receive this blessing from my arms, while they have yet strength to bestow her on thee."

Mr. Pelham, who from motives of the purest delicacy was absent at this eclaircissement, entered at the welcome summons. Mr. Dudley held his daughter's hand between his numbed and clammy palms, and raising his eyes with patriarchal dignity, thus bestowed her on her kneeling lover. "I give her to thee, a dear and solemn trust. Look down, Gracious Creator, and bless this worthy pair. Give them long life, love, and temporal felicity: and let their last moments enjoy the holy transport, the divine beatitude which I now enjoy."

Louisa sunk in speechless anguish as he spoke; Mr. Pelham supported her. His fond attentions recalled her fluttering senses. "Spare, oh spare, every expression of love and transport," said she. "My heart is entirely yours, but I can now attend to nothing but my father."

A serene, elevated smile, expressive of intellectual transport, beamed in Mr. Dudley's face. His agonies subsided. Instead of restless tossings and convulsive starts, he remained placidly composed. He received the most sacred rite of christianity with his beloved daughter and adopted son. As he tasted the consecrated chalice he again blessed them, the absent Marianne, and Mr. Clermont. He repeated to Louisa a parting charge for her sister; then sinking into a languid state, he dozed at intervals till the evening, when again calling his daughter to him, he drew his last breath in her arms.

CHAP. XXXIX.

Includes a greater portion of time than all the preceding narrative.

Miss Dudley, restraining her grief with sentiments of reverend awe, forbore to interrupt the departing soul. When the quivering pulse had stopped some moments, she pressed with pallid lips the honoured remains; and committing the corpse to the care of the attendants, with a request that every thing should be conducted with propriety, retired to her apartment.

Mr. Pelham followed her, he intended to have offered some topick of consolation, but his faultering voice disappointed his design, and he could only intreat her not to indulge her sorrow, lest it should affect her health. "In heart and in soul I resign him to his God," said the exalted mourner. "Ought I to sink in despair, because my beloved father is become an inhabitant of a better world? Yet allow me, Sir, to vent in privacy the fond regrets of nature, I wish to offer my first sorrows to my Maker; I trust he will enable me to support them."

Mr. Pelham acquiesced; but Mrs. Penelope was firmly of opinion that the young lady ought not to be left alone. It was expected my old friend's surprise at hearing Mr. Dudley was *really* dead, would be very great, as she even to the last perceived increasing marks of his amendment: but she happily recollected that she had administered her medicine *too* soon after Dr. L.'s last prescription, for her potion to exert its wonted efficacy. She now offered to visit Miss Dudley, and to talk her out of her melancholy, by arguments drawn from her favourite aphorisms, that "what must be will be," and "that Fate must govern all things;" but Mr. Pelham respected the sanctity of his Louisa's sorrows, and insisted that they should not be disturbed.

From the time of her father's death, till every thing was prepared for his funeral, Miss Dudley never left her chamber, except twice a day to visit the corpse. There, kneeling by the coffin, she poured forth the fulness of her affectionate grateful heart. There she accustomed herself to recollect all the invaluable precepts she had received from him, respecting her conduct in life, and lest her memory should fail, she committed them to writing. "These, my father," said she, apostrophising to his spirit, which she sublimely fancied ever present with her, "These, thy elevated sentiments, shall speak to me and console me, though the instructive voice which uttered them is mute, and the heart which prompted them no longer beats at thy highly favored child's approach. Yet let me reflect, though these eyes shine not upon me, they will no longer melt into tears; the human affections are indeed extinct; but sorrow will not come nigh thee. Thy tongue will never more console or instruct me, but the language of complaint has ceased for ever. Thine, my father, was an uneasy pilgrimage for thee; the change is blessed, therefore I will not mourn."

I will forbear from any further repetition of those sentiments of pious sorrow, by which Louisa and her worthy admirer expressed their unaffected grief. They were elevated and devout, and a feeling mind may easily conceive them. Nor will I circumstantially describe Mr. Pelham's behaviour, which was all that esteem, sympathy, and delicacy could prompt. The corpse was conveyed to Alderson manor, and interred in the family vault, close by Mrs. Dudley's coffin. Mr. Pelham attended Louisa on this sad occasion, and Mr. Clermont met her at the grave. Marianne could not join in the solemn obsequies. The intelligence of her father's danger, unwarily communicated, was more than her weakened spirits could support. A premature confinement was the consequence of the shock, by which not only Lord Clermont's anxious expectations of an heir were frustrated, but her own life was endangered, and the affections of her husband further[1] alienated.

Hitherto the behaviour of Mr. Pelham had been more indicative of the friend than the lover. He endeavoured to divert her grief by respectful attentions, or to soothe[2] it by sympathising in her loss; rather than to interrupt the train of her thoughts by unseasonable anticipations of expected happiness. At parting, reciprocal marks of tender regard appeared in each. He requested permission to write to her, which she readily granted; and while she accompanied Mr. Clermont to Stannadine, she perceived that all her liveliest affections were not buried in her father's grave.

The interview between the sisters presented a scene strikingly interesting.

The lovely form of Marianne, faded by sickness and distress, was supported by the amiable Louisa; who bending over her with matronly tenderness, joined in regret for a dear father's loss, and with firmer but not less feeling heart, recapitulated the affecting narrative of his sickness and death. Mrs. Clermont bitterly

1 In the second edition, "farther."
2 In the second edition, "sooth."

bewailed her absence; "and did he not," said she, "reproach his absent Marianne, and ask why she did not come to smooth the bed of death, and to wipe the faint dews from his honoured face? And you too, my Louisa, must surely condemn your unfeeling sister, for not hastening to assist you in those pious offices."

"I have *too* long known the virtues of that tender heart to doubt that some cruel necessity detained you from us. As for our father, unkind suspicion had no part in his character. Almost the last words which he spake were a prayer for you. Give, said he, emphatically, my dying blessing to my dear affectionate Marianne; and thou, all gracious Heaven, preserve her from real sorrow, and lessen her sense of the smaller evils of life. Bless Mr. Clermont too, and grant them many years of prosperity and *mutual* love."

"Vain were those pious prayers," cried Mrs. Clermont in an agony; "and yet they sometimes say the good man's dying wishes are fulfilled." She then related what a lamentable change had taken place in her husband's behaviour: Miss Dudley was distressed at the recital; yet she felt willing to hope that a too lively imagination had as usual aggravated the sombre lines of life; but her own observation during her stay at Stannadine fatally confirmed the fidelity of the portrait.

She now exerted all the sympathizing tenderness of her temper, and all the strong powers of her calm discretion, to support and console the mourner. She endeavoured to divert her from her own misfortunes by the exertion of those benevolent and active duties from which she had formerly derived pleasure. But the *spring* of Mrs. Clermont's mind was entirely broken. She pitied the distress of the poor, and when an object was *pointed* out, was willing to relieve them, but she had not vigour of soul sufficient to step out of herself, and to take a lively interest in the sorrows of others; her early and severe disappointment preyed upon her heart; she no longer felt any inclination for amusement, or any desire to excel, and her thoughts continually wandered within the gloomy pale of her own calamity.

Mr. Clermont (now commenced a man of the world) wandered from one place of publick resort to another; in pursuit of that fleeting happiness which still eluded his grasp. When disappointed he returned home; but it was only to contrast the *increased* pensiveness of his wife's behaviour with the gay scenes he had just forsaken, and he derived from her conduct a fresh desire to enjoy them.

Miss Dudley deeply felt for her sister's woes, but it was her *only* affliction. Her own prospects were peculiarly brilliant. Mr. Pelham's letters were dictated by that manly tenderness which shone in all his conduct; they were affectionate without insipidity, and polite without flattery. In one of them he informed her, that her business with the Spanish government was amicably settled; the whole property remitted to England, her father's debts discharged; and a surplus of five thousand pounds left at her disposal. "I rejoice at this event, said he, "as it will prevent your generous mind from feeling the pain of *supposed* obligation. And yet, my Louisa, should little pecuniary affairs ever disturb the felicity of *those* lovers, who are so happy as to be able to boast on *one* side elegant competence, and on the *other* transcendent worth?"

If Mr. Pelham had doubted as to the *actual* transfer of his heart from its *once* dear object, the sensations he experienced on revisiting Stannadine would have convinced him; he beheld the beauty of Mrs. Clermont withering under the worm of discontent, her features contracted by peevish melancholy, and her temper rendered irritable by disappointment. Though such an object moved his pity, admiration and love could only be awakened by the mild intelligence and unruffled sweetness of a Louisa. His impatience to call the meek-eyed angel his would scarcely permit him to wait the expiration of the twelve months, which she had devoted to the robes of mourning. At length the amiable pair plighted their mutual vows.

Immediately after their nuptials, Mr. Pelham conducted his bride to his country seat. As he led her the tour of his pleasure-grounds, she was particularly pleased with a long avenue of majestick oaks, sloping down the declivity of a hill, on the summit of which a fine Dorick temple was dedicated to Integrity and Fortitude. Mrs. Pelham admired the attick simplicity of the appropriate emblems; but her attention was suddenly arrested by

one object *superlatively* interesting; a fine bust of her father in
white marble, was placed at the upper end of the building, and on
a beautiful Etruscan urn under it, she read the following inscrip-
tion:

> Here, as to firm Integrity we kneel,
>   And light to Fortitude the votive flame,
> Thy memory, Dudley! animates our zeal,
>   And purer ardours kindle at thy name.
>
> Here, when we mourn the father and the friend,
>   Hope shall the funeral pall of sorrow raise;
> And selfish Grief its lamentations end,
>   Thy life to copy, and thy death to praise.
>
> Here, if we faint beneath the task of life,
>   Thy bright example shall new force supply;
> Arm our weak souls for renovated strife,
>   And point our just ambition to the sky.
>
> Oh, ever lov'd! while o'er thy sacred earth
>   Affection graves thy deeds, and drops a tear;
> Our future lives shall emulate thy worth:
>   Our future virtues prove that thou wert dear.

Mr. Pelham thus tenderly addressed her when she had recovered from her first emotion. "I propose myself many delightful
hours in this tranquil retreat. Here, my Louisa, we will often
retire to hold communications with our own hearts, and to form
a just estimate of life. We will not survey its *little sorrows* through
the gloom of misanthropy, nor will we judge of its *pleasures* from
the colourings of enthusiasm. We will recollect your father's precepts, and consider it as a chequered scene, from which the virtuous well regulated mind may derive many advantages. Here we
will converse with that ever-respected man; we will feast our eyes
with gazing upon his features, and our minds by recalling the
nobler likeness of the informing soul. We will think of him, not
with that useless regret which ends in pensive melancholy, much
less with that bold sorrow which audaciously dares to question
Providence; but our remembrance shall tend to meliorate our

own hearts, and our love prompt us to exercise those virtues which have glorified him, and will exalt us to equal happiness. Should any little error in the conduct of either, give pain to the susceptibility of fond attachment, here we will come, and fancy that marble animated, and that it repeats the excellent observations we have so often heard: *That imperfection is always mixed with human virtues, and infelicity with human bliss.*"

CHAP. XL.

The conclusion. Mrs. Prudentia ceremoniously takes leave of all her characters.

I have now brought my narrative to a period; but as Swift observes, that no well-bred modern author will omit the conclusion, I willingly subjoin one.

I once intended to have adopted supplicatory addresses to the candour and generosity of my *gentle* readers; but recollecting that there has *lately* been an uncommon demand for these qualities, and apprehending they must have been entirely worn out in the service of my sister novelists, I am under a necessity of depending upon the taste and discernment of the age, without even advancing the usual pleas of little leisure and painful interruptions. Indeed I am afraid readers care little about an author's private history, and after all the civil things we *can* say, only appreciate our merit by our ability to entertain and instruct *them*. Therefore, instead of obtruding myself upon the publick, the remaining pages shall be employed in describing the *present* situation of my principal characters.

Nearly three years have elapsed since Miss Dudley gave her hand to Mr. Pelham, and the enamoured husband *still* considers that event as the happiest of his life. She has fanned the torch of Love with such admirable dexterity, that it continues to burn with a calm steady flame; and with so little diminution of its pristine brightness, that Mr. Pelham is celebrated by all who know him, for being a polite, tender husband, to an unassuming wife. Her character rises in his estimation every hour, and she often surprises him by the discovery of some new virtue, or graceful accomplishment; which unobtrusive delicacy had hitherto concealed from his observation. Her excellent judgment, tempered by cheerful affability, induces him to confide in her as a friend, and to admire her as a companion; his high opinion of the superiority of *her* conduct, prompts him to be more observant of his *own*, and to guard with scrupulous care against his natural infirmities, lest they should prejudice him in her esteem. He is now acquainted with the preference which his Louisa felt for him, during the time of his attachment to Mrs. Clermont; and his greatness of soul induces him to admire the delicacy, that so closely concealed it from every eye, and the generosity, that resolved by conquering it to sacrifice every selfish wish to the good of others.

Mrs. Penelope Pelham, who was extremely averse to her nephew's connection with Miss Dudley, from a persuasion that he was deserving of a Duchess, and at last consented to the marriage because there is a fate in these things which cannot be withstood, is now completely reconciled.

She resides with the young couple, not only to see that every thing goes on right, but also to please Mr. Pelham, who she is convinced could not be happy without her. We have corresponded several years.

Her letters are now generally filled with the witticisms of master Pelham, who is just twenty months old, and by her account a prodigy. She sometimes speaks of her niece, allows her to be an obliging good-tempered young woman, and so well informed in housekeeping, that Mrs. Penelope has yielded the family affairs to her management, and they are now almost as well conducted as when she herself presided. She mentions amongst her niece's perfections, that she is an excellent milliner, and makes "mighty becoming bonnets" for ladies who are not very young. She has also learned to play at Tredrille.

Louisa has not deserted Seatondell. Indeed she is particularly attached to the little farm, which afforded an asylum to herself and her father in their adversity; and which was planted and decorated under his directions. Mrs. Arby and the rest of the neighbours are "prodigiously proud" when she honours them with a visit, and they discover many excellencies in Mrs. Pelham, which they overlooked in Louisa Dudley. I find she has enlarged the charitable institutions which she formerly founded, and it gives me particular pleasure to hear that Mr. Pelham has made poor Walden tolerably happy, by presenting him with a living.

Mr. Clermont is become a peer by his father's death, but the acquisition of a title has not contributed to his repose. The late Lord's sentiments in politicks were so violently in opposition to government, that they have operated as an antidote to his son; who being tired of the insipidity of a fashionable life, has entered into administration, with the sanguine hope of having *now* found the long-desired good. His features have acquired a cast of mystery, and his frank impassioned manner is changed into reserve and importance. He sometimes pays a short visit to his Lady at the Park, who welcomes him with tears, and endeavours to detain him by complaints. Her time passes very uncomfortably. She has in a great degree secluded herself from society, some of her neighbours say she is deranged, others think her intolerably proud; all blame her for living unhappily with a handsome, generous, well-behaved husband. Few can understand her sorrows, and fewer have courage to stem the torrent of publick opinion by pitying them.

The Dowager Lady Clermont is a convert to methodism, and is esteemed a *blessed* acquisition by that society.

Miss Milton's sense of her friend's injuries is so very acute, that she has rejected two unexceptionable offers, and transferring the faults of *one* man to the whole species, has declared herself a *determined* member of my sisterhood. Her resentment against the base, ungrateful, tyrannick sex is so great, that she entirely avoids the society of gentlemen. Her apartments are decorated with histories intended to describe their falshood;[1] and she spends her time in writing satires against perjured swains, and elegies upon deceived nymphs. Her favourite subject of conversation is to inveigh against Lord Clermont, and some of those censures have reached his Lordship, and contributed to increase the unkindness which she deplores.

---

1 In the second edition, "falsehood."

After several unsuccessful attempts to form a matrimonial connection with a woman of character, Sir William Milton has taken Miss Morton again into keeping. Their tempers are too violent for cordiality; scarce a day passes without a quarrel; and though he congratulates himself that he is not bound to the fury for life, she makes his haughty spirit bend to her controul. Nay, she affirms, that she may be Lady Milton when she pleases, and the bets in this particular are two to one against Sir William.

A very strange event has taken place at Danbury since I mentioned my favourite abode, and I beg my readers pardon for not informing them of it sooner. Could any one have believed that after thirty-five years of irreproachable conduct, Miss Cardamum should at last elope with Mr. Inkle. Though this match was completed under the auspices of Cupid, it does not prove to be a very happy one. Mr. Cardamum is inexorable in point of fortune, and as Mrs. Inkle positively refuses to go behind the counter, or to do any thing inconsistent with her dignity, I am afraid the young man is plagued with a well-bred wife, and a scanty income. We have excluded her from our genteel assembly: I am told she is much piqued at it, but such an unpardonable dereliction of all rules of decorum ought to be severely reprobated.

A great deal has been said lately respecting Captain Target's attention to Mrs. Eleanor Singleton. They have been surprised tête-a-tête at picquet;[1] and I saw him with my *own* eyes carry little Fido from church last Friday, for fear he should dirty his new pink sattin ribbon. I have a very good opinion of my friend's understanding, and I *hope* it was only a neighbourly action.

Since Mrs. Inkle's marriage, Mrs. Medium has laid strong siege to Mr. Alsop, and she manages the battery of her daughter Dolly's merits so admirably that I think his heart *must* surrender at discretion. His housekeeper, Mrs. Betty, is of a different opinion.

I shall conclude with a song lately composed by Mrs. Pelham; who still occasionally sacrifices to the Muses. My correspondent

---

1 Picquet (or piquet) is a card game for two players, with a pack of thirty-two cards (the two to the six of each suit being excluded), in which points are scored by making declarations and winning tricks.

Mrs. Penelope has luckily favoured me with a copy, just in time for publication:

> Go, daughters of Fashion, for pleasure repine,
> The joys ye pursue are not equal to mine;
> The humours of thousands for yours must agree,
> Mine centre in Henry, and Henry's in me.
>
> The rose thrice hath bloom'd on the chaplet of May,
> Since I bow'd at the altar, and vow'd to obey;
> Talk not of restrictions, the bond I approve,
> 'Tis sanction'd by reason, religion, and love.
>
> Gay carrols the lark as we rise in the morn,
> And at evening the blackbird chaunts sweet on the thorn,
> We join in the concert, why should we refrain?
> Our hearts are as grateful, as lively our strain.
>
> We bask in the sunshine which summer supplies,
> And count, fertile autumn! thy exquisite dies;
> No terror in ice-mantled winter we see,
> A book and a song still can conquer ennui.
>
> Domestick, yet cheerful, delighted to blend,
> By prudent attentions the lover and friend,
> In wedlock's full cup we some bitters expect,
> And allow for the frailties we try to correct.
>
> Though shunning the many, wild Comus's crew;
> For social enjoyment we chuse but a few:
> Those few round our table shall frequently meet,
> Sincere be the welcome, and simple the treat.
>
> Our boy on my bosom I cherish with pride,
> He calls to those duties we gladly divide;
> May he live when our limit of being is done,
> And our names and our virtues survive in our son.

THE END.

CPSIA information can be obtained
at www.ICGtesting.com
Printed in the USA
LVHW031235221121
704042LV00003B/350